The Zombie Sheriff Takes Tucson

A Love Story

Brian South

Copyright © 2015 by Brian South

This is a work of fiction. Any similarity to real persons, living or undead, is coincidental and not intended by the author.

All rights reserved. No part of this publication may be reproduced or transmitted in any form or by any means, electronic or mechanical, including photocopy, recording, or any information storage and retrieval system, without permission in writing from the author.

ISBN: 1505648645
ISBN-13: 978-1505648645

For Sarah

Acknowledgments

My thanks to Mitch Martin, Paul Otto, Dana Green, Rita Leganski, Milan Jovanovic and, most of all, to Sarah South

Contents

1.	Double Ambush at McGurley Pass	7
2.	Chester's Brigade	10
3.	The New Man in Town	16
4.	Of Nooses and Yo-Yo Strings	21
5.	Shadows in the Dark	31
6.	Everyone Goes to Peabody's	37
7.	Black is the New Pink	44
8.	Mission: LI 2C ME/I LWOO*M SFD	52
9.	Wilson's Tale	58
10.	In Which the Gentlemen Acquire Some Horses	67
11.	Fool's Errand	75
12.	A Fallen Log	83
13.	Of Vegetation and Folly	87
14.	Jorge Aromero	96
15.	Sleight of Arm	110
16.	Occurrence at Owl Creek Bridge	116
17.	The Magnificent Two	122
18.	The Battle of Owen's Folly	133

19.	Brought to You by the Fine Folks at Reading R.R.	149
20.	Kung Fu, Hustle	163
21.	Aurumania	168
22.	A Macabre Watermark	174
23.	Chester's Brigade Redux	179
24.	My Darling Jezebel	184
25.	A Man, a Plan, a Canal: Tucson	188
26.	Tucson Two-Step	193
27.	The Saviors	197
28.	Blood on the Moon	204
29.	The Wild Brunch	208
30.	Fear and Loathing in Tucson	219
31.	Wilson, P.I.	226
32.	Hamburgers with Gimmler-Heichman	240
33.	Lady Death	245
34.	The End of Dr. Friedrich Otto Gimmler-Heichman (SPOILER), That Dastardly Devil of Evil	259
	Epilogue	276

The Zombie Sheriff Takes Tucson

A Love Story

1.

DOUBLE AMBUSH AT McGURLEY PASS

Surprises have been known to lead to heart attacks, early labor, and being hit by an eco-friendly bus. This is why many people don't like surprises.

Some surprises, on the other hand, can lead to pleasant results. A winning lottery ticket, extra bacon with breakfast, the sudden death of one's enemy can all be surprises that brighten one's day.

The key, of course, to creating pleasant surprises is to expect the absolute worst from life. Did an article of clothing cost two times as much as it should, instead of three? Surprise! Did a loved one make it to fifty instead of forty before dying? Surprise! Did you make it to the final round of interviews before being turned down for a job, instead of being discounted outright? Surprise!

The toughest part about riding a horse is overcoming the urge to eat it. Many a reanimated cowboy has succumbed to the siren's call of fresh meat readily at hand without considering the unfortunate consequences, not the least of which is being stuck in the middle of the wilderness with only one's broken ankles for transportation.

While the sheriff, daring do-gooder, wily warrior, charitable champion of the oppressed, currently found himself without a horse, it wasn't because he had eaten it; he was much too smart for that (when he was first getting the hang of horseback riding, he had eaten his first three horses and had learned a hard lesson). The sheriff was horseless because a gang of slickskins had ambushed him at McGurley Pass, spraying bullets everywhere. Luckily most of the bullets had hit the sheriff in the upper torso, lodging themselves into his heart, lungs, and stomach. None of them had penetrated his skull and damaged his brain (which, as any knowledgeable ghoul-killer will tell you, is the only way to kill a ghoul; these were not knowledgeable ghoul-killers).

But a few bullets had hit his horse and the bundle hogtied across her rump. Chestnut, not being undead, promptly collapsed with a mournful neigh. The sheriff only had time to gnaw on her thigh a little before he found himself surrounded by slickskins, their guns raised to their shoulders like macabre fiddles.

"Now hold it right there, you devilish son of a bitch," said a man with a grizzled gray beard. "We've got you surrounded. Just you stay put and we'll make this quick." The man hadn't had a decent wash in weeks, nor had he gotten much sleep. He was grumpy.

"Pa, how many times do I have to tell you," said a younger man, "they ain't got no sense of understanding. Just shoot him and have done with it. We got bigger fish to fry." He spoke with the hard assurance of a man who had identified the current threat and felt he had it firmly in hand. Unfortunately for him, he was an idiot.

"What's that on him? There, on the pocket of his vest."

"Well, it looks like a tin star. Reckon he was a lawman before he turned."

"Damn shame. We could use a few more lawmen nowadays."

And just as the men carefully aimed their weapons and the sheriff silently mouthed his final prayers, salvation came. Over and around the surrounding hills, quietly at first, but then gaining in intensity, came the sound of dull, heartless moans.

The slickskins looked over their shoulders almost as one.

"Where are they?" said one.

"Anybody see them?" said another.

"Sounds like dozens, hundreds maybe," said a third.

Where before they had surrounded the sheriff in a loose circle, now the gang of men formed up a tight block, each looking this way and that, trying to spy the source of the moans and also to avoid wetting themselves. The sheriff was more or less ignored as he slowly raised his arms and took a few shuffling steps toward the closest of his assailants.

"There!" cried one of them.

Cresting the hill was a deathly black shadow, cast by the full moon in the distance, that slowly spread down the slope toward the men. There were only ten of them.

"Fire at that shadow!" one of them called, and they all turned to the hill and shot at the ever-widening darkness. But rather than retreat or even hesitate, the shadow seemed to redouble its efforts and spread, a tidal wave of black blood. The terrible moaning grew so loud the men could hear nothing else, and though they yelled at one another to concentrate their shots to a single point in a vain effort to break through, their calls were unintelligible.

The shadow, now so close that its members were identifiable, yet still quite faceless, swarmed over the men, who were able to dispatch a few of the horde before they were promptly eaten.

2.

CHESTER'S BRIGADE

What is a community? A community is a group brought together by a common bond. Friendship can form communities. Fear can form communities. A ravenous thirst for blood can form communities. I know it has in my case.

Whatever their cause, communities enable their members to accomplish things they wouldn't be able to accomplish alone. Examples include raising children, building houses, and catching and eating the elderly. In each of these cases it is possible to accomplish the task by oneself, but it is advisable to enlist the help of others to avoid fatal errors or stomachaches.

Communities were first formed in ancient times when people became afraid of imaginary monsters. These monsters would prowl about at night, eating the weak and vulnerable, and they were only defeated by gangs of fearless warriors or by clear, rational thought. Clear, rational thought was at a premium back then. It was safer to go with the gangs of fearless warriors.

Not much has changed.

It was the well-known western philosopher Bronk Sylvester who said, "Brains are the clouds of the mind. He who would seek the heavens need only look inside himself. And he who would eat the heavens need look inside others." Truer words have never been spoken.

The Zombie Sheriff Takes Tucson

The sheriff would often daydream about the lusciousness of gray matter: its seemingly infinite folds, its airy, doughy goodness. Sometimes he wished he could get a look—and maybe a taste—of his own brain, but he knew that was ridiculous.

One of the great things about brains is that you don't need a campfire to prepare them. Just pop the top and enjoy. Some who would call themselves civilized use cutlery to enjoy the delicacy. Some even use napkins. The sheriff wasn't that high and mighty. Why confine yourself to the trappings of civilization more than is needed? One of life's great pleasures is to go out into the wilderness, catch your dinner with your bare hands, and enjoy the fruits of your labor.

After an hour or so of chomping and gnawing and slurping, the sheriff turned to address his rescuers. "Thank you, gentlemen and ladies. I believe those wretched men meant to do me harm."

A figure that had been munching on the cartilage from the grizzled old man's unwashed knee straightened itself and looked at the sheriff. The sheriff noticed the ghoul was missing his left arm below the elbow, where the stump still leaked a little blood. "You are very welcome, sheriff. And we're glad we found you with those slickskins. We haven't had a true bite to eat in nearly a week. Armadillos and rattlesnakes hardly provide the strength for an honest day's work."

"Well, it profited all parties involved, then. Except for the slickskins, of course. But you're wounded," said the sheriff, gesturing to the man's arm, which was still dripping blood onto the ground. It had begun to pool around his leather boots. "Do you need medical attention?"

The man used his right hand to bring his left up for closer inspection, spraying some nearby feasters in the process. They didn't mind. "Oh, it's nothing, sheriff. I've had much worse, really."

"If you're sure." The sheriff extended his hand, and the man took it in a firm grip. "Pleasure."

"Mine. Name's Chester, and these are my friends and family," said Chester, leader of legions, terror of townspeople, gesturing to the mass of feeding beings. "Most call us Chester's Brigade, for want of a more creative title."

"A wholesome bunch if ever I saw one."

"Mighty kind of you to say, sheriff. What do you go by?"

"People tend to just call me sheriff."

"Ah, I see. Sort of like a ghoul-with-no-name kind of thing. Very tidy. What brings you to these parts?"

"Well, Chester, I've been tracking a no-good slickskin by the name of McFarland. He's been terrorizing the people of this region for longer than I'd like to say, and it's high time someone put a stop to it. The law's the law."

The sheriff produced a well-worn scrap of paper from inside his vest. "I've been interviewing people for months, and I've come up with this composite sketch of the bastard."

Chester examined the drawing for a long time. "It's so life-like," he said. "With this amount of detail I'm sure you'll catch the scoundrel in no time. And I can't think of anyone better suited to the job than you, sheriff."

"Too kind," said the sheriff, returning the paper to his pocket. "This McFarland is a mean one. Seems he takes particular pleasure in dispatching ghouls, and he's a crack shot to boot. One morning a man showed up at my door looking like he'd gone up and down a chimney. When I'd sat him down and gave him some stewed slickskin thigh meat, he told me a man named McFarland had killed his whole town. The whole thing—just wiped them out."

Chester gave a low whistle through two of his remaining teeth.

"Apparently McFarland and three of his friends—"

The sheriff cut off at the appearance of a small old woman. She seemed just barely able to walk, and there were only a few wisps of hair remaining atop her head. The muscles in her face had worn down so much that she appeared to be a talking skull. She had no teeth.

"Please, sheriff," she said, offering a cup of something with both hands. "After bringing us such a meal, it's the least I could do."

The sheriff took the cup and removed a small bundle of intestines that had been steeping in it.

"Blood tea," he said, blowing lightly into the cup. "My favorite. Much obliged, ma'am."

The old woman was overjoyed at his response and left to brew more tea. Old women tend to do that.

"Anyway," continued the sheriff. "McFarland and his friends had gotten mighty drunk one night and decided the world would be a better place without the town of Georgian Junction. So they made a wager: whichever one of them killed the most ghouls that night would get ten dollars from each of the other men. Didn't take them two hours to clear the town. No one saw it coming.

"I had been hearing stories about McFarland for years, but always from out west, too far for me to look him up, since he'd more than likely be gone by the time I got there. But he's here now. In my jurisdiction. And I'm fixing to do something about it."

"You're doing God's work, sheriff, God's own work."

"I had just apprehended one of McFarland's gang when I was waylaid by those heathens you rescued me from. But"—the sheriff gestured to the remains of Chestnut and her cargo—"as you can see, the slickskin was killed by one of his own kind. Have to start from square one.

"Enough about me, though. What's the story with your group here, the Brigade, as you call them? Why don't you settle down? You've got more than enough here for a decent settlement."

Chester's face fell. The sheriff had the impression Chester had been through unendurable hardship, and he felt an instant connection to the man. It was totally platonic, though. "We've been driven from our home," said Chester. "We're no Georgian Junction, mind you, but it sure felt like it. We lived in a handsome village, a bastion of civility and grace, for generations.

"Then they came. They didn't attack the town—I have the feeling we would have been too much for them. But they settled damn close to us. And any ghouls they saw wandering in small groups they'd pick off as thoughtlessly as shooting a bird or a deer. Their town grew and grew, while ours shrank. It got to the point where we were afraid if they had a mind, they could have wiped us out all at once. So we left."

"All of you?" asked the sheriff.

"All of us. What you see here, perhaps several dozen in number, is all that's left of the hundreds that made up the great city of Charon's Gate.

"But don't pity us too much. We don't pity ourselves. We get by. As I said, snakes and desert creatures aren't much of a meal, but they get the job done. When we're lucky we come across a decent piece of meat, and we take in all our bodies can handle." He gestured with his remaining hand at the corpses on the ground. "This is a banquet we haven't enjoyed in quite a while. My heart breaks for the little ones."

With the back of his hand the sheriff wiped one still-functioning eye. "That is a sad tale if ever I've heard one." And the sheriff had indeed heard his share of sad tales, so this wasn't a hollow declaration. Chester started to walk, and when he picked up his boots, a stringy trail of congealed blood followed after him, as did the sheriff, listening attentively.

"But we do what we can to survive. Our dream is to one day reclaim that fair land that we once called home."

As the sheriff followed Chester through the feasting horde, he saw the men, women, and children of Chester's Brigade, refugees from their rightful land, as part of his own family. After all, wasn't he a man without a home, just as they were? And he saw the slickskins as the evil menace they were—preying on his people, shooting on sight, unmerciful even toward women and children. The sheriff's resolve hardened. He would make a difference for these people.

He would find and kill McFarland, and after he'd done that, he'd see the people of Chester's Brigade got the home they deserved.

3.

The New Man in Town

The phoenix, like chivalry, is something that lives a full, ripe existence, burns itself up, and reincarnates from its own ashes. There are countless stories of phoenixes performing brave, heroic endeavors, sacrificing life and limb for the benefit of others. Then, as the phoenix nears death, a great flame engulfs it, reducing it to ashes. Amongst these ashes can be found a little heroic phoenix.

The phoenix, also like chivalry, is a myth.

Abernathy Jones, energetic everyman, devout deputy, above-average avenger, wrote on a sheet of paper in long, flowing letters:

> Nancy, I've arrived in Arizona and found to my pleasure some of the most welcoming people I've ever encountered. There seems to be a certain fascination with precious metals in the region as a whole, but the folks I have spoken with seem resentful that a few hundred fortune-seekers are giving the West a bad name. Indeed, I was welcomed at my current place of rest with a meat pie and a glass of whiskey, gratis. Please make a note in my permanent files that the town of Phoenix, Arizona might one day make a won-

derful vacation spot. But I wouldn't like spending too many summers here.

There has been no sign of him as of yet, but I still hold out hope. It is a wide world, but not so wide that one person may hide from another when the need is so great.

One last item. I know you will not be receiving this letter for some time, but when you do, would you mind sending along my special cane? Twice in the last week I have been accosted by roving packs of ghouls. I say packs because that's exactly what they were: it seems there are many more ghouls in the West, and more often than not they travel in groups. Very strange. If they were any more organized, the authorities would be facing undead militias! I'm sure this isn't a reflection on the quality of resident in the fair state of Arizona, but in case of further unfortunate incidents, my special cane may well be needed. You know how I abhor carrying any sort of firearm.

→ both sides think other is stupid

He blotted the ink, folded the paper carefully, and inserted it into an envelope. He folded the flap of the envelope down carefully and dabbed a bit of hot wax on to the overlapping portion. With the face of his signet ring, he pressed down into the cooling wax. He enjoyed the feeling of making an impression in the solidifying wax. He liked the idea that he could have some way of making his mark, however impermanently, on the physical world. Things done properly gave Abernathy a particular sense of satisfaction. It seemed a long while now that life had devolved into chaos; any mark of order he could impose upon it seemed a radical, albeit inconsequential victory.

Abernathy packed his writing implements into their valise, picked up the valise by its leather handle, and left the small, sparse room that had been his home for three days. He walked down the stairs listening to the clink of poker chips and watching the cigar smoke create chimerical images as it rose to the ceiling. He saw a sea horse, then a unicorn, then a six-shooter. At the bar downstairs he handed the sealed letter to the barkeep.

"Al, you wouldn't mind posting that for me, would you?" asked Abernathy, giving the young man a little money along with a smile so genuine it seemed fake. "This should cover it, and your trouble besides."

"Not a problem, Mr. Jones," said Al.

Abernathy tipped his hat and walked outside to find a street urchin on the front porch of the saloon. He flipped a coin into the lad's upturned hat, along with a small, stiff card.

The card read:

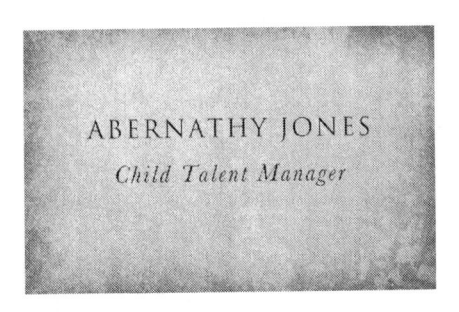

> ABERNATHY JONES
> *Child Talent Manager*

The boy read the card with great difficulty, turned it over to inspect the blank back side, and slipped it into a pocket.

"Ghoul! Ghoul!" yelled a shrill feminine voice from not too far off. Abernathy Jones, valise still in hand, ran toward the source of the call.

He found himself at the outskirts of town, where the sandy backyards of the buildings faded into the sandy wilderness. He had lost the sense of where the cry had come from. He looked about carefully, scanning for any movement in the area, but despite the stillness of the landscape, nothing stood out. Then:

"Help, oh please, help!"

The voice wasn't too far off—it had probably come from behind a nearby shed. Abernathy ran toward the shed, giving a wide berth to see what was going on behind it.

He saw a middle-aged woman in a long dress pressed up against the back of the shed. A few feet from her a frustrated-looking ghoul clearly intent on enjoying an early lunch was doing its best to reach the lady. The ghoul was missing its lower jaw, Abernathy noticed, revealing a crimson-colored moist hole that led all the way back to the creature's throat.

Trying to bite off more than he could chew, Abernathy thought to himself. The only thing preventing the ghoul from reaching the frantic woman was a small white parasol, with which she was frantically poking her assailant.

Abernathy smiled despite himself and calmly walked toward the distressed party. The woman, understandably, didn't seem to notice.

When he was close enough, Abernathy inhaled deeply, then like a discus thrower winding up for a throw, he twisted the valise behind his back. The world seemed stuck in time as Abernathy envisioned what he was about to do. Then all at once it happened:

Exhaling, Abernathy whipped the valise from behind his body to the front in a broad horizontal arc. At the point in the arc where the centrifugal force was greatest, the valise met the ghoul's face. The face was not pleased.

The ghoul's entire head (sans the absent lower jaw, of course) spun around several times on its trunk like a morbid game of spin the bottle. The head gradually slowed its spinning until it was once again facing the terrified woman. But the eyes of the monster were now lifeless, and the ghoul fell to the ground. As it did, the spinal column slipped out of the body like a snake shedding its skin.

The woman stood petrified, a look of pure horror frozen on her face. Small gasps left her mouth as she stared down at the ghoul's remains.

"Please, madam, make no mention of it," said Abernathy, wiping his valise clean with a handkerchief. "All in a day's work."

After perhaps an hour or two—long after her valiant rescuer had departed to accomplish other noble deeds—the woman regained enough of her senses to notice her hand was grasping a business card. Still dazed, she looked down at it.

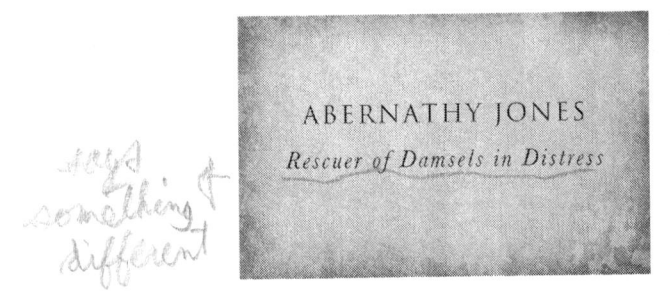

ABERNATHY JONES

Rescuer of Damsels in Distress

She bent down, a little unsteadily, and retrieved her fallen handbag. She opened it, removed a billfold, and firmly slid the business card into an unused pocket.

You never know when you'll need a rescuer.

4.

OF NOOSES AND YO-YO STRINGS

What's in a gesture? We gesture to the voluptuous barmaid to bring us another round. We gesture to animals to get out of our way or else face the wrath of our cart's wheel. We gesture to an enemy to suggest he do unfortunate things to his mother.

A gesture, then, is an extension of ourselves, a nonverbal, primal means of communicating something felt within our hearts. But gestures may be mistaken if the gesturer and the gesturee are not on a common page.

It is said that when Caesar looked upon the banks of the Rubicon and debated within himself one final time whether or not to cross, his resolve suddenly weakened, and he signaled to his centurions to fall back. But the centurions misread Caesar's gesture—or perhaps they were so certain of his intended course of action that they paid no attention—and they themselves cast the die for Caesar.

When Louis XVI had been presented with an inordinately long and unwieldy sandwich by his chef, he made a simple chopping gesture with his hand, indicating that he would like it cut into smaller pieces. What transpired, however, was a dizzying series of conferences, committee meetings, and public debates that eventually produced—through the tireless efforts of Joseph-Ignace Guillotin and Antoine Louis—a machine that went on to kill thousands of French. Rumor has it that Louis XVI's bodiless head mouthed with words *"Je voulais simplement mon sandwich couper"* (*"I just wanted my sandwich cut"*) as his head rested in the basket.

Gestures can be dangerous things, indeed.

The sheriff stayed with Chester's Brigade for a time, and he found before too long his initial reaction was correct; these people were his kind of people: hard-working, resilient, slickskin-devouring. They looked after one another like an extended family, and when a slickskin was sighted, they sprang into action like the ragtag yet lethal machine they were (there had actually been talk within the Brigade of forming an a cappella group called "Ragtag Lethal Machine," but as yet it had failed to take off).

The sheriff saw no better example of their ruthless efficiency than during an event that occurred after he had been with the Brigade for a few weeks. It was a crystal-clear night, the moon shining silvery down on the Brigade's ever-ravenous maws while the pinpricks of stars tried to keep up. The last meal the Brigade had been able to find—three days prior—was a group of about a dozen bighorn sheep, which they'd set into with neither enthusiasm nor delay. Nothing compared to the sweet tang of slickskin meat, the savor of slickskin blood, the tangible shock of slickskin terror. Their last taste of slickskin had come on the night the sheriff came aboard. It had been too long.

But on that night an advance scout had come back to Chester and the sheriff with more eagerness than an inmate on the eve of his first conjugal visit. "S-sir, I think I've spotted some, sir!" The words rushed out of the scout's mouth as quickly as words had ever left the mouth of any ghoul ever before. Which is to say, not particularly quickly.

"Whoa there, Randolph," said Chester, using the same tone he would use with an unruly horse, or his aging mother.

He placed his hand on the lad's shoulder. "Just slow down and tell me what 'some' you saw."

The sheriff couldn't help but crack a small smile at the scout's enthusiasm. It wasn't that long ago he himself had had all the energy in the world, after all. Now he had to rely more on his wits than his body.

Randolph took a steadying breath. He was a gaunt young man, and his temples seemed to protrude from his face, stretching his skin like the head of a drum. The clothes he wore were perhaps of a finer quality than that of most other ghouls—well-cut dark trousers and a billowy button-down shirt that at one time may have been a color resembling something close to white. Over his shirt Randolph wore a faded wool vest. He was, like any ghoul, covered from head to toe in grime, blood, and dirt.

After he had regained his composure, he began again. "I saw up ahead, maybe a mile or so, what looked like a dozen or more slickskins."

"Well that is good news, Randolph, and I thank you for reporting it to me. You said a mile up ahead—that wouldn't be by the old hanging tree, would it?"

Randolph thought for a moment and then said, "They may be making toward it, sir. They were headed that direction."

Chester removed his hand from the scout's shoulder and turned to the sheriff. "It may be that we've found your boy McFarland without too much of a fuss, after all, sheriff."

The sheriff's eye shone with the ache of undelivered justice. "Think so?"

"This hanging tree is a favorite of local bandits. They make their way to it in the middle of the night with some sorry soul they think has done them wrong. They put his neck in the noose and hang him from that tree until he's dead. It's usually an opportune time for an attack. The bandits are too busy with their hanging and drinking to keep much of a look out. I've had quite a few memorable meals under that tree."

"Sounds wonderful," said the sheriff. "Let's see what we can see."

"Excuse me, sir," said Randolph, "but why do the slickskin bandits hang their enemies from the tree until they die? Seems to me that might be a very long time. Don't slickskins live sixty, seventy years or more?" *longer then ghouls*

"They do under normal circumstances," said Chester, "but 'skins have to do this pesky thing called breathing, or else they die earlier. That's why they hang them—if they can't get air down their necks, they can't breathe."

"Oh. I've heard of breathing before. Don't we breathe, sir?"

"Ghouls sometimes bring air into their lungs and out again, yes, lad, but they don't really need to in order to live. But enough questions for now. Let's go see if these bandits are the same ones the sheriff's after."

"Of course, sir," said Randolph.

As Chester's Brigade made their way to the hanging tree, the trio outpaced the horde and reached the destination first. What they saw there made their mouths water.

There were twelve slickskins in all: ten crowded around a huge, stunted tree, and two standing under that tree, their arms bound behind their backs and their mouths gagged. The men's horses were tethered a few yards away.

The ten looked angry. The two looked scared. The horses looked bored.

Randolph led Chester and the sheriff to the cover of a small group of rocks near the tree. They hadn't been noticed.

"Thought you'd pulled one over on us didn't you, boys?" one of the slickskins was saying. "Thought you'd just leave our little band, eh? Well, let me tell you something. Mr. Larribee doesn't care for deserters. Before we do this thing, I just have one question for you sorry maggots. What on earth made you think you'd get away with it?"

The man, somewhat gratuitously, punched each of the captives in the stomach when they failed to speak. It was unclear whether he expected the bound men to respond despite their gags, or if he was just mean.

By now the Brigade had caught up to their leader, and like any well-trained group they awaited orders before taking what might be considered the obvious course of action. They were remarkably disciplined; only a few errant moans could be heard in the stillness of the night.

"You hear something?" asked one of the slickskins to another.

The other shrugged. He just wanted to get this over with and spend the rest of the night with his favorite whiskey bottle. "Lots of things out there tonight, Tommy," he replied. "Could be anything."

"As long as it isn't what I think it might be," said Tommy.

Chester was busy relaying signals to the Brigade using absurdly intricate hand gestures (which was especially impressive, given that he had only one hand).

After a while, Chester looked at the sheriff. "You think McFarland's there?"

The sheriff took out the scrap of paper from his vest and looked at it for the thousandth time.

He shook his head with regret. "I'd have seen him by now. These aren't his men. But nonetheless, they're lawbreakers, and they deserve what's coming to them. The law's the law."

Chester nodded and turned back to his people. After a rather forceful gesture that the sheriff reflected looked like an act better left to the domain of the bedroom, the Brigade seemed to disappear into the night. Try as he might, the sheriff couldn't see or hear anything of them.

"Get them ready," the leader of the slickskins was saying. The two captives had nooses placed around their necks and were made to step up onto long, thin rocks turned on their side, so that if either man lost his balance the rock would fall and the noose would draw tight around his neck.

But just as the leader was saying some very impolite final words to the two sorry souls, it happened.

From all directions ghouls tore into the clearing that housed the hanging tree, and they were on the slickskins so quickly that none of them had any chance to fight back, or indeed to give any reaction at all other than to let out terrified screams that sounded more like they came from toddlers than grown men.

But their terror was perhaps justified; Chester's Brigade set into their prey with practiced malice. Some of the more memorable actions undertaken:

- Limbs broken, mashed, pulverized (12 arms, 7 legs)
- Heads popped off—and ensuing mini-skirmishes to see who would win the treasured brain held within (all 10)
- Carotid arteries bitten into, causing spurts of blood to shoot like fireworks into the air (7 in total)
- Intestines pulled out of abdomens like string unwound from a yo-yo (24.5 feet in total length)
- Skin peeled off, as a triumphant doctor takes off a glove (2: once while the slickskin was protesting, once while he wasn't)

All in all, it was a pleasant evening.

The two sat by a fire. Some of the Brigade had brought them limbs to gnaw as they talked.

"Times are changing," said the sheriff, taking a large chunk out of a forearm. "It used to be a man could trust the world, trust that he wouldn't be taken advantage of, or worse. That's the tragic thing about all this. Since the slickskins started to fight back we've all been made to feel helpless.

"Slickskins don't care who you are, where you come from. Slickskins don't care what your story is, or what you aim to do. They see you, they kill you."

"I'm afraid you're right," said Chester. "That's where things are nowadays."

They both stared into the fire for a time.

"What do you suggest we do with them?" asked Chester, pointing to the two slickskins balanced precariously on the rocks, nooses still around their necks. Terror had been in their eyes long before the Brigade arrived. Now their pants were soaked with urine.

"Well, I don't see that they've done us any harm, and we've got plenty to eat. But on the other hand they have been or are currently outlaws. I think the proper course of action would be to leave them as we found them."

Chester tried unsuccessfully to hide his grin. "Anyone ever tell you you're a wise man, sheriff?"

The sheriff didn't respond.

He looked at the Brigade, most of whom were still enjoying their meal. His mind was made up. He shuffled over to a nearby tree stump and carefully climbed atop it.

"The problem is they won't let us live in peace," he said, as if continuing his conversation of a moment ago. Some of the Brigade took notice. "They think that we'll just fall over undead at the drop of a hat. Well, I say we won't. It's time we made a stand against all slickskins everywhere—not just those we find for food. I say it's time to show them that we aren't second-class citizens, that we're a force to be reckoned with. Who's with me?"

A low, grumbling moan went up from the Brigade. By now all of them were listening to the sheriff speak.

"And I say before you today that I will make it my life's mission to defeat the slickskins." He reached down and ruffled the hair of a young boy named Wilson, learner of lessons, clever conman, faithful friend. The lad's bright red hair matched the color of the blood coating his smiling mouth. "No matter where I have to go, no matter what hardships come my way, I won't rest until we have the respect of the slickskins, or there aren't any slickskins left."

A much louder moaning now greeted the sheriff's words. Heads bobbed unsteadily on necks, limbs and partial limbs waved in the cool night air.

"I urge you all to continue your good work. You have strength in numbers. Use that strength for our common goal. If you see a town overrun with slickskins, do what you can to remove the infestation. There are so many of you, the slickskins will run screaming into the night when they find you've come."

"But what about you?" Chester asked him. "Why don't you join us?"

The sheriff smiled down at Chester. "Believe me when I say that I wish I could. But I can't. No, my job is to settle some unfinished business. There's a very nasty slickskin who needs taking care of. The law's the law, after all. But if I find groups like yours, or even individuals in danger in the wilderness, like I was when you all found me, you can be sure I'll bring them into our cause. You won't be just a brigade then—you'll be an army."

He cleared his throat and adjusted his leather vest. "I've been thinking about us, about our people living like pigs and the slickskins in your beloved home of Charon's Gate while you roam aimless. Oh, I'm so full of wrath! There are a million of them, and a hundred thousand of us are starving. And I've been wondering if all our folks got together and moaned..."

"Sheriff, they'd drag you out and cut you down just like they done to us a thousand times," said Chester, concern thick in his voice.

"They'll drag me anyways. Sooner or later they'll get me for one thing if not for another. Until then—"

"Until then, you'll try to kill every last one of them!" shouted Wilson, looking up at the sheriff with something akin to adulation. The Brigade moaned their approval.

"You got that right, son! And I'm leaving those last two slickskins in their nooses as a parting gift. As long as I'm an outlaw to them, maybe I can do something, maybe I can find out something, scrounge around and maybe find out what it is that's wrong. And see if there's something that can be done about it."

"That sounds all right, sheriff, but will we ever see you again?" asked Chester.

"But I won't really be leaving you. I'll be all around in the dark—I'll be everywhere. Wherever you look—wherever there's a scuffle, so hungry ghouls can eat, I'll be there. Wherever there's a slickskin beating up a guy, I'll be there. I'll be in the way guys moan when they're mad. I'll be in the way kids laugh when they're hungry and they know supper's ready, and when the people are eating the limbs and stuff they tear off slickskins—I'll be there, too."

There wasn't a dry eye among all the Brigade after the sheriff had finished. The moans reached the bright, clear moon high above.

"Well, sheriff, I don't understand it, but I can appreciate it," said Chester when the sheriff had come down from the stump.

"Me neither, Chester, but—it's just something I've been thinking about."

5.

SHADOWS IN THE DARK

There is a legend about the harmonica. In the old days, before good music was discovered, a man used to go around blowing on random objects to see if they would make nice sounds. He blew on everything—rocks, trees, schoolhouses—but nothing seemed to do the trick.

Then one day, after the man had drunk a great deal of alcohol to bury his misery at not being able to blow on anything to have it make a nice sound, he discovered something quite by accident. He was allergic to pollen, and there was a lot of pollen in the air, so the man let out a great big sneeze—just across the opening of his bottle of alcohol.

Lo and behold, the man discovered a brilliant way of making a nice sound! All he had to do was blow wind across the opening of a bottle. The man fine-tuned his method, continuing to blow on bottles of various levels of fullness and creating different pitches for days at a time until his neighbor, who had just invented the harmonica, enraged by the constant blowing on bottles, came over and killed him.

And that is the legend of the harmonica.

The sheriff stayed with Chester's Brigade for a few days more, but his words that fateful night stuck with them like the sweet smell of death, and they all knew he had to leave them soon. It didn't make it easier for them to see him go. Chester was their leader, and they followed and loved him, but the message the sheriff brought was one they'd been waiting to hear all their undead lives.

The morning the sheriff was to leave he found Wilson waiting for him as he opened his eye from a slumber made restful by dreams of clouds of brain matter. Wilson had followed the sheriff around like an undead puppy the length of his stay with the Brigade, and the sheriff knew it would be hard on the boy when he left. In truth, he sort of enjoyed having him around. The kid never got in the way, and it was clear he had a good soul. And he was plucky.

Wilson had been taken in as a boy when the Brigade found him all on his own. Apparently his parents had fallen prey to slickskins. Even at such a young age Wilson had had the wherewithal to survive by himself. On the third day on his own he had waylaid a small family of slickskins who were picnicking under a tree. By the time he was finished with them, the only thing left was a checkered picnic blanket, a half-eaten ham sandwich, and the tree. Wilson didn't much care for ham.

"Today's the day, then?" Wilson asked the sheriff. "You're really leaving us?"

"I'm afraid so, son," said the sheriff.

The two walked over to a nearby campfire where a pot of something blood red was bubbling. The toothless old woman handed them bowls of the concoction.

"Much obliged," said the sheriff.

The sheriff and Wilson sat silently eating their breakfast, neither one of them wanting to say what was on his mind.

Finally, when they had almost finished their meal, the sheriff put down his bowl and said, "Look, Wilson—"

Without so much as a word, the boy darted off in tears, or would have had he been able to run. As it was, he sort of shuffled away in a reckless manner. He even fell down once.

Anyway, the boy was faster than most of the Brigade. Though still quite slow.

Shaken by the boy's abrupt departure, the sheriff knew that prolonging his departure would only cause similar wounds among the Brigade. It was time.

"I wish we had a horse to offer you," said Chester, after the sheriff had gathered his few belongings, "but we ate the last one three days ago."

All of Chester's Brigade had turned out to see him off. All of them but Wilson, that is. There was much crying and waving and gnashing of other people's teeth.

The sheriff looked them over one last time, and hope filled his heart. "Remember what I said. You are a force for good. Hunt down those slickskins until we get the rights we deserve. That's what I'll be doing."

They cheered him as he slowly shuffled off, alone.

The sheriff made good time that day, and he was a fair distance from the Brigade when he finally set up camp that evening. It was hard for the sheriff to leave the fine folks of Chester's Brigade, as had never liked being alone. As best he could recall this aversion came about when his own father had left him out in the wilderness to fend for himself for a week. He had said it was for his own good, but the sheriff had always suspected it was to find a new Mrs. Sheriff, or at least conduct multiple auditions.

Despite his survival on that earliest of missions, the most enduring lesson the sheriff learned was that he wasn't a solitary soul. There was no one to have meaningful silences with as you galloped across the countryside for days on end. There was no one to create a diversion while you ambushed a juicy slickskin for dinner. And there was no one to watch the campsite while you went to empty your bowels of undigested slickskin meat. Simply put, life was harder on your own. Incomplete, even.

So when the sheriff found himself the sole occupant of his campsite that night, he got out his harmonica and played a sad, sad tune. It was a melody of loss and redemption, of fondness and heartbreak, of campfires and brains.

But he heard something that made him stop playing. It was a rustling of some sort off in some bushes twenty or thirty yards away. Was it a meal? He had left the Brigade with quite a store of meats and vittles, but he would never turn down fresh food. And brains. He really loved brains.

Or was it a friend? His thoughts of loneliness returned to him, and for a moment he imagined that it might be Chester, out to bring him back to the Brigade. Or, dare he even dream of it, a female ghoul unattached to the encumbrances of love. But that thinking was foolish. He had left them to do their job, and he had to do his.

This was fresh meat, and by god, he was going to eat it.

Just as he was rising to his feet, the sheriff saw a shadow dart from the bush to a tree ten yards beside it. So much for a friend. No one from beyond the grave could move that fast without falling flat on their face. Probably a deer. He dared not hope that it would be a slickskin. His luck wasn't that good.

Just in case, though, he let out a low moan. That always seemed to petrify the slickskins.

And it worked. Just next to the tree a middle-aged woman stood terrified. The sheriff slowly moved toward her, arms outstretched, his sluggish salivary glands already starting to kick in. The woman was about to let out a scream—female slickskins have a bad habit of doing that—when all of a sudden she lost her head. Literally. One moment she was gearing up for the yell of her life (or death, as it were), and the next the sheriff was looking at a bloody stump.

Confused, he nonetheless continued toward the headless body, which was still a few yards away. When he reached the corpse and heard the gnawing, everything fell into place. Kneeling by the woman was a shadow. A small shadow.

"Evening, sheriff," it said.

"Evening, Wilson."

Before he could continue the conversation, the sheriff couldn't help himself—he crouched down next to the body and took an enormous bite out of its shoulder.

When the two had had a good, long meal the sheriff finally asked the obvious question. "Is there any brain left?"

Wilson looked down at the skull by his feet. "I do believe there is, sheriff. I was sort of saving it for you." He tossed the head to the sheriff. It looked up at him with a seductively blank gaze.

"Much obliged."

"Don't mention it."

The sheriff considered it a moment then all at once bit straight into its forehead, removing a sizeable portion of skull and skin. Then he tipped the head forward and ate the brains in three quick slurps.

"And Wilson," he said, wiping some of the gray matter from his cheek and depositing it into his mouth, "how is it you come to be a day's journey outside the Brigade camp?"

The boy looked sheepishly away and wiped a little of the blood off his mouth with his sleeve. "Being such an important sheriff and all, I just thought you'd need a deputy."

"I told you, son, this is something I just have to do alone. It's safer that way." But the thoughts he had had earlier in the evening came back to him. What was so wrong with having a little company? A deputy could come in damn handy now and then.

No. Wilson was just a boy—he couldn't be more than twelve or fourteen. He had so much to learn, and the sheriff couldn't be spending his valuable time teaching him. He had bigger fish to fry (the thought of frying up pieces of McFarland instantly set his mouth watering again). The boy needed a mentor, sure—but it wasn't going to be him.

"We can camp together tonight, but at daybreak you're on your way back."

Wilson hung his head, but to his credit he didn't protest.

6.

Everyone Goes to Peabody's

When asked what profession they like least, most people will give the obvious answer: clowns. Then they will offer up politicians and lawyers, usually in that order. But fourth on the list is a profession that perhaps is the most insidious of all: bankers.

What do bankers do? They take people's money—and they will do practically anything to avoid giving it back. Their greed extends so far that they often create vaults to keep people from retrieving their money.

What do they do with all this money? Sources say the Bankers' International Trust and Charter for Head Executive Services has been working tirelessly over the past decade to create a monopoly on air, especially the hot kind. Of course after the politicians and lawyers caught wind of this atmospheric coup, they mounted a concerted effort to ensure their right to use as much hot air as they please.

What about the clowns? Everyone's still scared as shit of clowns.

They laid out their bedrolls around the campfire that night, and the sheriff had just begun his nighttime regimen of gargling slickskin uric acid when Wilson said, "Sheriff, tell me a story."

The sheriff spat out his mouthful into the fire, and the flames rose in protest. "What kind of story?"

"Tell me a scary story. A really scary one."

The sheriff smiled. He himself had been one for scary stories in his youth. A lot about this boy reminded him of himself.

"You sure you're up for that, son? It's a black night. No telling what could be out there. Don't want to spook you."

"Oh, sheriff, cut it out. I'm not a kid anymore. I killed my share of slickskins."

"How old are you, anyway?"

"Old enough."

The sheriff gave him a half-smile and a knowing glance. "If you say so. A scary story, huh? Well, I only know one kind of story like that. It was a story my daddy told me when I was about your age."

"You had a daddy?"

"Course I did. Everyone's got a daddy."

"I don't have one," Wilson said quietly.

"You do too. You just don't know it." What was he saying? Why was he giving the kid false hope? "Anyway, you're the type that can take care of himself."

Wilson brightened visibly at that.

"Okay, back to the story. My daddy told this to me I don't know how many times, and each time he told it to me it was scarier than the last."

"What's it about?"

"Slickskins."

"No!"

"Sure is. You sure you want to hear it?"

"I sure am sure! Don't you go back on your word. You told me you'd tell me a scary story."

"All right, then. Just wanted to make sure you knew what you were getting yourself into. Well this story starts with a slickskin named Franklin. Franklin worked on his family's farm until he was about twelve or fourteen years old. His family had connections, so they sent him to apprentice at a bank. But Franklin didn't want to go.

"'I don't want to go to a stupid bank,' he told his parents.

"'You will go to that bank and you'll like it,'" his daddy told him. 'We had to call in a lot of favors to get you that position. There's a lot of money in banks.'

"But try as Franklin might, he couldn't convince his parents not to send him. He found himself packaged into a coach one morning with a trunk of his possessions, and after a tearful good-bye, a two-day ride, and a whole lot of dust, Franklin found himself in town."

"When's it get scary?" Wilson asked.

"Quiet, boy. I'm coming to it. You need to know this stuff for the scary stuff to make sense.

"As I was saying, Franklin found himself in town with only his trunk and his wits. He walked right into the bank and told the teller he was there to see Mr. Plimpton. The teller showed him into Plimpton's office, and there was Plimpton sitting behind his desk. He was a thin, short man with thin, short hair. He wore glasses that made his eyes look like a mole's.

"'Mr. Plimpton,' said Franklin, 'I'm to be your new apprentice.' And he handed the man a letter of introduction from his parents.

"Plimpton took the letter and brought it so close to his face his nose almost touched it. 'Ah, yes,' he said, 'Franklin the farmer. I remember now. Well, have a seat, lad. I need to explain some things to you. Banking is going to be a big change for you, but it does have some parallels to farming, I suppose. For instance, you must always start out with some seed if you want your crops to grow.'

"The banker looked at the boy from over his glasses. 'Seed. Heh heh. Do you like my analogy?'

"Plimpton showed Franklin his lodging and settled him in, and he began to train him on the basics of banking. The boy actually took to it very well. Every time Plimpton started to cover a new topic related to finance, Franklin seemed to be further and further ahead.

"After just a couple of months, Franklin had mastered all the fundamentals of banking, and Plimpton was very pleased. 'I must say, boy, you have a natural talent for this sort of thing. I am quite impressed. I've decided to see how you will do, given a little a freedom.'

"Plimpton explained that two local businesses, a coffin-maker and a dress-maker, had applied for loans from the bank, but the bank could only invest in one of the businesses at the moment, considering its other financial obligations. 'Your job is to evaluate which of the two businesses we should give the loan to. I will look at this as your first true test of banking. If you choose wisely, you will be given more responsibility—and a raise.'

"So Franklin set out interviewing the two businesses. Mr. Tulliver, the coffin-maker, was just seeing off a grieving family as Franklin arrived.

"'Don't you worry about a thing,' said the man. 'I'll make sure your dear mother will be handled in the gentlest possible way.

"'Oh, Mr. Tulliver, how can we ever thank you for your kindness?' said a young woman.

"'No need. No need at all. Here. Take this'—he gave her a few coins—'have yourself a few pints at Peabody's on me. That's where the wake will be, won't it? I wouldn't miss it for the world.'

"When Franklin questioned the man about the loan, he had this to say: 'The problem with my business is I can't afford to keep more coffins on hand or to keep up with demand. Sometimes families have to wait a week or more for a coffin, and that's not right. I need this loan to hire someone part time to help me out.'

"'A noble goal,' said Franklin. 'If this town can't bury its dead in a timely fashion, it can't be much of a town, can it? Thank you, Mr. Tulliver. I think I have all the information I need from you.'

"Next, Franklin paid a visit to Mrs. Wellington, the dress-maker. Upon entering her store, Franklin noticed something odd—there wasn't a scrap of fabric to be seen.

"'Mrs. Wellington?' he asked.

"'Yes?' said a middle-aged woman behind a counter.

"'The dress-maker?'

"'That's me. You must be from the bank. And from the expression on your face, you've learned why I need an investor so badly. I can't keep up with demand. Every bolt of fabric I order, every scrap of trim is sold before I can put out prices on them.'

"'Then why don't you raise prices?'

"'I have. Three times. The mayor's even come to see me about it. His wife told him he doesn't want prices any higher than they are, and I can't really blame them—I make a tidy profit as it is. But my profit would be much greater if I could keep fabric in stock. Now there's this dance planned for next month at the saloon. The whole town will be there, but only if they have something to wear. There's already been talk among the ladies of having another business brought in to stir up some competition, and the only way around that is to get more money to hold more inventory. Surely the bank can see how profitable this would be for them?'

"'Surely,' said Franklin. 'Thank you for your time.'

"Franklin reflected on all he had seen and heard, and when he had arrived at his decision, he went to see Plimpton in his office.

"'I've made my choice, sir,' he said. 'I know which business in town to invest in.'

"Plimpton peered over his glasses at the boy, mentally weighing his confidence in the matter. 'Proceed. Will it be the coffin-maker, who so desperately needs the funds so families in the town won't be further aggrieved during their mourning period, or will it be the dress-maker, who intends to single-handedly bring up the town's spirits?'

"At first Franklin was taken aback that the banker was so knowledgeable about the options, given that he had put Franklin in charge of making the determination. But it made sense. The man wanted to evaluate how competent his apprentice would be in making a major financial decision. How else would he know which was the better option to select, if he didn't know the particulars involved?

"With complete confidence, Franklin delivered his answer. 'Neither, sir.'

"Plimpton stared at the boy in disbelief. 'Neither?'

"'Neither business offers the best investment opportunity for this bank, Mr. Plimpton. You charged me with finding the best business for the bank's funds, and I have found it. And it isn't the coffin-maker, and it isn't the dress-maker.'

"'Well then what is it, lad?'

"'It's Peabody's saloon. In the first place, they need investment capital to expand onto the next property over. That means more customers, more card tables, and more rooms rented. Second, where do people go in this town? What is there to do? When someone dies, you go to the coffin-maker. When there's a party, you go to the dress-maker. But when either one happens, and many more things besides, you go to Peabody's.

"'What's more, I already talked with Peabody. He's willing to give us a substantial stake for not a lot of risk, given we're the only legal lender in town.'

"Plimpton digested what the boy told him for a moment, and then a broad smile crept across his face. He stood and walked around his desk, and taking the boy's hand, said,

'Welcome to the world of finance, my boy. You're going to go far.'

"And Franklin did go far. In just a few short years he was making practically every major financial decision at the bank. Like King Solomon of old, people would see him from far and wide, and they'd have to get his permission for a loan, or else they wouldn't get one. As Franklin became more and more confident in his position, his lending practices became more and more shrewd. He would only accept the most usurious of terms, and it wasn't unheard of that the bank would foreclose on businesses and homes when the payments weren't kept up.

"One day an old man and woman hobbled into his office at the bank and begged for a loan. The crops were failing, they said, and they just needed enough money to make it through the winter.

"'And what collateral do you offer?' Franklin asked.

"'The only thing of value we own,' said the man. 'Our farm.'

"Franklin wrote something down on a piece of paper. 'And just where is this farm?'

"The man told him.

"'That old dump? said Franklin. 'That farm wouldn't serve as collateral for half that loan!'

"'But son,' cried the man, 'couldn't you just help us through the winter? It isn't too much to ask!'

"'Certainly not,' replied Franklin. 'Do you think I've learned nothing as a banker?'"

Wilson sat trembling in his bedroll. When he could bring himself to speak, he said, "That's—that's horrifying."

"I told you it was scary," said the sheriff.

"You were right. I won't sleep for a week."

7.

BLACK IS THE NEW PINK

I like to make lists. Lists put things in their place. They help to make sense of life. Prioritize it. Like a grocery list, or a list of wanted criminals. You know what needs to get done, and you're not worried you'll miss something, because there it all is—on the list.

One thing that lists aren't is shy. They get right up in your face. What's first, they'll ask. Which thing's at the top? What comes next? Why didn't you put that one up there? Don't you love her anymore? Lists aren't afraid to ask these questions.

And lists have the potential for providing endless satisfaction. You know that feeling you get when you're able to cross something off your list? You can get that feeling whenever you want. Just add more things to the list.

Sometimes I add things to a list I've already done, just to be able to cross them off.

To sum up:

1. *Lists help to make sense of life*
2. *Lists aren't shy*
3. *Crossing off stuff is fun*

"Call," said Abernathy Jones calmly. He found himself, due to circumstances he could hardly discern, in the middle of a high-stakes poker game with three individuals he had just met that day. He had gone downstairs from his room to speak with the barkeeper, Al, a delightful man full of stories of events he had never taken part in, when all of a sudden he heard a rough voice calling to him from across the room.

It was late afternoon and the saloon was empty—or else Abernathy wouldn't have been there; he shied away from crowds—save for a table of three men of varying degrees of desperation and sobriety. He excused himself from Al's presence and took his drink over to the men.

"Good afternoon to you, gentlemen. How may I be of service?"

A gruff old man—older by far than the other two—gathered some mucus from the back of his throat and spat it onto the ground beside him. "Service? You may be of service by sitting down and losing all your money to us, lad!" Then he coughed his way through a paroxysm of laughter.

As Abernathy sat down one of the other players, a trim man who looked as though he had been out of work for some time, said, "Thanks, stranger. Our fourth had to get home to the wife and kids."

"Poker's just not fun with only three," said the other man, who could have been the trim man's brother, except that he was tremendously fat. "I'm Carl, and that's my brother, Carter. And this here's—well, we didn't quite catch your name, sir."

The old man couldn't answer, as he was still in a laughing fit. Or it could have been a coughing fit.

"Pleased to meet each of you. Abernathy Jones is my name. I'm afraid I haven't played poker in quite some time."

The brothers smiled at one another, while the old man continued to laugh.

"I'd be happy to partake in your game, but knowing my habits, I must place some limits on myself. This is all I'm comfortably willing to play with"—he set a modest amount of money onto the table—"and I will play until my money is gone or the hour is up." He gestured to the clock standing in the corner.

"Sounds like a man who doesn't like to get into trouble," Carter said with a smile.

"On the contrary," Abernathy replied, and he began shuffling the deck.

Over the next forty-five minutes Abernathy won hands and lost them, sipped at his drink, and tried to ignore the fact that Carl was blatantly pulling cards from his sleeve. He discovered that the old man, Martin Mansfield III was his name, had a wild-eyed way of looking at people and things, like a sea captain or a drunk toddler. Most of the time Martin was either laughing or staring intently across the room at nothing in particular.

But toward the end of Abernathy's allotted hour, just as he called the hand, Martin looked him straight in the eyes with that strange intensity.

"I know what you're after," he said.

"I beg your pardon?"

"I said that I know what you're after. I can smell it on you." Martin inhaled deeply, as if he was trying to sniff a flower from across the room. Gone was the raucous laughter of nearly an hour before. "You know you're playing a dangerous game, don't you?"

The two brothers glanced at each other uneasily.

"I'm sure I don't know what you're talking about," said Abernathy, looking quickly at the clock.

"I'm sure that you do. If you want to play that game, that's your wager. But a word of advance, mister. It ain't natural. You shouldn't be seeking them out. It's bad enough when they come to you."

"How do you know this?" asked Abernathy quietly.

"As a told you before, I can smell it on you."

"But you don't understand. I'm not going to—it's a job, see. It's something I have to do, something I signed up to do a long time ago."

The old man spat on the floor again. "I was over the border in earlier days, in a town I can't recall, in a saloon a lot like this one. A man there told me a story. He told me of a fellow who grew so sick of living in human civilization, so sick of talking with people and doing whatever everyone expects that he left. And before long he met up with them. And do you know what he did?"

"What did he do?"

"He stayed with them. He lived with them. Not as one of them, but as himself, you understand."

Silence hung over the table. The cards were forgotten.

"They didn't eat him?" asked Carl.

"No," said Martin. "They accepted him."

He looked straight at Abernathy again with that crazy gaze. "I don't know what would be worse."

Just then the clock chimed, and they threw down their cards as if automatons. Abernathy had the best hand. He added the pot to the rest of his money and counted it up.

It was exactly what he had started with. He had broken even.

Bill's General Store was nearly empty as Abernathy stepped across its threshold and was confronted by a large sack of barley. Two old women trying to decide whether to buy some fabric were the only patrons in the place. Abernathy listened to their conversation as he browsed the aisles, his gaze dancing from bull whips to snake oil, from coyote jerky to pre-owned chaps.

"I like the pattern," said a round woman with too many teeth, "but I'm not sure of the color."

"Oh, black is the new pink," said Bill, holding the bolt of fabric higher so the women could get a better look at all its fashionable qualities.

"I rather like it for a dress," said the other woman, who held a severe expression on her face. She wore a high-necked dress with a cameo at her throat—the only skin she allowed to show was her face and hands. "My husband would look wonderful in it."

Bill and the toothy woman stared with eyebrows raised, neither looking directly at the other woman. Bill's mouth had come open a bit, but before the woman with the free-spirited husband could notice, he gulped and said, "All right, then, I'll just wrap it up for you." He disappeared quickly into a back room with the bolt of fabric and reemerged with a tissue-wrapped package.

"Here you are," he said. "I don't know if your husband would be interested, but I just got in a shipment of heels from the East." He produced a delicate-looking shoe from behind the counter for them to admire.

"Well!" said the severe woman. "Whatever gave you the idea that my husband would be caught dead walking around in women's shoes?"

Bill's jaw once again lowered involuntarily. The woman said, "Come on, Martha. I'm sure we can find a store that's more respectful of its patrons!"

As Bill recovered from the shock of his unorthodox customers, Abernathy made his way unnoticed to the counter. He had to clear his throat twice before Bill looked up.

"Sorry, Abernathy," he said, taking his hand warmly and shaking it. "I just can't quite understand the people in this town."

"Sweetest citizens on earth," said Abernathy.

"Sweetest, maybe, but craziest, certainly."

"Oh, I don't know. The woman was just looking out for the interests of her husband. No harm in that."

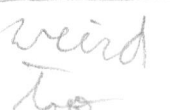

"You're a charitable man, Abernathy Jones. But I suppose I wouldn't have this shop if that weren't true."

Abernathy waved his hand as if shooing a fly. "It was just a little seed money. Besides, you did me any number of favors back home."

"And you've paid back any favors I did you a hundredfold." *modest (abernathy)*

"If you say so. By the way, any news on that fellow I was asking you about?"

"Funny you should ask. A fur trader was in here just yesterday said someone who basically matched the description you gave was out to the east, raising all kinds of ruckus. Said he was one mean son of a bitch."

"That sounds rather promising. I remember him as one mean son of a bitch. Where's this trader staying?"

"I'm afraid he was just passing through. Didn't even stay the night. He did say he would look in at the sheriff's office and file a report. You might want to try there."

"Much obliged, Bill," said Abernathy.

"Say, what line of work are you in now, anyway?"

Abernathy reached into the inner pocket of his duster and handed Bill a card. It read:

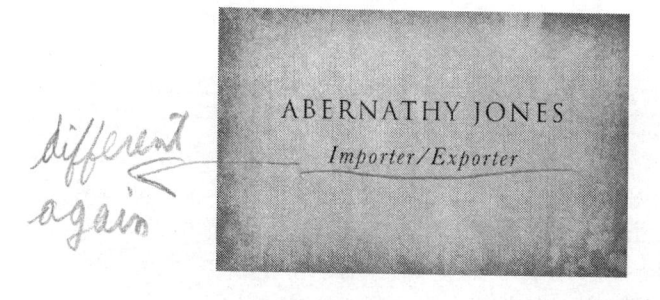

different again

ABERNATHY JONES
Importer/Exporter

Bill gave a low whistle as he read the business card. "That's luck for you and me both. I've been looking for an importer for a while now. Can't seem to keep chips in stock."

"Potato?"

"Poker."

"I'm your man," said Abernathy with a smile.

The Phoenix sheriff's office was perhaps bigger than most, but that didn't mean it was big. As a matter of fact it had just two cells, a desk for business, and a table for the boys to play cards. The only thing that made it bigger was the scrawniness of the deputies and the lack of pay.

"Fur trader?" said Sheriff Wilcox between puffs of his enormous cigar. "Sure, he passed through yesterday, said he was heading to California. Probably one of those gold-crazed loons. Said he wanted to do his civic duty or some such nonsense. I don't know why anyone would go to the bother of reporting those monsters, since anyone with half a brain and an ounce of compassion would shoot them on sight. But I took his statement. Even had Earl here draw up his portrait real nice and pretty."

Abernathy perked up at this news. "A portrait? Would you mind if I had a look?"

Sheriff Wilcox squinted at him with one eye. "You ain't trying anything funny, are you? I mean, you're not a—sympathizer, are you?"

Abernathy looked shocked, and a little insulted. "Far from it, sheriff. If I had my way they'd all be round up and shot."

The sheriff continued to squint for a moment, but then apparently decided Abernathy's intentions were true. "All right, then," he said, gesturing to a cork board on the wall. "There it is. Look all you want."

Abernathy made sure not to appear too excited as he walked over to the board and scanned the various wanted posters. And—

There it was. Third from the top. A rough portrait of a rough man, greasy hair, a sneer on his mouth. One eye. Beneath the man's picture in bold, uppercase letters:

The Zombie Sheriff Takes Tucson

<u>WANTED</u>

UNDEAD OR ALIVE

THE SHERIFF

"That him?" Abernathy jumped, the voice came from so near. He turned to see Sheriff Wilcox glancing at the poster from over his shoulder, a thin ribbon of cigar smoke cutting his face in two.

"It is," said Abernathy.

"Well, I don't know why you're looking for him, young man, but let me tell you. This one's no ordinary ghoul. I've been on the job here for more than twenty years, and I've never seen one so...intelligent. He knows what he's doing, somehow."

"Oh, the sheriff's intelligent, all right."

Again Sheriff Wilcox gave him the squint. "You talk like you know that thing."

"No, sir," said Abernathy quickly. "Just heard things. Like you."

"Well, make sure you keep it at just hearing. Because if something happens to you out there among those monsters, ain't nobody going to be there to save you."

8.

MISSION: LI 2C ME/I LWOO*M SFD

What—Love at first sight?
A myth espoused by sad fools?
No. It does doubt exist.

From cavemen and elk,
To Romeo and his Jules:
Love sans prior sight.

But what of today?
Can love last that with a glance
Begins? I think not.

The sheriff woke before dawn the next morning after a restful sleep. It was nice to have company out in the wild, even if it was just for one night. He thought about the evening before and the story of the evil banker he had told Wilson. He had warned the boy. If he hadn't slept, it was his own fault.

He looked over at the bedroll across the campfire and found it was empty. Where had the boy run off to so early?

The sheriff stretched his old limbs until he heard a few pops. He reflected that his body wasn't as young as it once was. He searched the campsite for Wilson. It was emptier than a slickskin's skull after the Brigade got done with it. He called for the boy but got no response. Then he saw it.

It was one of the smoking fire-sticks the slickskins used, and it was still smoldering. There was only one conclusion the sheriff could come to.

Wilson was a slickskin. *impossible—eats brains*

Or, on second thought, maybe the slickskins had found Wilson, captured him, and were off doing nefarious things to him. After some reflection the sheriff conceded that the second conclusion was perhaps more likely.

Slowly, very slowly, the sheriff took the tin star from his vest, spat on it, and shined it on the cuff of his sleeve. He reattached it.

He had a job to do. He would find Wilson if it meant searching till the end of his days. Or at least until he found some slickskins and got hungry. But he would find him. The law's the law, after all.

As quickly as he could the sheriff gathered his few belongings and broke camp. It would be fiendishly hard to track down Wilson without a horse, but maybe, just maybe, the slickskins didn't have horses either. They would still have the proper use of their ankles, however, which made the need for urgency all the more pressing.

After an hour of tracking the faint footfalls of his prey, the sheriff was satisfied there weren't any horses in the party, and he was heartened by another sign. Every once in a while the sheriff came across a long scuffling mark, and the sheriff hadn't met a slickskin yet who walked like that. It could only be Wilson—alive (or at least not dead again). They were marching him somewhere. Although he was relieved at his friend's continued undead existence, chills ran up the sheriff's spine at the thought of what the slickskins might do to him. He hastened his pace.

The sheriff knew it would be a challenge to catch up to his prey, but he had a huge advantage. Slickskins had to stop at night to rest, due to their delicate immune system, whereas a member of the undead only slept as a luxury, or out of boredom. Or sometimes after sex. He was therefore convinced that he would gain on them, however slow his pace might be compared to theirs, and if their destination was far enough away, he would catch them.

A little after noon on the second day his theory was validated when he came across a campsite. The fire had long since gone cold, but beside it he found two helpful clues. The first was another of the fire-sticks of the slickskins; the second, a hastily scrawled note. The note read:

LI 2C ME/I LWOO*M SFD, DSF IMLS-E F HHJ4
—Wilson

The sheriff was overcome with joy. His pursuit was not in vain; the boy was alive and clever enough to steal a scrap of paper and write a note on it! His resolve hardened. Also he would have to teach the boy some spelling once he caught up to him.

The next few days were uneventful save that the sheriff repeatedly found those same smoking fire-sticks. Eventually they even began to feel warm, as if the night's chill hadn't fallen on them.

It was days and days of constant tracking before the sheriff knew he was finally getting close to the party of slickskins. One morning, for the first time, he came across a fire-stick that still let off smoke. He slowly bent over, picked it up, and took a few puffs.

And coughed uncontrollably. How the slickskins enjoyed these things was beyond him. He was afraid the thing would kill him—and he was already dead.

His damned spirit soaring at this new, life-threatening sign of good fortune, the sheriff set off with renewed vigor, and it wasn't long before his tenacity was rewarded.

The Zombie Sheriff Takes Tucson

A few hours after the discovery of the smoking fire-stick he started to hear voices in the distance. As he drew closer he began to discern that they were arguing over something. Trying to keep his moaning to a minimum, the sheriff peered over a rise at the small party of slickskins below. What he saw made what little blood that was still circulating in his body boil.

The party of slickskins seemed to be in disagreement and had split in two. The nearer group, maybe five or six in number, had a small captive—which could only be Wilson—with his arms tied behind his back, and a length of rope tied around his neck like a leash. The farther group, of about the same size, also had a captive.

(A short note on the sheriff's romantic life over the past twenty years might be appropriate at this juncture. In sum, he had none to speak of. His task of tirelessly upholding truth and justice had kept him from making any meaningful attachment with the fairer sex, but it did nothing to quell the desire for it. He was no prude; when he rode into town after a long mission he might frequent the ladies of the night at the local brothel now and again, but he had never had the social structure built into his life to make the acquaintance of a truly refined gentlewoman.)

Before him now, however—the other captive...

She was the most beautiful creature the sheriff had ever seen. Long blond hair framed her begrimed face, two luminous gray eyes bracketed a hollow nasal cavity, and her crimson lips were torn away on the right side, revealing teeth as white as pearls. She was perfection itself.

Unbidden, images from out of the past—seeped—into the sheriff's visual conscious, visions he hadn't recalled in nearly twenty years. An image of a thinner sheriff, bashful and awkward still with youth. A lithe girl in a meadow, her dewy white skin flushed with the exertions of a country hike. A dinner at the house of her father—chicken and potatoes.

The echoes superimposed themselves on what the sheriff was seeing now.

Fate, it seemed, had decided to take a hand—and place such a lady before him at this very moment. So love-struck was he that he nearly forgot about his original purpose—the rescue of Wilson—completely.

Meanwhile, the two groups of slickskins were arguing more and more vociferously. A tall, thin man in the nearer group shouted, "We need to end this here! The longer we take these things with us, the more danger we put ourselves in."

A man with red side-whiskers from the farther group answered him, "They are paying good money. How could they harm us? There's a boy and a woman with half her face missing—and we've got both of them tied up."

The remark concerning the lady drew the sheriff's attention once again to the lovely being in the farther group. She was beautiful indeed. And yet her eyes seemed to carry a great sadness. How he yearned to relieve her of that sadness!

"What was that?"

Without meaning to, the sheriff had let out a loud meandering moan while thinking of his lady. The men had heard.

The closer group seemed to turn as one, and guns bristled from their midst. The farther group, however—they were fleeing! And with them, that gorgeous specimen of womanhood!

The sheriff stumbled down the hill as quickly as he could, arms before him in supplication. His moans grew louder and more sorrowful. He would have yelled, Wait! Wait! but for the emotion pouring from his lips.

He was vaguely aware that the remaining slickskins had begun firing on him, but he didn't care. As it happened, they were particularly poor shots and most of their bullets fell into the earth or lodged into his legs.

The Zombie Sheriff Takes Tucson

When he reached the group of slickskins he tore into them as savagely as ever he had. It was a maelstrom of limbs and blood and bones and more blood. But the sheriff wasn't even paying attention to the fight. His eyes were on the horizon, where already the tiny form of his ladylove was disappearing into the sunset.

The slickskins had all been obliterated, until it was difficult not only to discern where individual bodies began and ended, but also from what part of the body individual limbs had come.

In the midst of the carnage, splattered in buckets of blood, calmly stood Wilson, his arms still tied behind his back.

"Thanks for rescuing me, sheriff."

"You're welcome, kid," said the sheriff, almost as an afterthought.

9.

Wilson's Tale

The word 'package' starts with the letter P. It is a deceptive word. 'Pack' implies something placed somewhere for some purpose. But 'age' adds a very different connotation to the word. What is in this mysterious package, and how long has it been in there? What, exactly, is its 'age'?

These are questions that can never be answered. Timeless questions that have been asked since the first husband was shamed into putting the first inadequate gift into the first box to give to his upset wife. Packages are attempts, but they are rarely successes.

'Penitent' also starts with the letter P.

After he had loosed the boy's bonds and the two feasted on the half dozen mutilated corpses for a time, the sheriff's grief finally overcame him. He wandered over to a rock and collapsed against it. A glazed look came into his eye. At first Wilson was too busy devouring his former captives' corpses to notice the absence of the sheriff, but then he saw the sorrowful posture taken up by the most heroic of men.

"You hurt, sheriff?" asked the boy.

"I sure am, Wilson. I'm hurt real bad. Hurt where you can't see the wound."

Wilson, as a still relatively inexperienced member of the undead race, had no idea what the man was talking about. "They get you in the balls?"

"No, son. Much worse than that. They got me in the heart."

Now Wilson was really confused. He had personally known at least five people whose hearts had been completely removed from their bodies, whether through fights with slickskins or general decay, who had gone on to live perfectly normal undead lives. It couldn't have been such a big thing for the sheriff to lose his heart.

"Well, sheriff...I'm real sorry to hear that. You can have my heart if you want. It's a little small, but we can probably make it fit."

The sheriff's visage softened at Wilson's words. "You're a good man, you know that?" The boy puffed up at the unlooked-for compliment.

"I've traveled far and wide around these parts, Wilson. I've seen all kinds of women—thin, fat, fair, dark, tall, short. But I haven't ever seen a woman as beautiful as the one I've seen today."

"I see. What makes her so attractive?"

Again the flashes of the pale girl in the meadow.

"Well, she's beautiful on the outside, of course. Long golden locks. A face to die for. But what really gets me is her inner beauty. Oh, you may say, how can you know she has inner beauty when you haven't even talked to the woman? But I know. I know the way you know about a good brain.

"I love that she gets cold when it's 91 degrees out. I love that it takes her an hour and a half to eat a tendon. I love that she gets a little crinkle above her nose when she's thinking about eating some slickskin's brain. I love that after I spend just a few minutes with her, I can still smell her unique odor of decay on my clothes. And I love that she is the last person I want to talk to before I go to sleep at night.

And it's not because I'm lonely, and it's not because it's All Hallows' Eve. I've got to find her, because when you realize you want to spend the rest of your life with somebody, you want the rest of your life to start as soon as possible."

"It's All Hallows' Eve?" asked Wilson.

"I think so."

"Well, sheriff, I'm happy you found someone you're so in love with. Everyone deserves to find happiness, and you most of all. What's her name?"

"I don't know."

"You don't know her name? And you've never spoken to her? Wait a minute—are you talking about Jezebel? The woman they captured along with me?"

"Jezebel. What a lovely name. Yes, Wilson, if Jezebel is the woman who was with that other gang of slickskins that so cowardishly ran off, then Jezebel is my love."

"Nice choice."

"I'm glad you approve. But please, if my friendship has meant anything to you, tell me all your story, every second from the time you left our camp to this moment."

"Every second? Like when I went to the bathroom and stuff?"

"You can leave that out, I suppose, but please, tell me what happened."

"Well, it all started when I woke up that morning and saw you were still sleeping. I said to myself, 'Maybe, just maybe, if I surprise the sheriff with a nice fresh breakfast he'll reconsider and make me his deputy after all.' I didn't think you really would just because I brought you breakfast, but I was trying to show you how useful I could be.

"But it sort of came out the opposite—instead of being a use to you I caused you a whole heck of a lot of trouble. And for that I'm sorry, sheriff, I truly am.

"It wasn't long that I was out tracking, trying to find a coyote or maybe a nice javelina, when I heard something rustle a ways away. I thought that was my moment, so I crept up on it from the side to get a look at it, and wouldn't you know—it was a slickskin! He was just an average-looking slickskin, not too young, not too old. Juicy. My mouth started watering just thinking about him. Then I thought how impressive it would be, me bringing you back a whole slickskin for breakfast. You were sure to make me a deputy for that.

"I guess my enthusiasm kind of got away from me, because I forgot the first rule of slickskin hunting—they never travel alone. I just went straight for the guy, arms out, wailing away with excitement.

"I tell you, sheriff, the guy just turned and looked at me coming at him, even had a little smile on his face, like he knew I was there the whole time. And I bet he did, too, because just before I was within arm's reach of him, I was ambushed. There were two or three other slickskins hiding out in a tree just above, and they threw down a weighted net right on top of me.

"Well, after the net, I couldn't tell you too much about where they took me, as they put this hood or some such over my head, tied my hands up real good behind my back, and put a rope around my neck. I didn't know what to think. Who ever heard of slickskins taking somebody captive? What were they going to do with me? Welcome me into their rotten, good-for-nothing society? I found out soon enough.

"They marched me for at least two days. I could tell because they seemed to camp for a bit at night, but it wasn't a very long rest, even by slickskin standards.

"Then, about noon on the third day, we stopped. I wasn't too clear on the particulars, but it seemed we were waiting for something. I remember a man with a real gruff voice, who I sort of worked out was their leader or something saying, 'By God, if they're much later, I'm giving up this whole thing. We'll put an end to it right here, I swear.' I couldn't see anything at all, but he seemed pretty upset.

"We did wait longer—quite a bit longer, it seemed to me, but of course I couldn't be sure. But then I heard it. It was that sound slickskins make when they aren't trying to be sneaky—you can hear them from miles around.

"Old gruff voice said, 'About damn time your crew showed, Anderson! We've been waiting here hours. Beginning to think we should rename this spot; "rendezvous point" doesn't sound quite right when there isn't any rendezvous.'

"'McFarland,' said a voice from farther off, 'if I say I'm going to be somewheres, I'm damn sure going to be there, you can be sure of it! Let's stop the chatter and talk about why we're really here. You have your package?'"

"Wait a second," said the sheriff. "Did you say McFarland?"

"Yeah. At least I think that was his name."

The sheriff's face had brightened, and he said almost savagely, "Go on."

"Then the Anderson guy said, 'Course we do. You have yours?'

"'Signed, sealed, and delivered. Let's see what you got.'

"Suddenly I felt a tremendous tug on the rope around my neck. I was pretty used to it by then, since they never touched me, just used that leash to lead me around like a dog.

"When I had taken maybe two dozen steps, the hood they had put over my head was yanked off, and I was blinded in that noontime sun.

"I got a sense that the slickskins around me drew back a bit. You know how they're always afraid, even when they have the numbers, the cowards. McFarland said, 'But you got yourself just a baby one. I thought orders was to come back with a full-sized man-eater?'

The Zombie Sheriff Takes Tucson

"'He'll do just fine,' said Anderson. 'He's nearly full size anyway. Let's see yours.'

"By this time my vision had adjusted and I could make out the vile slickskins all around me. There were six in the group that brought me there, and the same number in the group that had just arrived. They all looked like they'd been traveling for weeks—not like normal slickskins who wallow in a pool of water every day when they're in a town. Most of these men had dirt caked on them."

"So you saw him then, when they took off your hood?" interrupted the sheriff. "You actually saw McFarland?"

"Yeah, I guess I did."

The sheriff reached into his vest and brought out the sketch. "Did he look like this?"

Wilson only had to look at the drawing for a moment. "That's him, all right. Near perfect likeness."

The sheriff nodded. "Go on."

"After Anderson asked to see the other ghoul, the men of McFarland's group shifted a bit, and out came a figure in the same condition as me: hands tied behind the back, rope around the neck. She still had her hood on, though.

"And when they removed it, there was Jezebel. I don't need to describe her, since you've seen her, sheriff, but she was sure a sight for sore eyes. I didn't pay much attention to what the slickskins said after that, as I had some words with Miss Jezebel. Not sure why they let us speak to one another, but I was sure glad of it.

"'Hi, there. Name's Wilson,' I said to her.

"'Jezebel. Pleased to make your acquaintance.' She had a pretty little voice. Not too high pitched like some women you come across. Hers was sweet, like honey.

"'Well, Miss Jezebel, we're in a tight spot. How'd they capture you?'

Her jaw tightened as the memories came back. "'I was just feeding the hens on my father's farm when I saw this big old cloud of dust coming up the lane. I thought to myself, "This can't be good." And it wasn't.

"'Before I even had time to scream, they were on me. They roped me like a common steer, put this big sack over my head. I reckon I haven't seen the light of day since, until this very hour. But I know what they did next—I could hear the sound of what they did to Daddy, and I could smell the burning of the farm. The monsters!'

"'Well that's horrible,' I said, 'them doing that to a lady. I can tolerate it myself, since I'm a man and all, but it just ain't right to handle a lady rough like that.'

"At these words, the corner of her mouth went up in half a smile. Which I guess was a whole smile for her, seeing as she only had one side of her mouth.

"'But did you hear them talking at all? Do you know what they want with us?'

"'I did hear them now and again,' said Jezebel. 'It seems they are being paid to bring us in.'

"'Paid? What slickskin would pay to get one of us? The only interest I've ever seen them have with us is using us for target practice. Not that I mind, that is, since I'm really good at eluding attacks and whatnot.'

"Jezebel glanced over at the slickskins, but they still weren't paying any attention to us. 'I think they mentioned his name once, the man who they're bringing us to. Dr. Gimple-Heckman or something like that.'

"'Gimple-Heckman?' I said. 'Must be a Chinaman. I don't trust Chinamen. You never know what they're going to do next. We've got to get out of here, Jezebel.'

"'Oh? I was sort of enjoying being held against my will.'

"'You were?'

"'No, I was being sarcastic. What's your plan for getting us out of here?'

"'Okay, here's what we'll do—'

"Just then the slickskins began yelling at one another. The man with the gruff voice shouted, 'You realize what Gimmler-Heichman's going to do to these things? Do you know what he's trying to accomplish?'

"Another man, who seemed just as upset as the first man, shouted back, 'I don't care what he's going to do with them. It's not my job to care!

"'We need to end this here! The longer we take these things with us, the more danger we put ourselves in.'

"'Why'd you sign up for the job if you didn't want to see it through? They're paying good money. Besides, how could they do us any harm? There's a boy and a woman with half her face missing—and we've got both of them tied up.'

"But then all the slickskins turned toward a nearby hillside. And that's where you come in. Before I even knew what happened, that group of slickskins absconded with Jezebel and you were down that hill and mauling slickskins left and right.

"And that's the story, front to back. What do you make of it, sheriff?"

The sheriff thought about it for a long while, stroking his chin in concentration. Finally he seemed to reach some conclusion.

"We're going to need some horses," was all he said.

10.

In Which the Gentlemen Acquire Some Horses

At first glance, most flowers appear to be innocuous. What's not to like? They smell good. They come in a wide variety of colors. Women swoon for them. But there is a darker, more sinister side to flowers that most haven't even dreamed of.

In truth, flowers are an ancient sign of evil that persists to this day. Clowns wear them in their lapels, offering small children the chance to take a fragrant whiff, until—BAM!—water in the face. Sometimes it's acid.

An evil warlock of old created the seemingly harmless tradition of he-loves-me-he-loves-me-not, raising the hopes of thousands of young girls. But he knew full well that all the flowers in the area had an even number of petals. Suicides shot sky high.

Then there is the siren orchid of Panama, which has petals of intoxicating beauty. When an admirer is drawn too close, however, a malodorous baboon—with which the siren orchid has developed a symbiotic relationship—swings down from the trees and clubs the admirer over the head.

This is why it is important never to pick or smell flowers, and to always wear headgear when admiring them.

* * *

The sheriff reflected on all the boy had said once they started after Jezebel. Who was this Gimmler-Heichman, and what did he want with the undead? Whatever it was, the sheriff was sure he didn't want Jezebel to be the one to find out. Beauties like that come along once in a lifetime. He could still see her missing cheek when he closed his eye, and he longed to gently kiss it, to softly run his hand along her skin, now smooth, now decaying, now smooth again.

The plan was to go as far as they had to on foot until they could find at least one horse to significantly speed up their pursuit. Neither the sheriff nor Wilson knew the terrain here very well, but they knew they were headed in the direction of Tucson, and they knew they'd get to where they were going a lot faster atop a horse or two.

"Now Wilson," said the sheriff, "have you ever ridden a horse before?"

"Of course I have, sheriff. Just a few weeks ago the Brigade found a small group of slickskins with horses. I got up on that horse for a good five minutes, trotting around, galloping. You know, riding it."

"And why only five minutes?" the sheriff asked knowingly.

"Well, I, er, got sort of hungry."

"That's exactly why I bring this up. If you're going to ride a horse, you have to have willpower. You can't look at the horse as an animal; you have to see it only as transportation. Transportation that we need right now."

Wilson ducked his head a bit. He knew this might be a problem for him. It was just that riding a horse, with the feel of living meat right there beneath you, was too much to bear. How could you help but take a bite? And of course if you've taken one bite, the horse isn't likely to last too much longer, so you might as well finish it off.

A thought struck him. "Sheriff, how is it that the slickskins are able to not eat their horses?"

The Zombie Sheriff Takes Tucson

[handwritten: very smart & knowledgeable. Not]

"The only slickskins that eat their horses are the French."

"Oh. The slickskins around here aren't French?"

"They sure aren't."

"If you say so."

Suddenly Wilson stopped in his tracks and cocked his head to one side. "Hey! What's that?"

"What's what?"

"Listen."

Sure enough, once the sheriff concentrated enough he heard the faint clip-clop of horses' hooves gradually getting louder.

"Boy, you'll be a deputy yet. Well done. Let's hide behind these trees and try to get the jump on them."

The sheriff led Wilson to a small clump of trees beside the faint trail they'd been following. "Now be ready to jump out as quick as you can. We should come out before they're on us to give ourselves time to get at the horses. Otherwise they'll just run us over."

"You got it, sheriff."

They could feel the hoof beats through the ground now as well as hear them. The sheriff tingled with anticipation. Wilson tingled with hunger.

Then all at once they could make out the pair of horses racing toward them, the two slickskins riding them without a care in the world. With a low moan the sheriff stumbled out of the trees and shuffled as quickly as he could toward the horses with Wilson in hot pursuit.

The horses reared up on their hind legs, and it was all the riders could do to avoid being bucked off. "Whoa!" they cried, ignorant of the cause of their horses' distress. When the horses had regained their footing, the slickskins got a look at their two assailants and let out a stream of expletives. One let out a stream into his pants.

The riders forsook the path completely, riding directly into the rocky terrain that surrounded them. This was something the sheriff, always the linear thinker, hadn't accounted for.

"After them!" he shouted, furious that his prey had eluded him.

the title

Charles and Edgar Gardner were brothers brought up a few days' ride from Tucson in a small cabin in the woods. When their parents died in a tragic flower-picking incident, the two brothers were just barely old enough in the eyes of the state to continue living in the cabin without guardians.

This arrangement became much more awkward three years later when Charles married Lucinda, a young woman from the next town over. Throughout their engagement Charles and Lucinda dropped hints to Edgar that it might be time for him to find his own place, or at the very least to construct an addition to their cramped living conditions, but Edgar, whether through willful ignorance or natural stupidity, failed to receive this message.

The wedding came and went and Lucinda found herself moving into a one-room cabin with her husband and her brother-in-law both, and the only privacy afforded the newlyweds was a sheet draped from the ceiling that didn't even touch the floor.

It was the third week of wedded bliss, and Lucinda sat tending the supper fire alone while she waited for Charles and Edgar to return from a nearby village. It had been a rough three weeks, there was no doubt about it. Between Edgar's farting and belching, it was nearly impossible to focus on her new life with Charles. It was the stinkiest cabin she'd ever entered. And now it was her home.

She nodded to herself as she made the decision. When the men returned, she would take Charles aside and tell him it was either Edgar or her—she wouldn't sleep one more night under the same roof with that dullard. She nodded again. That's what she would say, just like that—wouldn't sleep one more night—

Her head shot up, the image of the fire still burned on her vision in reverse. Surely those were the men now. But why in such a hurry? She'd never heard hoofbeats that quick before, not just outside her own door anyway. Were the fools racing each other home?

The door burst open and there was Charles with a look of madness in his eyes, Edgar right behind him.

"The hammer. My hammer, woman—where is it?"

"What? Charles, what's the matter?"

"Never mind. Where is my hammer?" Even as he asked the question he had taken up the hammer and a fistful of nails and started to examine the doorframe.

Edgar meanwhile took one of the chairs by its back, hoisted it above his head, and smashed it into the ground, sending bits of wood everywhere.

"Edgar, what on earth are you doing?"

Instead of a response, Edgar selected a solid piece from the chair's remains and silently handed it to his brother. Charles took up the plank and began nailing it diagonally across the corner of the door. Edgar began rummaging through the scraps again, looking for another suitable piece.

"Will someone please tell me what is going on!" Lucinda demanded.

After a moment, Charles turned to her. "Go to the window," he said. "Let me know if you see anything."

Lucinda did as she was instructed, pulling the curtains back from the window and looking out into the dusk. She didn't see anything out of the ordinary, just their humble little property and the two horses hitched out front.

"What am I supposed to be looking for? I don't see anything."

"You will soon enough," said Edgar, taking up another of the chairs and smashing it to pieces.

"We were followed coming back from town," said Charles.

"Followed? Not the Turner boys again? You'd think they'd have learned their lesson the last time."

"Not the Turner boys. Worse."

"Worse? You mean you're in some kind of trouble with the law? Or gamblers? Not outlaws!"

"Not those," said Charles. "Worse."

"Worse than...no! You can't mean it."

"I do. We saw two of them right in the middle of the path, arms out, moaning like their arses were on fire. We left the path as quick as we could, but they caught our scent."

"And once they catch your scent," said Edgar, "supposedly they won't let up until you're dead or they are—again."

"But I thought it was just a ghost story, something to tell the neighborhood children into going back home before sundown?"

"Is that what you thought?" asked Charles, starting to board up one of the windows. "Put out that fire."

Lucinda did as she was told. Now the only light came from a hurricane lantern whose door was nearly shut. The men continued their work until the door and both windows were boarded up completely except for a small sliver in one of the windows.

"I still don't see any sign of them," said Edgar, coming away from the crack.

"Maybe they didn't follow you after all," said Lucinda.

"They followed us, sure enough. They turned into the brush once we did and started in our direction."

Charles got the rifle down from the mantle and made sure it was loaded.

"There they are!" called Edgar. "I see them, clear as day." He could see a tall figure in a vest and another, shorter shape, both of them slowly stumbling toward the cabin.

"Let me have a look," said Lucinda. She shouldered him aside and looked out. "Oh, it's so horrible! God save us!"

After she retreated to the far corner of the cabin, her husband peered out at their attackers.

"It shouldn't be long now before they get to the house and start at the door. We need to be ready." He checked again that the rifle was loaded.

"Here," said Charles, and he handed his brother an axe.

An idea slowly formed in Lucinda's mind. "Oh, Lord, Lord, who will protect me? The horribleness of it all! Who will save me from this demon spawn?"

Charles walked over to her and placed a hand on her shoulder. "Lucinda, I'll protect you. I'll make sure they never lay a finger on you."

"And we're just supposed to sit here, trapped like animals waiting for slaughter?"

Charles's resolve hardened. "Edgar, open the door. I'm going out there. I don't know how many more of them there might be, but Lucinda is right. I need to protect my family."

"No!" Lucinda shrieked. "Don't you leave me!"

"Well, what do you want from me, woman?"

"I want you to stay here with me, to protect me. If only there was someone else who could venture out and save us from those beasts before they even reach the house."

She looked over at Edgar, who was peering out the window.

"Someone brave enough to face the danger," she continued in Edgar's direction, a little louder. "While my husband protects me here."

Edgar finally heard her entreaties. "I'll do it," he said, as if volunteering from a group of dozens. He stepped toward them and took the rifle from Charles. You both have been so kind to me, letting me stay on here after you got married, treating me as close as can be. It's the least I can do."

"But not the rifle!" said Lucinda. "You'll draw any number of those things toward us!"

"Fine." Edgar returned the rifle to Charles and took back the axe.

"Edgar, you are such a gentleman," said Lucinda. "Of course you don't need to do this to repay us; it's been our pleasure having you here, and we wouldn't have it any other way. God bless you for going out there, in the face of near certain death."

While Lucinda was speaking, Charles took his place at the window. "I—I think they're leaving."

"What?" asked his wife.

"I said I think they're leaving—I can't see too clearly, but their shadows look a lot farther down the road. Oh! Would you look at that?"

"What?" shouted Lucinda, pushing him aside to look out the window.

"They just disappeared. That was quick. Thought they couldn't walk that well."

"But you said once they caught our scent they would never let up until we died!"

"I don't know what to tell you. Guess I was wrong."

Lucinda tore open the door and looked out into the night. There was nothing there.

"Where'd they go?" she asked, half-crazed. She called again into the darkness, louder. "Where'd they go!"

Charles took her roughly by the shoulders and shushed her. "What are you trying to do, bring them back?"

Behind them, silhouetted in the doorway, Edgar asked, "Hey! Where are the horses?"

11.

Fool's Errand

There was a young man named Isaac. He traveled the world, did Isaac, meeting the people and seeing the sights. But when Isaac had made his way to Spain, he saw something he had never seen before: the most beautiful woman in the world.

Hyperbole is frequently used to refer to beautiful people and things, but in this case, hyperbole has no part of it. Isabella was quite literally the most beautiful woman in the world. Everyone who ever saw her freely admitted it, and marriage proposals came in almost daily.

The problem—and there is always a problem—is that Isabella's father was fully aware of the beauty he had created and was loathe to give it up. So he made a public decree. Anyone marrying his daughter would be slaughtered the day after the wedding.

Still, men from across the country couldn't help themselves: the proposals continued to pour in. Isabella, terrified what her father would do to the man if she accepted a proposal, rejected all the suitors.

Then came Isaac. There is a connection between two people who are meant to be together, a spark that ignites of its own accord. Isaac was far from the most handsome man in the world, but to Isabella it didn't matter.

So she said yes. They were married within a month, and the ceremony, a grand affair with no expense spared, was attended by not a few jealous young bachelors.

Isaac and Isabella spent one blissful night together. Then Isabella's father killed Isaac with an axe.

Sometimes the thing one wants most is the very thing that will get him killed with an axe.

Abernathy always started his day with a preparatory checklist. If any of the items on the list were missing, nothing could be accomplished that day to any degree of satisfaction until the missing items were rectified. In order of importance, the items on the checklist were:

1. A clean pair of underpants. Even when Abernathy ventured into the wilderness for weeks at a time, he was sure to bring enough clean undergarments, or enough soap for the job.
2. A long drink of water.
3. Seven minutes of deep meditation. To clear the mind; usually accompanied by heavy breathing, and occasionally by fluttering eyelids.
4. A few short words of thanks to his dear departed mother. He wasn't stupid enough to think that she could actually hear him, but it made him calmer all the same.
5. Urination. Self-explanatory.

Two days after his illuminating conversation with Sheriff Wilcox regarding the infamous sheriff, Abernathy had just finished his seven minutes of meditation and was beginning to explain to his mother why he preferred looser, less restricting underpants to the more binding alternative when his monologue was broken by three sharp raps at the door of his room.

The Zombie Sheriff Takes Tucson

Abernathy's eyes slid open in curiosity as he considered the door, still vibrating from the force of the knocks. Of course he could answer the door and see what his visitor wanted; but then his morning checklist would be put on hold, and nothing good came of delaying the checklist—he'd learned nothing in life if he hadn't learned that. He could just as easily ignore the apparently powerful person on the other side of the door, continue the rather odd topic of conversation that had popped into his mind that morning, and then gain the deep satisfaction of relieving himself in Al's fine outhouse.

The balance of the equation shifted as the knocking resumed, this time shivering some splinters out of the doorframe.

"All right then," said Abernathy. "Half a moment."

He unfolded himself from his position on the floor, unlocked the door, and opened it.

It was Sheriff Wilcox. "Sheriff, what a pleasant surprise!"

The sheriff gave him a look that said no one had ever viewed his presence as any kind of surprise but an unpleasant one.

"Right," he said. "I just got a cable from Tucson. Sheriff there tells me there's been trouble."

"Trouble? That's too bad."

"Ghoul trouble. Said he's never seen the undead stirred up so much. They're even organizing."

"Organizing? What do you mean?"

"You heard me. They've wandered around in groups before and happened upon helpless men and women, but now it's different. According to the Tucson sheriff, they're seeking out their prey with strategy in mind."

"You can't be serious."

"I can be serious, Mr. Jones, and I am. I came to you because you were asking about that particular ghoul that trader told of. He's behind all this."

Abernathy felt the blood drain from his face, and suddenly he wanted to repeat the second item on his checklist. He tried his hardest to forestall the fifth. Abernathy wanted the sheriff to be wrong, but he knew he wasn't. "But how can you know?"

"There's only one ghoul who has shown any sort of ability for this sort of thing. And he's been sighted."

"The sheriff?"

"The sheriff. A survivor ran into the Tucson sheriff's office, said she saw a ghoul with a vest and tin star wearing a duster. Couldn't be any other."

Abernathy heard himself take a deep breath. This was a stroke of luck, he told himself. He'd been looking for this ghoul—tracking him—for what seemed like years. There was a score to settle. So why didn't he feel lucky?

"I appreciate your taking the time to let me know, sheriff," he said.

Sheriff Wilcox made as if to leave, but hesitated at the door. "I won't pretend to think you aren't going after that thing. Maybe that's why I passed on the information. Maybe somebody needs to go hunting for that menace. Or maybe it's a fool's errand. I don't know."

He extended his hand, which Abernathy took. "But in any event, good luck."

When Sheriff Wilcox had departed, Abernathy waited a suitable amount of time for him to exit the building, and then ran down the stairs and straight to the outhouse. He found he would need a second pair of clean underpants that morning.

Later that day, Abernathy handed Al, the barkeep, a card that read in finely printed letters:

The Zombie Sheriff Takes Tucson

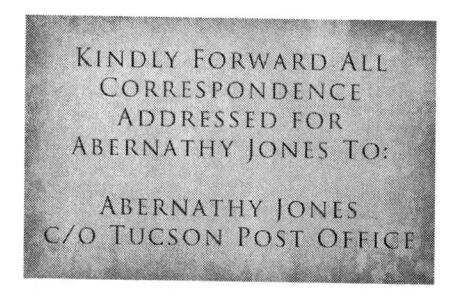

> Kindly Forward All Correspondence Addressed for Abernathy Jones To:
>
> Abernathy Jones
> c/o Tucson Post Office

Al, after reading over the card slowly, looked Abernathy in the eye and said, "Well, Abe, we're sure going to miss you around here."

"I can honestly say the feeling is mutual, Al." Abernathy extended his hand and shook Al's warmly.

"You'll be visiting?" asked Al.

"Count on it."

"Oh! I almost forgot. Don't go anywhere!" Al scrambled into the storeroom and came back with a long, narrow package. "This came for you just this morning."

"Nancy, you've outdone yourself once again," Abernathy said to himself. He took the parcel to an empty table and carefully unwrapped it. Contained within a box were five pair of new underpants, the current issue of *Typography Today*, and a jet-black cane.

"That's Nancy," he said.

Abernathy gave Al a letter for that very person. The letter read:

> Nancy, I finally have some positive news to report. Besides the general happy demeanor of the residents of Phoenix, they have helped me to a breakthrough in my quest to find the sheriff. Apparently he has been causing some problems for the fine people of Tucson.

Needless to say, my next destination will be that very same fair Tucson. Please send any future correspondence to the Tucson Post Office until I can establish myself at one of the what I'm sure will be more than adequate local accommodations. I will also leave a forwarding address with the proprietor of the Phoenix saloon from which I am departing. He is a pleasant man named Al.

As always, Nancy, your assistance is more than essential to the work I'm doing. Without your aid, I would probably still find myself in the admittedly charming state of New Jersey.

Upstairs Abernathy carefully packed the items Nancy had sent him with the rest of his belongings and checked to see that the cane was in proper order. Before bring his two bags downstairs, he left a card on the side table:

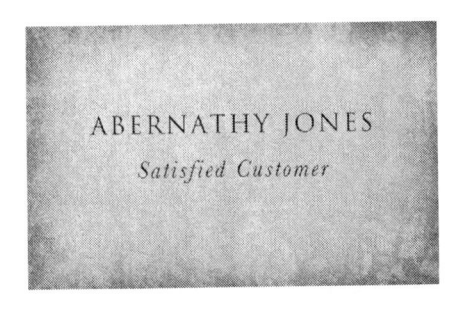

> ABERNATHY JONES
> *Satisfied Customer*

Out on the porch a youthful voice shouted, "Well there he is! The very man!" Abernathy looked over to see a crowd of people gathered around the orphan, who was playing a guitar as effortlessly as breathing. In front of him lay an overturned hat with a considerable amount of money in it.

"Mister, I don't know how to thank you," said the orphan. He turned back to his audience. "This is the man I

The Zombie Sheriff Takes Tucson

was telling you about. Somehow he knew I should be playing this guitar, and was he ever right!"

He walked over to Abernathy and held out a thick envelope. "I want you to have this. It's the least I can do to repay you."

"I wouldn't dream of it," said Abernathy. "Enjoy it."

"Sir, you are one of a kind," said the boy.

"You're too generous," said Abernathy.

Outside Bill's General Store Abernathy noticed a large pallet of boxes. He smiled to himself and entered the store.

"How are those poker chips working out for you?" he asked.

Bill gave him a bright smile. "You sure know business, Abe. I haven't seen poker chips move this quickly since the Poker Boom of '43. I'm getting another shipment next week, and I don't expect them to last more than a few days."

"That's fine," said Abernathy. "The other day you inquired about the possibility of exporting cactus liqueur to the East."

"I sure did. Any word?"

"I'll say. I have four buyers just wanting you to name your price and they'll take as much as you can give them."

Bill walked out from behind the counter and hugged Abernathy—who was unaccustomed to being hugged—quite vehemently. "You are a saint. We agreed on a 15% cut of profits for you?"

"Let's make it 5%."

"But—why?"

"One of my many mottoes is not to be too greedy. Would you mind keeping my funds for me until I return? Use it as a reserve. If times get tough, you'll have a little extra. If they don't, well, no harm done."

"Take this," he said, handing Bill a card. "This has the contact information of my assistant, Nancy. She can tell you where and how to send your liqueur, and I'm sure she can help you much more competently than I can."

Before Bill could go in for another hug, Abernathy shoved his hand toward the man and shook his.

"It's been a pleasure, Abe."

"All mine," he responded. "Oh, Bill? You wouldn't have a horse for sale, would you?"

12.

A Fallen Log

The hardest part of losing your leg is not feeling the wind blow through your leg hair anymore. It sounds silly, but I remember—back when I had both legs—arising early one fine spring morning and going on a walk through the countryside in short pants. The slight breeze made the tangled hairs on my calf rustle gently, small goose bumps appeared on the exposed skin, and the morning dew gloriously wet my boots. A wooden peg just doesn't give you the same experience.

I try the same walk nowadays and all I get is one leg with goose bumps and the other stuck in the mud. I know onlookers like to laugh. I would too if I were in their shoe(s). That's just human nature.

That's the thing about one-leggers—we attract more than a few gawkers. People—slickskins, that is—aren't shy about staring at your stump as you make your way down the road or pull up to the bar for a libation. To them it's a spectacle, something new, different, never-to-be-seen-again. Until next month, when they come across the man in the mining accident who lost his leg at his knee: then, again, it's a spectacle, something new, different, never-to-be-seen-again. They never consider the sorry fella they're staring at, let alone the feelings of the poor stump.

Horse riding takes some getting used to, but it's possible with time and patience. The benefits, of course, are enormous, since pedal locomotion has become such an inefficient shore. Having the use of a fine steed cuts travel time into a small fraction of what it would be, and it can provide a strong sense of accomplishment. Helps to get a horse that's been through his share of misfortune, too. After a while the horse even starts to feel sorry for you, especially if you decide not to attach a spur to the stump.

In general, ladies steer clear of a man with a peg leg. Most admit, rightly or wrongly, to an at least subconscious comparison to a different kind of stump. Alas—lonely are the nights of the one-legged man, unless he has money or luck, or both.

Some women do, however, view it as a kind of novelty. You wouldn't believe the kinds of things that can be done with a stump in the hands of the right woman. If you're curious, visit San Antonio. Sand the stump first.

There are other benefits to an artificial leg as well. Some manufacturers are starting to get clever and are building various compartments into their peg legs. Stumps R Us, one of the oldest names in handcrafted prosthetic legs, has just released a model that is completely hollow. When the mood strikes, it is possible to unscrew the stump and pour out a favorite spirit. Other variations include a peg leg with a custom niche for the concealment of a firearm or throwing knife and a model that retains its bark and a few branches for that woodsy feel.

Most long-time peg leg wearers will admit that hobbling around all day can take its toll on one's hip, so some have customized the stump with various gadgets, such as a roller skate or spring. I once saw a man bounce from his place of residence all the way to the saloon. He was too drunk to bounce back.

Peg legs can be made of any sort of wood, from fallen logs to the finest California redwood. A general rule, though, is to opt only for as good a quality wood as you're willing to defend. Stump thieves have made off with many a man's leg in the middle of the night, leaving him to shame-facedly hop down the stairs and ask for an ordinary old crutch. The black market for peg legs is so lu-

crative that bandits' attacks are getting more and more brazen by the day.

Pegleggers are famous for being isolationists. For instance, at the most recent PegConSW, the semi-annual peg leg convention for the southwestern United States, only three people were in attendance, and one turned out to be a salesman peddling wood polish.

There is a legend of an influential sea captain, Captain Longwood. He was a captain seasoned on the high seas. It was on a ship that he toddled as a toddler, ladded as a lad, and it was a ship he manned as a man. The exact details are as murky as the captain's soul, but as rumor has it, Captain Longwood became obsessed with tracking down a certain white dolphin that, no doubt in a bout of carefree dolphin debauchery that is their wont, enraged the captain by waving its tail at him in an exceptionally lewd manner. The captain was so offended that he tripped over some cargo and shattered his leg, which he proceeded to saw off himself with a rusty belt knife. After briefly passing out he cauterized the wound, fashioned a crude peg leg from some of the unfortunate cargo, and gave the order to pursue the dolphin at all costs.

Of course the dolphin had long since departed, but the crew tried valiantly to follow its trail nonetheless (water tracking is much more sophisticated an art than is land tracking). After nearly a decade of doggedly hunting his great nemesis, Captain Longwood one day raised a great cry and commanded he be lowered in a small boat into the water. Spying a school of dolphins (which had frequently made appearances during the captain's decade-long quest), he rowed the boat directly toward it.

"Aha!" he cried. "I have you now!" And he took the peg leg from his stump and hurled it like a javelin directly into the school. As the water filled with blood, Captain Longwood dove after his peg leg, and when he retrieved it he proudly showed his onlooking crew that with the end of it he had successfully pierced the eye of one of the dolphins, penetrating deep into its brain and killing it *instantly. The dolphin was white. Happily the captain removed the peg leg and reattached it to his stump.*

Ever since, stories have been told of Captain Longwood's magical peg leg that helped him kill a white dolphin that had done him wrong ten years prior (or at least one that looked very similar).

Captain Longwood's peg leg had a reputation only eclipsed by that of his sexual prowess. Women wanted to do him, and men wanted to do women like he did. It is said the captain, in the mad throes of his stupendous quest for vengeance, once put into a remote harbor and spent an energetic weekend in the town's saloons and brothels. He enjoyed himself, needless to say, and that weekend the echo of his peg leg sounded down every darkened alley.

A year later, after he had found the blasted beast and put an end to its miserable carefree existence, Captain Longwood once again visited the harbor. As he walked down the gangplank and breathed in the air of land once more, finally relieved to be free of the curse that had been hounding him for so many years, he was struck by the staggering amount of one-year-old children, many of whom bore a close resemblance to him. Then, while he made his way through the city streets to his favorite brothel, the captain noticed something even more striking: all the men of the town had peg legs.

Captain Longwood was indeed a charismatic man.

The sheriff and Wilson rode on past a fallen log, their backs toward the east, having finally rediscovered the trail of McFarland, venomous villain, inconstant incendiary, devious doer of evil, and his gang.

13.

Of Vegetation and Folly

The largest doctor ever recorded was found off the shores of the Rio Grande. Eyewitnesses say the man was nearly seven feet tall, and his medical bag was a full three feet wide. He was spotted rowing a dinghy with a female companion.

"His arm-span was enormous," said Sawyer, one of the men who discovered the huge healer. "The way he worked those oars— I bet he was amazing in surgery." Others speculated that perhaps his above-average quantity of blood would aid him in providing infusions to his patients, or that some of his extra meat could be used to repair damaged limbs.

The doctor was in fact caught and stuffed, and is now being studied at the Bureau for the Retention and Investigation of Non-natural Slickskins until August, when it will be part of a traveling exhibit and put on display in museums across the country.

The sheriff reckoned they had lost a good two or three days' time trying to find horses, but now that they had them the time could be made up quickly. Wilson admired the sheriff's courage and his ability to see past the present. Who would have thought taking valuable time finding horses would pay off in the long run? It goes against common sense.

But Wilson saw the logic in it, now that the sheriff had explained it to him.

Another thing the sheriff had to keep reminding him was that the horse he was riding was not a meal. Several times an hour Wilson found himself leaning down in the saddle and smelling the smooth, oily horsey smell of the beast of which he was atop, and more than once the sheriff had to shout at him when he slowly opened his mouth to get a soft taste of the glossy mane. It was something completely foreign to Wilson to actually use an animal for a purpose other than sustenance. It made the same sort of sense as taking the time to hunt down the horses in the first place. You take time now, you save time later; you don't eat your horse now, there's a bigger reward later. Wilson could understand it if he didn't think about it too hard.

They were now coming upon a fairly odd sort of country. Where most of the foliage around the area was dry and brambly, this area seemed lush, like it was infused with an underground water source or a mist descending nightly from the heavens. The sheriff had never seen anything like it, and it made him uneasy. Had his pursuit ventured here on purpose to throw him off the track? He couldn't even tell what some of these plants were.

Giant sucker pods grew on a vine that trailed up a cactus. Mushrooms the size of saddlebags dotted the landscape on either side of the path. A large, hairy plant that looked like a four-foot-tall Venus flytrap glared down at him through the haze. The sheriff didn't like what he saw.

All of a sudden he heard a dull thud and a grunt, and he looked back to see Wilson's horse Wilsonless. He looked all along the trail, but there was no sign of the boy.

Not again.

Slowly, carefully, the sheriff dismounted, and when he reached Wilson's horse he saw the animal had caught its hoof in a vine—it was nearly wrapped all the way around the leg. He gingerly freed the animal of its encumbrance, and he tied both beasts to a branch jutting out into the path. "Wilson!" he called. "Wilson, where are you, boy?"

He listened to the night, and he thought he heard only the dimmest of responses over the whistling of the wind. Or was that the wind?

"Wilson! You all right?"

Again, he heard a faint call as if in response, and nothing else except the whistle of the wind.

He moved off in what he thought was the direction of the return call, but still he could see barely anything through the mist all about him.

He felt a sharp tap on his forehead, just above his right eye. "Ow! Wilson, was that you?" He bent over to inspect the projectile. It was some sort of pod—it looked a little like a pea, but it was larger and more firm.

"Wilson? You out there, boy?"

"Errr!"

Now he had definitely heard that, and it was definitely Wilson—and nearby. The sheriff took a few more steps in the direction of the voice and was assaulted with three more of the pods, once more right to the head.

"Jesus! Wilson, if you think this is some idea of a joke..."

"Errrrrrrrr!"

The sound had come from just beside him. He peered into the darkness and could just barely make out the form of Wilson intertwined with dozens of vines. The boy was contorted in a very unnatural position, his one hand extended nearly full length above his head, while both legs were ramrod straight.

"Wilson!" The sheriff pried at one of the vines with all of his strength, but he could just barely move the thing. For his efforts, he got dozens of peapods shot straight into his face.

"That's quite enough," he said, and took an enormous bite out of the vine. It broke clean in two, and Wilson's arm came free. The sheriff took a few more bites, and it seemed that the entire vine recoiled back into the night, leaving the boy in a heap on the ground.

"What happened?" asked Wilson, rubbing his eyes.

"You tell me. One minute we're riding after Jezebel, and the next you're gone."

"I don't remember. I felt a hard fall and then a bunch of hands."

"Bunch of hands, huh? More like a bunch of vines. But let's get out of here. This place gives me the creeps. My grandmother used to tell me ghost stories of mutant plants. I've had nightmares tamer than this."

That morning brought with it a landscape so pristine it was hard to imagine the events of the previous night occurring. The sheriff looked back the way they had come to where the mist would have been, but all he could make out was one long stretch of beautiful, sunny countryside.

They skipped breakfast and rode on.

Two days of hard riding saw them much nearer their prey. "McFarland and Jezebel can't be too much farther, can they, sheriff?" asked Wilson.

"I can't see how they could be. Those tracks in the stream look no more than a day old, if that."

Wilson broke into a broad grin and said, "We're going to get those sons of bitches."

While completely unaware of it, Wilson was repeating a phrase that has brought those who utter it bad luck throughout history.

A recent example came when Adolf Hitler made the befuddling move of opening up a second front by attacking Russia. He famously declared at a Nazi Youth rally, "Wir werden diese Hurensöhne bekommen," or, "we will get those sons of bitches."

On the eve of the Battle of Trafalgar, Admiral Horatio Nelson was thought famously to remark to his second in command, "I am going to see that we get those sons of bitches if it is the last thing I do." And while Nelson famously did get the sons of bitches, it was in fact the last thing he did.

The phrase was also said to be uttered by the Incan ruler Atahualpa just before the Battle of Cajamarca, which led to thousands of his followers being slaughtered and his kidnapping (and eventual death) at the hands of the Spanish conquistador Francisco Pizarro. It's unclear exactly what Atahualpa had said, but Pizarro's journal is riddled with the quotation "hijo de una puta."

Finally, modern scholarship into cave etchings found in Mesopotamia seems to prove that in a drawing a hunter is exclaiming "We will get you, you sons of whores" to a herd of long-horned elk, while in the next drawing in the progression the same hunter is shown gored by a very irritated-looking elk.

Surely Wilson would have selected a different phrase had he known the pedigree of this particular saying.

The fresh tracks in the riverbed were just outside a small town that looked like it hadn't been lived in for years. Windows were missing, shrubs grew in the middle of the road, and buildings were missing entire walls. Rather than going through this unkempt town, however, the tracks led up a steep incline to a path that the sheriff could see ended at a few cabins in the far distance. If he were looking for a place to make a defensive stand in these parts, he would pick those cabins.

"They're in the cabins," said the sheriff. "There's no doubt in my mind. But we can't charge up there like two hotshot gunslingers. This calls for a more subtle approach. Let's go through this town and up that ridge, see if we can come at them from the other side. They'd be much more vulnerable there."

"Whatever you say, sheriff," said Wilson. "You're the sheriff."

On the way into town they passed a wooden sign that creaked in the breeze. They could barely make out the words "Owen's Folly" burned into it.

"Well hello, sheriff," said a friendly voice. "What brings you to these parts?"

The owner of the voice was a large man with spectacles that only had one lens. He was very pale and scraggly dark hair lay matted over his enormous head. It looked like he was wearing a lab coat that was once, long, long ago, perhaps somewhat close to the color white.

"Morning," said the sheriff, tipping his hat to the man. "We're tracking some outlaws who have absconded with a young lady. Their marks seem to lead to those cabins outside of town."

"I'm his deputy," put in Wilson.

"More of an apprentice," said the sheriff. "Know anything about those cabins?"

The man wiped a meaty paw across his hair and looked over the glasses at the visitors. "Fascinating! Those cabins are the reason I'm on guard duty. In those cabins is a band of slickskins like you've never seen. They've been terrorizing our fair town for months now. If you say more slickskins just joined them, well, I don't know what to say to that. It's been all we could do to keep them out of the town as it is. With reinforcements, I'm afraid we're done for."

"This is a dire situation, Mr...."

"Callahan. Arthur T. Callahan, M.D. I serve as Owen's Folly's resident doctor."

"Doctor who?"

"Dr. Callahan. I just told you my name."

"Sorry. Dr. Callahan, my apprentice and I would like to offer our services to you and Owen's Folly."

The Zombie Sheriff Takes Tucson

Dr. Callahan, medico of miracles, kindly caregiver, diffident defender, grinned so wide the sheriff thought he might have been given the prestigious Glasgow smile. "You would?" asked the doctor. "That's marvelous! Marvelous!" He took up the sheriff's hand and shook it violently. "We've long thought they have us dead to rights. The town owes you a great deal of debt."

"But I can't do it alone, doctor."

The hand shaking stopped abruptly. "Unfortunately, Owen's Folly hasn't had any sort of law enforcement since that gang arrived. That's why I'm out here, you see. Like I said, I'm just a doctor. The town's residents take shifts keeping a look out. If they come this way, the alarm is sounded and we all take cover."

The sheriff thought for a moment and nodded. "I understand. Let me think on it a bit. I'd like to talk to your townspeople tomorrow morning. Do you think you can arrange that?"

"Of course, of course," said Dr. Callahan. "Just you go to Mungo's, and he'll fix you something delicious while I spread the word."

"Mungo's?"

"The finest dining establishment in our fair town."

The sheriff looked out on the rotting buildings, sagging roofs, and overgrown playgrounds, and he felt the soft pang in his heart of forgotten youth. Owen's Folly reminded him of something, long ago, so long ago that what he had forgotten was itself only a memory of a memory, an echo of a time that didn't hound him so insistently, didn't pant with such furious pace as did this era of bloodlust. He could get used to a town like Owen's Folly.

"It is a fair town," he said.

As the sheriff pushed through with many a creak the swinging doors of Mungo's, he couldn't help but feel a little impressed. It was everything a ghoul saloon should be. There was a long wooden bar with a great mirror behind it that reflected the decaying faces of the patrons sitting on stools. Those thirsty denizens slowly brought glasses of red murky liquid up to their mouths and occasionally talked to one another in low, raspy voices, giving further character to the broken melody that emanated from the tinny piano next to the bar. The piano player swayed back and forth with supernatural energy as he played rags and famous old tunes, his skill doubly impressive in that his left arm ended in a jagged fragment of bone that he used to play single bass notes in accompaniment to the melody. Curls of harsh smoke floated to the second-floor ceiling, devotedly puffed from pipes made from slickskin bone, the smokers, like the tables in the establishment, strewn all about the place.

The sheriff and Wilson had just sat down at one of the few empty tables when a ghoul who could only be the eponymous Mungo, cheeky chewer, purveyor of provisions, cuisinier of cartilage, wearing an apron splattered with blood and upon which the self-evident moniker "MUNGO" was stitched in barely visible crimson, handed them each a menu and set down two blood beers in front of them.

"Welcome to Mungo's," said the proprietor. "Dr. Callahan tells me you're here to deal with those nasty slickskins outside town. Least I can do to give you a meal on the house."

"Much obliged," said the sheriff, "but it isn't necessary. The law's the law. Wilson and I are just doing our jobs."

"Nonsense! Let me tell you the specials. You know, brains are the fruit of the mind. You can barbecue them, boil them, broil them, bake them, sauté them. We've got brains-kabobs, brains Creole, brains gumbo. Pan fried, deep fried, and stir-fried brains. There's pineapple brains, lemon brains, coconut brains, pepper brains, brains soup, brains stew, brains salad, brains and potatoes, brains burger, and brains sandwich. I think that's it. But if you can think of any other dish with brains, I'm sure we could whip it up for you."

"That's a lot of different kinds of brains," said the sheriff. "And they're all specials?" His mouth was watering just thinking about them all, and he noticed that at some point during Mungo's monologue Wilson had begun to moan with delight.

"Sure are," said Mungo. "Brains are always special at Mungo's. We've been cooking in Owen's Folly since before Owen. I grew up cooking brains, my mama cooked brains. And my mama before her cooked brains and her mama before her mama cooked brains, too. My family knows everything there is to know about brains."

"I believe it."

"So what'll you have?"

"Brains, I guess," he said, handing the menus back to Mungo.

14.

Jorge Aromero

Every so often you'll come across something that doesn't seem to belong. An old woman at the poker table. A mule out running with the horses. A politician out of jail.

But what does it mean to belong, anyway? I guess you might say that belonging is being where you're supposed to be. The problem is when people from the outside—people who don't really understand—make a judgment about your being some place they don't think you're supposed to be when in fact you're right where you belong.

But what do people know? People are stupid.

They were into their third different course of brains—this one was broasted brains on a bed of pureed brains—when the sheriff noticed something across the room.

"If I didn't know better," he said to Wilson, "I'd say that man is a slickskin."

"A slickskin?" said Wilson. "In the middle of a ghoul bar and grill in the middle of a village of ghouls?"

But then Wilson took a closer look. The man in question was of very short stature and was rather round—he reminded Wilson somewhat of a toad—and his mustachioed face was worn with age, but not necessarily with decay. The boy also noticed that despite a wooden leg he moved slightly faster than the rest of the crowd as he brought back to his table a pitcher of blood beer from the bar. He wore a hat that made Wilson think he would be more at home driving a horse and buggy in some city than enjoying a warm blood beer at Mungo's.

"Now that you mention it, sheriff, I do feel oddly drawn to the man. I sort of want to...bite him."

"Of course you do," said Mungo, arriving with the next course. "Jorge's a slickskin. This here is brain shish kebob. You can make out the brain clear enough, but that in between is stewed cartilage. I've found the toughness of the cartilage makes a nice contrast with the fluffiness of the brains. And it's finished off with special spices from the Orient."

"But—a slickskin?" asked the sheriff. "Here? Why aren't people tackling him to the ground and pulling out his entrails?"

Mungo let out a great belly laugh. "Tackle Jorge Aromero? Eat his entrails? That's priceless!" Mungo attempted to say more on the matter but his laughter escalated so quickly that it devolved into a debilitating bout of choking.

As the laughter-turned-choking continued Wilson found himself increasingly annoyed. "But why aren't they? And why is he drinking blood beer?"

Reasonably recovered, Mungo was able to reply, "That's quite a long story, lad, and one Jorge thoroughly enjoys telling to newcomers himself. I'll just call him over—"

"No, no, that's quite all right," said the sheriff, worried that despite having already eaten an enormous amount of brains, he and Wilson would be unable to control themselves. "We don't want to bother him."

But it was too late. Jorge, corpse chewer, friend of fiends, had apparently seen the proprietor speaking with the two newcomers, and the frequency with which each of the communicants glanced over at him left no mystery as to the topic of their conversation.

"Greetings," said Jorge warmly, as he took a seat at their table. He brought his blood beer up to his mouth, and when he lowered it a thick line of clotted red clung to his mustache. "How are you folks today?"

The sheriff and Wilson looked uncomfortably at one another. "Fine," said the sheriff. "How are you, sir?"

"Splendid, sheriff. Name's Aromero. Jorge Aromero." He extended his hand, which the sheriff took. It required every ounce of self control not to bite it off.

"Pleasure. This here's Wilson."

"Nice to meet you, youngster."

Wilson froze. He didn't trust himself to say anything. He didn't trust himself to move. Silence hung at the table stronger than the stench of death. Then slowly, ever so slowly, he leaned toward Jorge until he was nearly falling out of his chair. His face was inches away from Jorge's bicep. Then, just as slowly, Wilson opened his mouth, and gently bit Jorge's arm.

"Wilson!" said the sheriff. "I'm so sorry, Jorge. I've only just taken the lad under my wing, and clearly he needs further lessons in proper manners."

"Happens all the time," said Jorge, glancing down at Wilson not unkindly.

Wilson looked at both of them with apology in his eyes. But his teeth were still attached to Jorge's arm, all but breaking the skin.

Then, all of a sudden, Wilson jerked back from Jorge and spat on the ground. "Pah! Pleh! Ugh, you taste disgusting!" said Wilson.

"I sure do, young man."

"And—your skin is so tough. I wasn't really trying to, but if I was, I bet I could just barely break through the skin."

"That sounds about right."

"But why? Why are you here with all these ghouls, and why do you taste like that?"

"Well, son—"

"Wait!" cried Mungo, and he darted from the table. He reemerged just as suddenly with four shot glasses and a bottle marked "Blood Whiskey" and began pouring.

"Top shelf," proclaimed the barkeep with pride. Wilson, quite unaccustomed to the hard stuff, eyed the bottle nervously.

Mungo saw the boy's evident discomfort. "Oh, do you prefer your whiskey without pulp?" he asked. "Myself, I like the smoky aftertaste."

"No, no," said Wilson, "it's all right." And he took a small sip of the beverage, found that it was delightful, and gulped the rest down.

Refilling the boy's glass, Mungo said, "Please Jorge, forgive the interruption. Do Continue."

Jorge appeared not at all put off by the delay. If anything, he seemed more composed.

"If you really want to hear about it, the first thing you'll probably want to know is where I was born, and what my lousy childhood was like, and how my parents were occupied and all before they had me, and all that David Copperfield kind of crap, but I don't feel like going into it, if you want to know the truth.

"I'd rather enjoy a nice warm blood beer in peace. But I've always made it my policy to be kind to strangers, so I'll oblige you and your mentor, young one, since I can tell you're genuinely curious. Only the naturally curious can truly know the world.

"I was the elder of two children, and my brother and I always got along quite well. In our youth Esteban and I would do everything together: climb trees, swim in the river, throw rocks at girls. By the time my brother was ten—and I eleven—we were inseparable. It was an idyllic sort of brotherhood you only read about in poorly written books or Greek mythology.

"About this time, my parents sat me down at the table while my brother was allowed to go out and play.

"'Jorge,' said my mother, 'we have noticed you have been eating less and less these past few weeks. We are concerned.'

"'We are concerned, Jorge,' continued my father—my parents frequently worked in tandem. 'You are becoming skinny and pale. You do want to become big and strong like your papa, don't you? And perhaps work in the mill one day?'

"It was an obvious but well-played ploy. I often spoke of my desire to follow in my father's footsteps and work in the mill as soon as I was old enough.

"'But Mama, Papa,' I said, 'you know I want nothing more than to work in the mill. I too have noticed my appetite dwindling, but alas, I have no explanation for you. I see the food set before me, and despite that it was made by your loving hands, Mama, and that I know it must be delicious, I cannot take more than but two bites. I cannot explain it; my appetite is simply gone.'

"My mother and father conferred for quite a while in private after I told them of my declining interest in food. I have found that when parents care very much for their children, nothing can stand in the way of their devotion. There is a tale of a man whose small son had wandered away from a family picnic. When the man realized his son was missing he quickly followed the way he must have gone, only to see the son standing in the middle of a road with a stagecoach making directly for him at breakneck speed. To any observer it would appear the stagecoach would reach the young child in just seconds, and the idea the man could reach him in time would be hopeless fancy. But it is said the man ran faster than any human ever has, stopped directly in front of the oncoming horses, delivered such devastating punches to the jaws of the horses that they were instantly killed, and absorbed the inertia of the following coach. After giving the startled stagecoach driver a dirty look, the man retrieved his son and rejoined his wife to complete the picnic. Such is the devotion of parents for their children.

"When my parents returned from their deliberations they bore expressions of grave concern on their faces.

"'Jorge,' said my mother, 'we appreciate your honesty. You have always been a good boy. But we beg of you, we plead with you, eat the food, whether you find it appealing or not. You need your strength, or you will waste away and be carried off in the wind.'

"'We will give you one week,' said my father, concern dripping from his words, 'but after this week we will be forced to employ more assertive measures to make sure you are taken care of. And, Jorge, we do not want to do that.'

"I could see the pain I was causing my parents, and I resolved to try as best I could to eat at the next meal, and I told them so.

"I left the house to find Esteban swinging on the tree swing all by himself. It was one of our favorite games: we would try to see how high we'd dare go, shouting, 'Higher! Higher!' as the other struggled to push hard enough to fulfill the demand. By himself, Esteban seemed to barely leave the ground.

"'Hey,' I said, taking my place behind him and starting to push.

"'Hey,' said Esteban, kicking out his feet a little to aid the momentum. 'What were you and Mama and Papa talking about for so long?'

"'Nothing. I mean, they wanted to know if I was serious about working in the mill, and maybe I could work there earlier. That's what they were asking me about.'

"Esteban always had about twice my intelligence, but he only needed to be half as smart as me to see through this one. He knew I'd been losing weight. I couldn't see his face, but from his silence I knew he was working it all through in his head.

"Finally he just said, 'Oh. That's swell. You've always wanted to work in the mill. That's swell.'

"Then, after a moment of reflective silence, Esteban said, 'Higher. Push me higher, Jorge.'

"I pushed him higher, but soon he said again, 'Higher!'

"Now at the height of the arc Esteban was parallel to the ground, and I could see the wind making his hair into a dark blur. Neither of us had ever swung this high before.

"Then Esteban said, 'Higher.'

"'Are you sure? I don't know if that's safe.'

"'Yes,' he said. 'I'm sure. Push me higher.'

"At first it was glorious. Esteban went up so quickly that for a moment it seemed like he was on his way to the sun. He let out a great squeal of glee and his legs shot out and locked in place.

"But Esteban swung so high that the tension of the rope swing went slack, and instead of gliding back down in an arc, the swing snapped down. Esteban fell out of the swing and crumpled into a pile of innocent boyhood on the ground. Some of his limbs appeared to be assuming angles not normally possible.

"I heard of a widow who had gone into town to do some shopping. When she returned home, she found one of the front windows was ajar. The lady was sure—absolutely sure—that when she had left that window had been closed and therefore someone must have broken into the house while she had been away.

"So what did she do? She didn't go get the local lawman, or go to the neighbors for help. She started a small fire, took out a smoldering piece of kindling, and burned the house to the ground.

"When no human remains were found among the ashes, the widow said she didn't care. She never would have felt safe there again.

"Well there I was, standing not three feet from my brother, whose arm had bent too far backward and whose leg had a gash so deep that I could see the bone.

"To really understand how out of character what I did next was, you have to understand how I was an eleven-year-old boy, how on any given day of the week I would run from the sight of the carcass of the smallest rodent. But who among us could truly hope to perceive a previous version of themselves, let alone convey that perception to strangers?

"What I did was this: heedless of the blood, heedless of the exposed bone, I heroically took Esteban up in my arms and ran as fast as I could to the house. I laid him on the kitchen table and found Mama and Papa sitting in the living room. Through a collection of gibberish and wild physical exhortations I was able to give them the vague idea that something terrible had happened. When they saw Esteban in the kitchen, neither said a word; my mother covered her mouth and my father darted away to borrow the neighbor's horse and cart. Seven minutes later, Esteban was speeding along toward the nearest doctor.

"I looked with sorrow and guilt at my mother, who still had said nothing. Finally, as I began to walk toward her to comfort her, she fled the room with a whimper.

"It was then that I noticed I was mostly covered in blood. There was blood on my hands and arms. There was blood on my shirt and pants. Blood had even splattered on my face and onto my lips. I could taste its iron and saltiness.

"It was an odd taste, my brother's blood. I had tasted blood before, of course, when I had pricked a finger and sucked on the resulting sore, or when I bit my tongue the first time I really rode a horse at a gallop.

"But this taste was different. There was something—

"I brought the back of my hand up to my mouth and softly licked it. Yes, it was a sweetness I had never tasted before in my own blood, or anywhere else. I licked my hand again, then again, and then my arm as well.

"As I moved on to the other arm, a sound made me look up. I saw my mother standing in the doorway watching me silently. I had no idea how long she had been watching me, but she had an odd look on her face, a sort of mixture of horror and sadness. As I looked up, she left the room.

"Papa didn't come back again until the next day, but he brought with him good news. Esteban was going to be okay. He would always have a nasty scar on his leg, but the doctor had set his arm and pronounced that if he progressed as expected over the next day, he would be allowed to return home to complete his convalescence.

"My mother was overjoyed at the news, and a smile became a permanent fixture on her face over the next few hours. I kept waiting for her to tell father what she had seen me doing, but she never did.

"The next morning I was sent out of the house while my mother gave it a thorough cleaning. She said she didn't want to take anymore chance of infection than she had to. I had a suspicion she just didn't want to be around me.

"With my natural playmate gone, most of my regular occupations were not available. There was no one to swing with. There was no one to throw rocks at tin cans with. There was no one to look through the neighbor's fourteen-year-old daughter's curtains with.

"I ended up wandering out away from the house with no clear direction in mind. Before me stretched a wide landscape composed mostly of harsh vegetation, rocks, and gritty dirt. I walked along a narrow dirt road I had seldom taken before; there was no important destination in this direction for another hundred miles or more.

"The sun was hot overhead, and I stopped to take a drink from my canteen, which had a dent in it from the time Esteban and I had run out of tin cans. All of a sudden I heard a tremendous cry, which I knew must have come from a horse. It was the sound of an animal that had encountered something so terrifying that it had lost all sense of safety.

"I rushed down the dirt road to see something retreat into the nearby brush, but my attention was quickly drawn to the scene of horror that lay before me. The horse, having fallen after giving that terrifying scream, was just rising to its feet, seemingly unscathed. As it moved off some distance, what had lain beneath it was revealed to me: it was the rider, twisted in some inhuman way. At first I thought he must have been killed by the horse's fall, but then I noticed something missing.

"The rider's arms. And his head.

"Despite the growing sense of nausea I was somehow drawn to the corpse; I remember taking step after unconscious step, the scene becoming clearer to me with each tread. When I reached the body, I realized one of the arms was not missing after all—it was off to the side, about three feet from the rider.

"'A headless horseman,' I said to myself, and I considered the scene. The body lay like a turkey ready for cooking, wings torn off prematurely. Blood was everywhere. The horse had meandered a bit down the path. I thought about the movement I had seen as I arrived.

"I crouched down beside the body and looked at all the blood on it. There was quite a lot. Slowly I extended my hand and dipped my fingers into the blood. I brought them up to my mouth. Again I felt the curious sweetness, felt the euphoria.

"I repeated the action again and again: I dipped my hand into the blood then licked it clean, then dipped my hand in it again, and again licked it clean. Soon I stopped using my hand and went directly to the source.

"After a while I couldn't take it anymore. I wondered at what I had done, though it didn't horrify me like it would have most slickskins. And I was eleven. All I knew was it tasted good.

"I wondered again about what I had seen when I got to the scene: some flash of movement disappearing into the brush. I didn't know what it could have been—some sort of animal, maybe—though in hindsight it was pretty clear it was just a ghoul that needed a fourth for brainball and a snack for the trip back.

"I looked at that arm laying there, taken cleanly out of its socket. It too was speckled with blood. I could see the oily skin covered in the soft down of hair. I could see the space at the end where it had been disconnected from its body, the muscles and veins and blood, all gross-looking.

"And yet, for some reason, it wasn't gross at all. It was—inviting. I remembered what my parents had said about eating, about getting my strength up.

"I picked up the arm and started back home.

"I threw the bones, picked clean, into one of the neighbor's yards and washed up at the well. Esteban should be home by now.

"Mother and Father were cooing over him and making sure every pillow was fluffed.

"'Hey,' I said to him. 'You all right?'

"'Yeah,' he said, and gave me a smile. That was just like Esteban. He would sooner give up looking at the neighbor's daughter than blame me for what had happened.

"'Good,' I said. 'I'm sorry about—the accident. I shouldn't have pushed you so high.'

"'Wasn't your fault,' said Esteban. 'I asked you to.'

"'All the same, I shouldn't have—'

"That's when I saw it. I had looked away from Esteban's face for a moment, and my gaze had come upon his bandaged leg. Some blood had seeped through the bandage.

"I could feel my mouth begin to water.

"'You shouldn't have what?' prompted my father. 'Jorge?'

"Uh, um, I shouldn't have done it,' I said, snapping back to the conversation at hand. 'Like I said, I shouldn't have pushed him so high.'

"For some reason Mother and Father seemed greatly relieved, though Esteban seemed genuinely to have forgiven me.

"But my eyes were once again drawn to the bandage. I could imagine what it looked like underneath, the skin sewed shut but still oozing blood, blood which was trying its hardest to stave off infection and to help the muscles reunite underneath that skin, bright pink muscles that pulsed with the blood and—

"'Jorge?' It was my mother.

"'Jorge, I said, let's let Esteban have some quiet time!'

"I sheepishly bowed my head to my mother and followed them out the room.

"When we were out of earshot of my brother's room, my mother rounded on me.

"'Jorge, you have got to take better care of your brother. I don't know what you were thinking, pushing him that high. He could have been killed, his brains knocked out of his head. Is that what you want?'

"Another image forced its way into my thoughts: my brother's lifeless head cracked open, me with a spoon kneeling behind him. Savoring every bite.

"This wasn't right. Normal eleven-year-olds didn't have these types of thoughts.

"I looked at both my parents and considered telling them everything I had done, everything I had imagined doing. But instead of my parents, all I saw was meat.

"Followed by their protests, I ran out of the house without uttering a word. I kept repeating to myself, 'It's for their own good. It's for their own good.'

"That was the last time I ever saw my family.

"Except some years later, when I returned and ate them.

The sheriff looked at Wilson to see a mix of surprise and admiration on the boy's face.

"Well, Mr. Aromero, sir," said the sheriff. "I learned something today. I learned I have something in common with a slickskin."

"You sure do," said Jorge, topping off the sheriff's glass with the last of the blood beer from the pitcher. He raised his own glass to the sheriff and drank it down.

"But what about your skin?" asked Wilson. "How did it get to be so tough and foul-tasting? And your leg—why are you missing part of it?"

"Well, son, after I left my family, I wandered from place to place, and soon enough it became clear to me that a slickskin community didn't exist that would tolerate me. One day I ran into a couple of ghouls munching on an old lady, and at the time I had made it a practice to avoid ghouls as any sane slickskin would do, but I was so hungry I joined right in. As you know, old women are probably at the bottom of the appetizing list, but I wasn't in a position to be picky.

"When I started in on the lady, those two ghouls recoiled at first, then when they saw I was a slickskin they turned on me instead. One of them took a huge chunk out of my calf"—Jorge knocked on his wooden stump—"right here, and spat it out just as quick. Then they just stood there looking at me. They didn't know what to do.

"As you can imagine, I was in a fair bit of pain due to that bite, and it was clear I was going to have to lose the lower portion of my leg if I wanted to live. So I did."

"But how did you survive?" asked Wilson.

"Like I said, I chopped off the leg. It's really not that hard, you just have to ignore the pain."

"No, I mean, how did you survive? You weren't turned into a ghoul."

"I've noticed that," said Jorge. "And I don't have a good explanation for you. I guess it might have something to do with all the slickskin meat I've eaten over the years. It's been suggested that it's given me some sort of immunity, and that it's made me taste rotten."

"That's certain," said Wilson.

"After that little mishap, the ghouls seemed to accept me. I was able to communicate with them a little bit, and they led me here, to Owen's Folly. Most wouldn't believe I didn't taste good, but when they sunk their teeth in a little, as you did, youngster, they found out soon enough. And I've been here ever since."

"That is certainly a unique story," said the sheriff.

"It sure is," said Wilson.

15.

SLEIGHT OF ARM

What you'll find in this one:

1. *Finite volumes*
2. *A low-down, rotten, cowardly devil*
3. *A pouched forearm*
4. *A lurch for the exits*
5. *Fools in the middle of a showdown*
6. *Red and green flags*
7. *A small dog*
8. *Frenzy*
9. *Sage advice*
10. *More brains*

Enjoy.

--Jorge

After gorging themselves before, during, and after Jorge's peculiar story on every different kind of brains they could imagine, and many they couldn't, the sheriff and Wilson finally gave in. There was a finite volume their bodies could physically hold, and they had reached that threshold—

though it seemed that Wilson had kept up suspiciously well despite his much smaller size.

Letting out an enormous belch, the sheriff noticed that Dr. Callahan was sitting off to the corner of the room. "Why, doctor," he called, "how long have you been there?"

"Oh, not long," responded Dr. Callahan. "I just came to tell you that as you requested all the able-bodied men and women of Owen's Folly will be ready for you tomorrow, sure as Sunday morning."

"Excellent. I appreciate the—"

But the sheriff's appreciation was cut short by a commotion across the room. The sheriff saw a well-dressed ghoul standing at a round table forcefully addressing the ghoul sitting across from him. As the patrons of Mungo's became aware of the scene, glasses were lowered, cards were set down, and the tinny piano music ceased. The sheriff began to make out what the agitated man was saying.

"...Low-down, rotten, cowardly devil," said the man. "I may have looked the other way before, but this is the last time you cheat me at cards, you hear?"

"What'd you see, Jonathon?" asked one of the seated men at the table who hadn't incurred the wrath of the well-dressed player.

"He's been cheating the whole time," the ghoul responded. "I thought I imagined it at first, but I just saw it plain as day. He's got cards up his arm."

"Up his arm?"

"Yes, sir. He's got a slit in the skin of his forearm, right there," said Jonathon, pointing at the offending limb. "He's got a stash of cards in there and he's been pulling them out while no one's looking."

Until that point the accused man had said or done nothing. But all at once he made his response clear: he stood up from his chair with such violence that the table threatened to topple. The half-drunk pints of blood beer sloshed to and fro, and (perhaps with a greater potential for tragedy) also threatened to topple.

"You would accuse me of cheating, would you, Jonathon? After we've known each other for how many years? Well, this won't go unanswered."

"It better not, Davidson. It better not."

Then all at once without a further word spoken, all of Mungo's seemed to lurch for the exits, led by the two gentlemen in conflict. The sheriff turned to Dr. Callahan, who had just risen to his feet, with a questioning glance.

"Owen's Folly had been the epitome of law and order for the longest time, sheriff," explained the doctor, "but as you can see when we lost our lawman, the less desirable aspects of the community began to come out. It isn't usually quite as bad as this, though. Usually folks settle their differences without violence."

The sheriff and Wilson found themselves swept out of Mungo's and into the village square to join what felt like the whole town. A circle had formed around the two men, Jonathon and Davidson, who stood facing one another some thirty yards apart. They were as still as death.

Wilson had been caught up in the emotion of it all along with the rest of the town, but in the stillness he had time to reflect. He looked up at the sheriff and said, "Hadn't you better go out there and stop them, sheriff? Before they get too hurt?"

"Only a fool gets in the middle of a showdown, Wilson. If these men want to break the law, trying to stop them will only get somebody killed. And the only ones threatened are themselves. Sometimes these things have to play out first."

Wilson nodded to himself, satisfied he had done his civic duty. If the sheriff said he wouldn't intervene, then that was the way it was. He looked out at the two aggrieved men, still standing as if they had been there since the dawn of time. Their eyes were small slits as the wind blew across their faces, and flaps of decomposing skin waved gently like red and green flags. Their arms hung at their sides, their hands held at the ready inches above their hips. Wilson thought the scene looked like a monument to something, something that had been memorable, or would be memorable one day. He imagined hearing music as the men stared at one another, frozen in the heat, trumpets blaring and guitars strumming and shakers shaking. The song started softly, like wheat, and built up with wavering intensity, the tension rising and falling, but always rising. Wilson thought it was almost unbearable. When would the spell be broken? Who would make the first move? How much longer would the music play?

Just as the clock inside Mungo's chimed high noon, a small dog wandered across the spectacle, unnoticed by anyone in attendance.

Then all of a sudden one of the men—which it was didn't really matter—dropped his hand and took a slow, stuttering step toward the other, and soon both men were stumbling at one another at break-neck speed. When, minutes later, they reached one another, what transpired was not a sight for sensitive eyes.

A haze of red mist seemed to envelope the men as they attacked one another, their arms scratching and clawing at a speed of almost a foot per second. Skin and scabs sprayed the onlookers, and wounds new and old alike were opened up. The stench of decay permeated the crowd (at which point several of the onlookers returned to Mungo's to order a meal).

It was a frenzy.

As the duel went on, a substantive casualty made an appearance: one of Davidson's arms fell to the ground and, ever faithful to its owner, continued trying to tear at Jonathon. Playing cards scattered about on the dirt.

Wilson felt rather than saw the sheriff shift beside him.

"Gone on long enough," said the sheriff. "Any more and someone's really going to get hurt." He cut through the crowd and into the circle, and with an ease that surprised just about everyone, separated the two men.

"That'll do. You've done yourselves enough harm. Dr. Callahan, if you wouldn't mind getting this fellow patched up, I'll take this one to your sheriff's office."

"Aw, we was just having a scuffle," said Davidson. "There's no need for legal intervention."

"The law's the law," said the sheriff. "You were fighting in a public place, and from the looks of it cheating at cards to boot. You'll answer for both."

An hour later, thanks to Dr. Callahan's handiwork, Davidson's swindling arm had been reattached—the cards having been removed beforehand—and he was taken to join Jonathon in the jail cell.

"What do you have to say for yourselves?" asked the sheriff. Wilson sat in the corner trying not to be noticed, lest he be shooed away.

Jonathon looked at Davidson, then back at the sheriff. "This one got a little too liberal with his cards. He needed to be taught a lesson. And he was."

"I'll agree, sheriff," said Davidson. "What I done was wrong, and I've paid for it." Davidson nodded down to his reattached limb, which had been put on backward, so his right arm was now facing behind him. "I won't be card sharping anymore, I can tell you that." He knocked on the cell wall behind him.

"I suppose you won't, Davidson. And you, Jonathon? What do you propose for your punishment?"

"Well, sheriff, like I said, what was done needed doing. I've known this man for more years than I care to tell, and he got what had been a long time coming to him—and I'm glad I was the one who got to give it to him. But I understand that actions have consequences. I've been around long enough. Whatever you think is fair I'll abide, sheriff."

"Well said." The sheriff looked over at Wilson. "You hear that, son? Sage advice. There are very few men in this world who are truly bad."

He turned back to the men. "Davidson, as for your misdeeds at the card table, you'll be punished for the rest of your life. And for the both of you, I think a night with each other behind these bars would fit the bill. I'll let you out in the morning."

"As you say, sheriff," said Davidson.

"Come on, Wilson," said the sheriff, ushering the boy from the building. "They've got some thinking to do."

"You think Mungo has anymore brains?" said the boy.

16.

Occurrence at Owl Creek Bridge

Pumpkins.

The very word still strikes terror into the heart of many a Mexican (though for some odd reason they call the things calabazas*). For the memory of the Pumpkin Pestilence, though long past, still lingers in the tormented dreams of those who experienced its terrible curse.*

Manuel de la Gourd was the first to encounter the Pestilence. One day as he was returning home from a long day of labor as a janitorial supply closet stocker, Manuel saw a pumpkin by the side of the road. He thought nothing of it and went home to make passionate love to his wife. The following evening, after a day made frustrating by a nationwide plunger shortage, Manuel returned home to find two pumpkins resting on his kitchen table, each with a crude smile carved into it. His wife was as surprised to see them as he was. On the third day four pumpkins appeared in the men's room of Big Al's Boracho Burrito Restaurante. The next day Manuel went to bed to find eight pumpkins pressing up through the mattress. On the sixth day there were sixteen pumpkins sitting on the roof of his house. On the seventh day thirty-two pumpkins rolled down a steep embankment just after Manuel passed. The eighth day saw sixty-four pumpkins fall from the sky, each narrowly missing Manuel as he sprinted to work.

The Zombie Sheriff Takes Tucson

Then came the fateful ninth day. Manuel's wife went to the outhouse in the middle of the night, and when she returned, she received the shock of her life. She opened the bedroom door, and dozens and dozens of pumpkins rolled out—the room was filled with them from floor to ceiling. She dug through them until she reached her husband.

Manuel lay in bed, surrounded by pumpkins, but atop his neck, where his head should be, was another pumpkin. Manuel's wife, thinking the pumpkin had been forced over her husband's head, quickly pulled the pumpkin off.

But she was wrong. The pumpkin wasn't atop Manuel's head. It had replaced his head. Consequently, blood spewed out in a crimson geyser, impacting the wife like a fire hose of gore. She was soon swept out of the house and carried out of town, never to be seen again.

Similar stories started cropping up all over Mexico—a man who died when a whole pumpkin mysteriously appeared in his stomach, a woman who died from shock when instead of giving birth to a child, she produced a bouncing baby gourd.

After three months of pumpkin-related horror, the Pumpkin Pestilence came to a welcome and wholly unexplained stop. No more pumpkins appeared in people's living rooms, no pumpkins chased people down narrow paths.

But don't mention pumpkins to the people of Mexico. To this day they dare not say that word, for fear that just as suddenly as the Pumpkin Pestilence ceased, it may one day begin again.

Nancy, please forgive the very poor penmanship, but in the interest of time I am composing this letter on horseback. Don't mistake me: the horse Bill let me have—for a very reasonable price, please note—rides quite well, and if I weren't trying to write a letter while riding I'm sure I would be having a wonderful and very enjoyable experience, especially since there would be no ink with which the rocky, winding roads could stain my saddle.

It is with a heavy heart that I leave Phoenix. I already miss the dear acquaintances I have made there: Bill, whose friendship I renewed; Al, who was always on hand with a willing ear and a strong cup of coffee; Sheriff Wilcox, whose gruff demeanor no doubt hides a soft emotional center and a heart of gold; Nameless Orphan, who I believe I have somehow turned into a musical phenom, despite the fact that I never learned his name. All of these citizens and more have caused me to regard Phoenix with nothing but the fondest of memories.

I should have noted earlier: I received the package you sent, and once again you have outdone yourself, Nancy, both in the speed with which you work and in the clairvoyance with which you anticipate my needs.

I am just now noticing: most of this letter is perhaps unreadable, as much of the ink has run down the extent of the paper—but it would not surprise me in the least if you were able to decipher all or most of its meaning (see previous paragraph).

And now it appears I must cut this note short, as a few vaguely menacing shapes have begun to emerge out of a river I am approaching. Let us see to what extent my old cane is still reliable.

The road Abernathy had been following led to a bridge that spanned the length of the river, and perhaps he could have galloped ahead and avoided the four ghouls that had just now fully emerged from the water, but he wanted to test himself and—as he had noted to Nancy—his cane.

He tied his charcoal-gray horse, which Bill had regrettably named Alabaster, to a small tree and removed his cane from the saddlebags. He took up the cane in both hands, then extended his hands vertically above his head and stretched them as far back as they would go. He performed a few more stretches, gave a great yawn, and walked the rest of the way to the bridge.

The ghouls, excited by the prospect of fresh human meat, had begun a dull chorus of moans. Abernathy became mildly irritated.

He saw that one of the ghouls had separated itself and was closer to him than the other three. It was a ghoul of average build, with minimal decay. From afar it might have appeared to be one of those modern youths who dawdle around town, making nuisances of themselves (and in truth there is little difference between the two). It shambled toward him as all ghouls shamble, and its reach seemed no serious impediment.

Abernathy walked confidently forward to meet this first ghoul. When he was a few paces away, he grasped the cane firmly with both hands and raised it into the air.

Then, he waited.

The ghoul seemed unaware of the menacing stance Abernathy had assumed, for it made no change in either its pace or direction. So when the leading ghoul wandered into range, Abernathy swung the cane horizontally with all his might. It crashed into the ghoul's head just at its left ear and shattered its skull, creating a sound that resembled an enormous tree being felled. At the moment of impact, the ghoul's eyes popped out of their sockets and dropped to the ground, twin spurts of crimson blood accompanying them on the way down.

When Abernathy removed the cane from the ghoul's skull, he noticed he had created a cavity that reached almost halfway through the ghoul's head; he could see gray brain matter splotched here and there with green tumors. He tossed a card on the corpse:

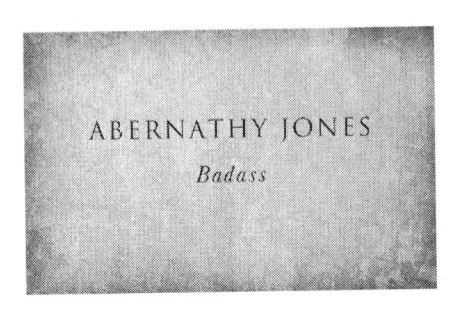

> ABERNATHY JONES
> *Badass*

He brought the cane up once more, this time holding it directly above his head, and smashed it down with so much force that the blow cut down far enough to meet the first wound. This second cut effectively halved the ghoul's skull and brain, and as Abernathy once more removed the cane, the entire left hemisphere of the ghoul's head fell to the ground next to the eyes.

The ghoul began walking progressively faster in a shallow circle until it eventually collapsed in a pool of foam that oozed out of its brain and mouth.

This threat removed, Abernathy sized up the remaining ghouls. They seemed not to have noticed what had befallen their comrade as they walked slowly and stiffly, still in a line, directly toward Abernathy.

This time Abernathy bent his knees until he was in a slight crouch. One hand held the handle of the cane while the other gripped it about eight inches farther down.

Again he waited.

When the ghouls had sufficiently approached, with one fluid motion Abernathy rose out of his crouch, gave the handle of his cane a half-turn, pulled out from its casing a thin, razor-sharp blade, and cut through each of the ghouls' necks. He remained frozen, the blade behind his back glistening with blood, as the heads of the three ghouls first tottered, then fell heavily to the ground. The bodies fell just after.

Abernathy considered the still-moaning heads for a moment then wiped the blade clean on one of the bodies. He returned the blade to its sheath, once again gave the handle a half-turn then smashed the cane down on each of the heads in turn.

They exploded like pumpkins.

17.

THE MAGNIFICENT TWO

The motto of the Boy Scouts of America is "Be Prepared." But be prepared for what? What aren't the Boy Scouts telling us?

Some have speculated the Boy Scouts are not the virtuous do-gooders they seem, but rather something much more terrifying. Horrible, horrible rumors swirl about deep-woods games of Who-Can-Be-The-Nicest and Pin-The-Compliment-On-The-Stranger. Details are sketchy at best, and many questions remain.

What have they done with all of the female Scouts? Where do they receive funding for their lavish, booze-filled parties? What of the rumor of the secret Platypus rank?

The world may never know—until it's too late.

That morning, after letting the duelists out of their cell and eating a hearty breakfast (of brains) at Mungo's, the sheriff and Wilson made their way out to the village square to find about a hundred townspeople gathered. He stood on the rickety top step and looked out at them. They weren't fighters physically, he could see that, but there was something about them, something hard to put into words. These people had seen hardship, had seen harassment. They might not be natural fighters, but they were hard. Most importantly, they were trainable.

"Citizens of Owen's Folly," he called to them. "I hear you have a bandit problem."

A few wry chuckles from the crowd greeted his remark.

"I'm here to fix it for you."

Moans of cheering erupted from them, surprisingly loud given the size of the group.

"But I can't do it alone. There are just too many of them for me and my apprentice—"

"Deputy!"

"—apprentice to take care of on our own. These are mean bastards, and Dr. Callahan tells me that unlike most slickskins, they know to shoot for the head.

"Now you've got about twenty of them holed up in those cabins, I'm told, plus the six that came in yesterday. The people of Owen's Folly have done a great job holding off these sons of bitches, but even though we outnumber them four to one, we're going to need to come up with a devious plan to defeat them.

"We come at them en masse and they're liable to have themselves a ghoul bonfire. Like I said, these are no ordinary slickskins. They seem to know more about us than most do, and that means trouble. That also means we have to behave differently than we normally would. Now over the next two days my apprentice, Wilson, and I are going to be training you on some tactics, as well as preparing Owen's Folly for the fight of its life. These slickskins may be clever, but I have a few tricks up my sleeve.

"But in general, you want to know how to get these slickskins? They pull a gun, you pull off their arm. One of them dies, you send him right back at them until he's dead again. That's the Owen's Folly way! And that's how you get slickskins. Now do you want to do that? Are you ready to do that? I'm offering you a deal. Do you want this deal?

The moans of elation rose to the heavens.

"Well, you've heard it all, but I can't do this without you. This is your town, and you need to decide if you're going to let people take it from you. How about it? Who wants to create our own Night of the Dead! Who's with me?"

The moans grew so loud that the sheriff was afraid the slickskin outlaws would hear them. No, on second thought, he hoped they would hear them, so they'd know what was coming for them.

The next morning Dr. Callahan gave the sheriff and Wilson a tour of the village. It wasn't a hard place to understand, as small as it was, but they hadn't been out long when they were interrupted.

"Sheriff!" A young woman came stumbling up to them with terror in her eyes. "Sheriff, you've got to help. Some of those slickskins are at it again!"

"Now calm down, darling," said the sheriff, putting a hand on her shoulder. "Everything's going to be all right. Just you tell me exactly what it is those slickskins are at again."

Just as she (her name was Florence; born and raised in Arizona, she had roamed around with her parents from place to place before establishing residence in Owen's Folly and taking up the piccolo to play in the community band and hopefully to find a young man to settle down with) was opening her mouth to reply, a loud shot was heard and her face exploded.

As Dr. Callahan, the sheriff, and Wilson wiped what remained of Florence's youthful visage off their own, the doctor explained, "She means—or meant—that the slickskins are shooting at us again."

"I see. Thank you, doctor. Take cover!" shouted the sheriff to anyone stupid enough to remain outside—and there were a few.

He found himself inside Mungo's with more than half the citizens of Owen's Folly. They were all chatting together nervously, and as he surveyed the room the piano player slunk onto his bench and began to play a few tentative bars. The citizens appeared scared, but it also looked as though they had done this before. They seemed resigned.

"Away from that window!" the sheriff barked at a woman peering outside, her hand held to her brow to shade her eyes. She jerked back at the sheriff's remonstration and looked at him, startled.

"You folks need direction," said the sheriff to no one in particular, just as a bullet came through the window and embedded itself harmless into a table. "You've got the heart. You need direction. Wilson, are you around here?"

"Sure am, sheriff."

"Good."

"You want me to go on a mission with you? Ravage some slickskins?"

"No. Stay here. Make sure these people don't get themselves killed."

"But sheriff—"

"I don't want to hear it." The sheriff knelt beside Wilson and lowered his voice. "You're the only one I really trust around here—now please, make sure these people don't get killed. They're good people."

The sheriff straightened. "Who can tell me what they know about these slickskins?"

The woman who had been at the window spoke up. "I can, sheriff. The name's Beverly, and I've seen them at it before. There's usually just two of them—always a different two—we call them Tweedledum and Tweedleshithead. They have a tree they like to sit in and try to pick a few of us off. They'd be much better shots if they weren't drunk. Eventually they get tired and go back to their cabins."

"I see. Thank you, madam. Is there a back way out of this place? Good. Doctor, you're with me. The rest of you, just relax. And stay away from the windows."

Mungo showed the sheriff and Dr. Callahan out the back of the saloon. "You sure I can't join you, sheriff?"

"I—I don't know if I'm the best man for the job, sheriff," added Dr. Callahan.

"Nonsense," said the sheriff, waving off both men with a flick of his hand. "We only need two for this job, and the doctor here is more than capable. Right, doctor?"

The sheriff and Dr. Callahan cautiously made their way through the decrepit village until they were behind the tree in which the two slickskins were roosting. They were so close, in fact, that they could hear the sloshing of the bottle as they passed it back and forth between them, punctuated by belches of some prodigious magnitude that it was a wonder the men didn't fall out of the tree onto their sweet, tender behinds.

"See there?" breathed the sheriff to Dr. Callahan. "They've only got one gun between them, and they keep exchanging the gun and the bottle. Looks like Beverly was right—their shots are getting more and more off the mark. They're probably more than a little intoxicated at this point."

"It does look that way, doesn't it, sheriff? Funny how 'skins sway when they imbibe too much. See how the one on the left has to support himself with that branch? Looks like a country lad at his first church social."

The sheriff suppressed a smile and nodded. The doctor's comparisons and sayings were beginning to grow on him. "Give me a hand here," he said, snapping off some dry branches from a fallen tree.

"Whatever you say, sheriff." Soon the two ghouls had broken off more kindling than they could carry.

"All right, doc. Grab as much as you can, but however much you take make sure you can be silent while carrying it."

"You don't mean..." Dr. Callahan trailed off and nodded at the slickskins. "We're not going to..."

"We sure are."

Dr. Callahan looked as if someone had just told him his favorite horse had been eaten—and none had been saved for him. "But burn them out? We'd have to get so close to them. And I don't usually care for cooked meat, though I do hear some of the more modern restaurants are experimenting with it."

"It's the safest way, doctor—as long as we can keep quiet. Those slickskins are blind drunk and facing the other way. If we come at them from any other direction they'll see us, and I'm not very good at climbing. The worst that can happen is the fire goes out and they get smoke in their eyes and start crying."

"With all due respect, sheriff, the worst that can happen is that they hear us coming and blow our heads off like two dandelions in the wind."

"But they won't hear us coming, will they?"

"I hope to Betsy they don't."

"Who's Betsy?"

"My mother. She was killed trying to sneak up on some slickskins."

So the sheriff and Dr. Callahan gathered as much kindling as they dared and began to make their way to the slickskin's tree, which was perhaps fifty yards away. At first they made wonderful progress, and the doctor began to think they might actually survive this half-brained mission. But then tragedy struck. Dr. Callahan stumbled, and three branches fell from his cradling arms, clattering onto the hard earth below. The ghouls both froze. Perhaps if the slickskins were drunk enough they would think the two to be foul-smelling, half-decayed trees.

Fortune was smiling upon them that day. The slickskin with the gun had just taken aim and fired at Florence's corpse for perhaps the tenth time (whether he was sadistic or extremely drunk to keep firing at the same body is unknown), and the echo of the shot still hung heavily in the air as Dr. Callahan's load lightened. The other slickskin—the one with the bottle—looked around a bit at the sound, but it was clear his main focus was on the contents of the bottle and not a sound that very probably he had imagined. The other slickskin gave no sign of hearing anything out of the ordinary.

The two ghouls remained in place for what seemed like hours until finally it was clear the slickskins suspected nothing (they traded accessories, and the other slickskin was now taking aim at Florence's corpse). The sheriff nodded to Dr. Callahan, and they continued on their trek.

Tweedleshithead had just handed over the rifle in exchange for the bottle once again, but he wasn't sure it was a fair trade anymore. Alcohol had certainly got him through more than a couple tough times in his life, and it had usually served to make even the good times better, but Tweedleshithead suspected he was encountering that mythical realm that one rarely remembers approaching. He thought he had had too much.

The feeling started when Tweedledum had the bottle last, and he had the rifle. It was marvelous. He couldn't miss a shot. Ghoul after ghoul dropped dead (again) before the awesome power of his marksmanship. But then he started to ask himself: didn't quite a few of the ghouls have on that dark, dingy dress with one sleeve missing? And didn't they all seem to drop in that same place, right there in the village square? Just what were the odds that a dozen ghouls in this area were wearing black dresses with the left sleeve missing and that they all happened to fall in precisely the same spot? And to his eye (admittedly blurry now), there seemed to be only a few—one?—corpses on the ground in the square. Where were the others?

Tweedledum seemed not to have noticed. He would often take a swig of the whiskey and remark, "nice shot!" or "dead on!" Sometimes Tweedleshithead hadn't even taken a shot.

And now the tree had started to sway a bit—the oddest thing—so he steadied himself with the hand not grasping the bottle like a pickpocket's throat. Better. The tree seemed rooted—rooted, as it was!—to the ground now, not hardly shaking at all.

Tweedledum fired another shot at the ghouls and to the resulting puff of smoke he proclaimed victory and notched another tally in his branch. Others from the cabins had been up here, and there were initials and notches throughout the tree. Tweedledum vaguely wondered how many of the notches represented ghouls and how many puffs of smoke.

That was the thing about being this far south—the heat. Sometimes it was unbearable. Sometimes you'd go days not remembering what it felt like not to sweat. Then other times—like now—you'd be out in the middle of the day and it wouldn't be so bad. It would be almost bearable, then all of a sudden a heat wave hits you. And not just any heat wave, like the sun comes out from behind some clouds, but a full on inferno, like someone lit a fire underneath you. Beads of sweat start to form on your brow. Wisps of steamy smoke come up from the ground like cracks have been opened into hell. The bottle, forgotten, drops from your hand.

It's so hot you just want to sleep, right here in this tree. You look over and there's Tweedledum, already asleep, and his skin looks red and irritated and maybe a little cracked, maybe even melting a little, and you figure, why not have a little siesta? You'll feel better when you wake.

Then the ground falls on your head.

*   *   *

Owen's Folly, though fallen into significant disrepair since the days of its founding by the great Jedidiah Owen, was nonetheless planned and laid out immaculately. The town—village, really—nestled to the north and west into a very rocky and treacherous stretch of foothills, which made traffic to and from the city in those directions practically impossible. The southeastern corner of the village just touched the river to which the sheriff and Wilson had tracked the McFarland gang and its precious hostage. The river was crossed by two roads, one coming from the east, one the south, and these two roads formed the main roads of the village. Where they intersected, in the heart of the city, was a village square in which a statue of the illustrious Owen had long stood proudly. The rest of the village was laid out on a grid. The largest of the dozen or so major buildings was Mungo's, at the extreme north of the village.

The sheriff took in all this and more as he devised his plans, assisted by the faithful Wilson. "You see, Wilson," he said, "the key to any battle is understanding the terrain. Any good general can tell you that. For the best chance at victory, you've got to use the terrain to your advantage. In this particular situation, our targets are already in the best possible defensive position up there in those cabins. If we attacked, they would have the high ground, which is quite a problem. The trick is to take what we know about the land and make it work for us."

"How do you plan to do that?"

"By putting ourselves on the defensive."

"But that means the slickskins would have to attack us—we'd be the ones in danger."

"Exactly. And if you know the land well enough, you can turn that danger around on your attackers."

The Zombie Sheriff Takes Tucson

The preparations took more than a day and a half, and by their end every undead soul in Owen's Folly was exhausted.

The townspeople were divided into four platoons, each roughly twenty-five strong and headed by a captain. The sheriff's platoon was to lie in wait near the east entrance to the village. Mungo's and Wilson's platoons were each slated to start out at Mungo's, but for very different reasons. Finally, Dr. Callahan's platoon would be sent off to attack the enemy.

Ever since the sheriff had named him a platoon captain, Wilson had been glowing. "I won't let you down, sheriff," he said.

The sheriff put an arm across the boy's slim shoulders. "I know you won't, son." In many ways, Wilson's job was the most important, and the sheriff wanted someone he could trust in charge.

Mungo was happy to have a platoon—he said he could make sure his crew could avoid damaging the slickskins' brains so he could try out some new recipes—but Dr. Callahan was less enthusiastic.

"I'm not good at this sort of thing," he said, worry splayed all over his enormous face. "Damn it, sheriff, I'm a doctor, not a slickskin hunter. I've never been one to whistle past the graveyard. I usually whistle in the graveyard, as a matter of fact."

"I know that, doc," said the sheriff. "That's why I put you in the platoon that should see the least fighting."

"But you said we were to attack the slickskins head on. I don't understand."

"Then let me explain it to you," said the sheriff, and he went on to lay out the plan for Dr. Callahan's platoon in painstaking detail as they walked around the village square.

After the plan had been fully explained for him—three times—Dr. Callahan was much relieved. "Thank you, sheriff, thank you," he said, shaking the sheriff's hand.

"There's still going to be danger, doctor. You're still putting yourself at risk."

"I know. But this is a risk I feel comfortable taking."

"Glad to hear you say that, doc. Now let's get ready."

After the sheriff drilled the townspeople in offensive and defensive attack strategies, the platoon leaders met with their charges to explain their specific objectives.

It was night when the preparations had been completed—the perfect time to launch the assault. The slickskins wouldn't be seeing the light of day again.

18.

The Battle of Owen's Folly

Communication. A long word for a very simple concept. The understanding of one another. But perhaps the concept isn't so simple after all. For how many times have men tried—and failed—to express themselves to one another, hindered by some unforeseeable circumstance? Can anyone truly comprehend the thoughts in one's own head? Is it ever possible to convey meaning exactly as one desires, to put into words or actions the precise idea one wishes to share?

Yes, but only thirteen-year-old boys can do it.

Wilson and his platoon assembled in Mungo's restaurant just before the sheriff gave the order for the attack to commence. He looked over his troops: men and women from all walks of death, none of them experienced in battle, but they did share one thing that was very important to their present mission. They were all trustworthy. He could see it in their eyes—each of them would see this mission to its completion no matter what. Wilson wondered how the sheriff was able to pick these ghouls in particular from among all the townspeople.

But the sheriff had indeed known what he was doing when he put together this unit. Their objective was almost as important as that of the sheriff's own platoon, and the sheriff might even say it was more important. They were going to rescue Jezebel.

Behind Mungo's were impenetrable rocky foothills that spanned the village's entire west and north borders, then continued on to the northeast, eventually reaching the cabins where McFarland and his men were hiding out. The plan was to use a little-known tunnel that ran from Mungo's cellar through the foothills and to a spot just above the cabins. From there, traveling single-file, the platoon could take a very narrow path down the cliff face to the back of the cabins. Then they were to locate Jezebel and bring her back.

Wilson approached the training of his platoon in the short amount of time he had with the seriousness he brought to all the tasks in his life he wasn't sure he could accomplish but really, really wanted to: he tried making it happen through sheer force of will. Within three minutes he had memorized all his platoon members' names. Within ten minutes he had assigned the platoon a theme song (The Battle Hymn of the Republic), a secret handshake (three snaps, a fist bump, and an explosion), and a mascot (the chupacabra). Within an hour he had learned the family histories of each member of the platoon, taught them basic first aid, and showed them how to move so quietly that only the most able-eared slickskin would hear them coming. By the end of their training, Wilson's platoon knew eight different attack moves, four different defensive ones, and the fundamentals of ancient philosophy.

"I still don't understand relativism," asked Margaret, the baker's wife. She was very good at tearing apart victims, but she was dreadfully stupid.

"It's just the theory that there is no absolute conception of good in the world," calmly repeated Wilson. "What's right for one group of people might not be right for another."

"Oh, I think I understand," said Margaret. "So like it's okay for us to kill slickskins, but it's not okay for them to kill us?"

The platoon gave a hearty chuckle at Margaret's question.

"Oh, Margaret!" said her husband, Fred. "You're just too much!"

Wilson was proud he had put together such a skilled, cohesive platoon in such a short time, but he was concerned about something. He asked the sheriff how he expected him to take on a group of almost thirty intelligent slickskins with just his platoon. The sheriff smiled.

"What, you can't handle a few slickskins?" The sheriff waited for a response, as if he had told a very funny joke. When none came, he said, "I expect there to be no more than five or six slickskins in those cabins by the time you get there."

"Why do you expect that?" asked Wilson.

"You'll see," was all the sheriff would say.

Everything went according to plan at first. Mungo showed them the trapdoor in the cellar that led to the tunnels, and they were off. Wilson had the town barber, Bub, defender of decency, ignorant instigator, slickskin slasher, hold a torch at the front of the group to light the way, while the other twenty members of the platoon followed closely behind. Margaret and Fred volunteered to bring up the rear.

They hadn't gone far into the tunnel before Wilson started noticing passages off to the left and right.

"Reckon lead anywhere?" Bub asked him, doing his best to feign intelligence.

"I don't plan to find out," said Wilson. "Our objective is to get in, get Jezebel, and get out as quickly as possible, and to do that, we go straight."

Bub nodded sagely in the torchlight.

They had been walking nearly twenty minutes, and were perhaps halfway through the tunnel, when a shout made Wilson and Bub stop.

"What's the matter?" asked Wilson.

"Margaret and Fred," said Tom, the youngest member of the platoon. "They're gone."

"What do you mean 'gone?'"

"I turned around to say something to Fred, and he just wasn't there."

Wilson found himself faced with his very first command decision. Should he continue on with the mission, which had been timed out so precisely, or should he go back to look for the baker and his wife?

"We need to keep moving," he said. "We have to be out of this cave and down the hill in thirty minutes, and we'll be lucky if we can make that. Besides, they'll still be in the tunnels when we're making our way back. That shouldn't be much longer than an hour."

The platoon nodded, and most of them appeared to think Wilson's assessment was a fair one.

Ten minutes later it was discovered that four more platoon members were missing. Wilson grew frustrated. This was his big chance to prove himself, to show the sheriff that he could be a real deputy. He didn't want to screw it up.

"Everyone stay together," he said. "This shouldn't be difficult. We're walking in a straight line. Don't go anywhere else."

When the remaining members of Wilson's platoon had almost made it to the end of the tunnel something terrible happened.

Bub pointed into the distance and said, "What that?"

To Wilson it looked like a mound of rocks, but as they got closer they discovered they weren't rocks. They were bodies.

The platoon gathered around the pile and began to recognize pieces of clothing. "That's Ned's tunic," said one member dismally. "There's a scrap of Margaret's dress," said another. "But if these bodies are our people, then where are the heads?"

With a chill Wilson realized why they didn't recognize any of their former platoon members. "Their faces have been smashed in with some sort of blunt weapon. If they had used firearms, we would have heard it."

"If they took them from behind us," asked Tom, "then how did they end up here? And where are the slickskins now?"

To a man they turned to look back the way they had come, but all they could see was darkness. And all they could hear was silence—not a drop of water, not the scurrying of rodents. Nothing.

They waited for what seemed an eon, seeing and hearing nothing at all, until finally Wilson said, "We have to go on. There's nothing we can do for them now, and the slickskins who did this are long gone. We have a mission to complete."

"Aaaaaaaahhhhhhhh!" A great roar sounded suddenly from just beside Wilson. They all turned quickly to face the new threat.

But it was Bub, letting out a bellow that echoed down the length of the tunnels and back again. "Damn right have a mission accomplish," he said. "Going get those 'skins, every last of them, and going rip puny little limbs off and feast feast feast until nothing left but dust bones."

"And save Jezebel, right?" asked Wilson.

"And save Jezebel, right," said Bub. Bub turned and barreled down the tunnel past the pile of their fallen platoon members, letting out another tremendous "Aaaaaaaaahhhhhh!" as he went. He moved surprisingly quickly for a member of the undead, and it was all the rest of the platoon could do to keep up with him. They had to—he still held the torch.

When they finally emerged from the tunnels they found the narrow path that wound down through the rocky foothills to the rear of the cabins, and Bub took it without hesitation, throwing down the torch, and moving just as quickly as he had in the tunnels.

"Careful, Bub," said Wilson. "One wrong step and you'll fall all the way down." The drop of a hundred feet might not kill a member of the undead, but it wouldn't be pleasant.

But Bub and the rest of the platoon made it safely down the path, and Wilson was happy to see that Bub had stopped once he had reached the bottom.

He peered out into the open area in front of the cabins. No one was around—just a freshly made campfire. He gathered the remaining members of his platoon together.

"Okay. Just as we discussed. Three cabins, three teams. We all go in at the same time. Watch me for the mark."

The platoon broke into the three teams efficiently, and Wilson was proud to see at least this had gone according to plan. But the real test was to see how they'd do against those slickskins.

The three groups moved in front of the cabins and signaled to Wilson they were ready. He stood beside Bub and savored the adrenaline coursing through him. The promise of a job well done. The promise of fresh meat. All that was standing between him and success was a flimsy wooden door.

He would show the sheriff he could be trusted. He slowly raised his hand and made sure the other two teams saw him.

He lowered his hand. All three teams crashed through the cabin doors as one, a testament to their training. In front of him, Bub splintered the door ferociously and almost leapt into the room. Wilson was right behind him

What he saw struck terror deep into his soul.

The Zombie Sheriff Takes Tucson

* * *

Dr. Callahan had no idea how he had gotten himself into this position. Just two days ago he was reattaching Mrs. Harrington's arm for what was probably the fourth time. Sure, the old lady wouldn't be able to use it anymore, but she wanted it sewn back on all the same. It was a cosmetic concern, she explained. How was she supposed to attract another husband if she didn't look her best?

He would much rather be dealing with Mrs. Harrington and her cosmetic concerns than doing what he was doing now. Which was hunting slickskins.

He wasn't a killer. Of course he enjoyed the pungent taste of fresh meat just like everyone else, but when there was a slickskin or a large mammal nearby, he'd let someone else do the killing. He just didn't enjoy the hunt. It wasn't in his nature.

But it wasn't entirely correct to say Dr. Callahan was hunting slickskins. More accurately, he was luring them. He told himself he could do that. All he had to do was walk to the cabins and walk back, right? That shouldn't be too much trouble. But what if the slickskins caught up to them? What if they had long-range weapons they hadn't revealed yet? What if their aim was even better than everyone said? What would he do then?

Kristen must have noticed his preoccupation. "What's bothering you, Doc?"

They had just crossed the east bridge leading out of the village. It would only be a forty-minute shuffle to the cabins.

"Nothing. I just..."

"It's the slickskins, isn't it? We all know you're not much of a fighter. Don't worry. The sheriff says we shouldn't see too much bloodshed—we're just the bait."

"Dammit, Kristen, I'm a doctor, not a fishing lure."

"The sheriff put only the fastest of us in this platoon. We're not even going to get close to those cabins."

"You're right, you're right—I know you're right. But I'm uneasy all the same."

Dr. Callahan stopped his platoon when they could just make out the campfire burning outside the three cabins.

"There's no telling how many are out of the cabins," said Kristen, "but I'm betting there will be at least a few. We may not have to get any closer than this."

With all his rotting heart, Dr. Callahan hoped she was right. He dispatched three scouts to alert the platoon when their prey had taken up the scent. When he was sure they had reached their posts, he said, "Begin."

Faintly at first, but growing in intensity, Dr. Callahan's platoon let out a haunting, soulless moan. It sounded a little like a prospective mother-in-law inspecting the boyfriend's bathroom and finding mold. It was, like, really scary.

Moans had long been the primary means of communication between ghouls, but moaning was, of course, not their exclusive domain.

Slickskin children, for one, learn from an early age that embellishing a simple scrape or fall with moans will almost certainly elicit extra sympathy or ameliorative treats from adult slickskins. Later in life slickskins use this same logic perhaps subconsciously to augment pleasure during amorous play. Slickskins have also been known to let out moans while in their death throes, again possibly to elicit sympathy and/or guilt from relatives and close friends they feel have done them wrong.

After seven minutes of moaning with no sign from the sentries, Dr. Callahan said to Kristen, "I would have thought them to be blood-thirsty enough to come after us at that. I guess we should get closer."

They moved about two hundred yards closer to the cabins and began again. After another seven minutes, Dr. Callahan looked at Kristen. "None the worse for wear so far," he said. She shrugged her shoulders and appeared on the verge of speaking when a projectile flew through the platoon and right into Kristen's head. Blood, skulls fragments, and bits of decayed brain went in all directions, coating those closest to her with a slimy residue.

"Run!" shouted Dr. Callahan, wiping what looked like part of Kristen's eye from his forehead.

As the entire platoon went into retreat (the command "Run!" of course being a figurative one; the best many of the ghouls could manage would be considered a spirited walk by slickskin standards), one of the sentries caught up with Dr. Callahan. "There was only one slickskin out of the cabin, sir. He was on the roof with some sort of long-range rifle. Did he hit any of our—" He stopped as he saw the side of Dr. Callahan's face covered in blood.

"Kristen."

The man's face fell. "I'm sorry. But the good news is the rest of the slickskins were inside the cabins. It wasn't an ambush, just a slickskin who got a lucky shot. Er, unlucky shot. It did the trick, though. They're all after us now."

Dr. Callahan's platoon needed every ounce of energy it had to stay ahead of McFarland's gang, and at first it looked as though they would make it back without further damage. But just as they reached the outskirts of the village, Dr. Callahan looked down at his forearm. A hole an inch thick had suddenly appeared—he could see straight through it.

Around him he saw other ghouls hesitate as bullets passed through them. Then one fell. That bullet had found its mark. Then another.

They were nearly there. Ahead, the village square loomed with the silence of a graveyard. If they could just make it a little farther.

"Onward!" Dr. Callahan yelled. In hindsight, after the heat of battle had long left his festering limbs, Dr. Callahan reflected that perhaps it was a wise decision on the sheriff's part to place the ghoul with the greatest fear of slickskins in charge of the platoon that needed to travel the fastest. Clever sheriff.

The platoon had reached the town center with no more fatalities, but their work wasn't finished yet. They pressed on through the square, many of them limping much more than they had when the mission began.

Finally, as they reached the southwestern corner of the square, Dr. Callahan shouted, "Halt!"

The platoon froze.

"About face!"

The platoon turned around.

"Commence—laughter!"

The platoon pointed at the slickskins, just now becoming visible as they neared the center of the square, and let out a horrific round of belly laughter that shocked the slickskins to a standstill.

When the last echoes of the laughter faded into the night and silence fell down upon the village square once more, and when the slickskins again began to advance on Dr. Callahan's platoon, it happened.

Piles of debris on the north side of the square began to shake. A hand missing three fingers emerged from the center of a large pool of mud. Out of the dirty waters of the trough outside Mungo's restaurant peered a half-intact skull. A ghoul burst from a rotting barrel, shivering splitters and muck in every direction. From the remains of a burnt-out stagecoach Mungo popped up. He looked around, saw to his satisfaction that his troops were right on schedule, and let out a tremendous moan.

"BRAINS!!!!"

This was Mungo's platoon. Their job was simple: wait until Dr. Callahan's platoon led the slickskins into the center of the village square and then push them back.

Scaring slickskins was one of Mungo's specialties. As a young ghoul he would be sent out to harvest brains for his father—but he wouldn't just kill the slickskins. He would make sure to surprise them each time in a new and terrible way. Sometimes he would just drop out of trees. Other times he would trail a slickskin for hours—just out of sight. His favorite way of striking fear deep into the hearts of his prey was to hollow out the corpse of a particularly rotund slickskin, climb carefully inside, and pop out once someone came to check on the victim.

He had spent most of the preparation time training his platoon to be as menacing as possible, because if there was one thing Mungo knew about slickskins, it was that when they were scared they were easy prey. Their behavior turned erratic. Their aim became unsteady. They often fell down. Some even wet themselves, which made them that much easier to track (and provided a unique marinade when their loins were prepared).

So when Dr. Callahan and his troops led McFarland's gang to the center of the village square, Mungo's platoon was ready. They emerged in all manner of ways, some of them quite ludicrous, but always as slowly as possible. For Mungo had found that for some reason slickskins became more frightened the slower the menace, which to him was rather counterintuitive.

They advanced upon the slickskins, who now found themselves facing two fronts of the undead: Dr. Callahan's platoon in the southwestern corner of the square and Mungo's platoon from the north. Both fronts were advancing.

Despite being deadly, experienced, and well-trained slickskins, McFarland's men were still slickskins, and therefore they were afraid. They were facing twice the number of ghouls than had originally been present, and they were now outnumbered almost two to one.

Most of the slickskins kept their cool, but all of them began to retreat back the way they had come. They walked backwards, warily watching the ghouls to make sure they didn't suddenly learn how to run. The ghouls, meanwhile, continued advancing, and the two platoons joined up to form a continuous line of slowly advancing undead. It was when the slickskins had almost made it out of the eastern side of the square that the last piece of the sheriff's macabre puzzle was put into place.

The river running along the eastern edge of the town square had a single bridge as a means of crossing. It was a stone bridge, and one of the few pieces of architecture in Owen's Folly not to have grown unreliable with the passage of time. As the slickskins turned they welcomed the sight of it, as the ghouls would have to form a much narrower column if they were to continue their pursuit across the bridge. They smiled at one another and hurried toward their freedom.

But as they neared the bridge they noticed the water become disturbed, first here, now there, then in many places. As they looked on in horror, two dozen heads began to emerge from the river, and those heads quickly became full-sized ghouls. The ghouls made their way with deceptive quickness up the bank of the river and covered the mouth of the bridge. The slickskins were completely surrounded.

Though it wasn't without some unique characteristics, what happened next has had many precedents throughout history. The Juarez Nacho Massacre of '23 immediately comes to mind, of course, but a more careful examination of the slickskins' imminent peril also draws parallels to:

- The Great Wildflower Cull of '07—occurred when hundreds of married men found themselves in the doghouse at the same time.
- The Mariachi Massacre of '16—occurred when a group of very gloomy ex-convicts stumbled into a major regional mariachi convention.
- The Slaughter of Sagacity (16th century)—occurred when Gutenberg and his minions first made it possible for a tract written by any average Joe (or Josef), no matter how idiotic, to find its way into print, thereby infecting untold thousands (or hundreds) with the same idiocy.

As the slickskins emptied their last remaining ammunition into the tightening circle with minimal success, the sheriff silently congratulated himself on a job well done. Owen's Folly had been a tough test of his command and strategic prowess. But his thoughts kept coming back to Wilson and his beloved Jezebel. Had the boy succeeded? He would surely have earned the title of deputy then. Heck, he'd give the kid his own star and call him emperor if he wanted, so long as he brought back Jezebel safe and sound. And what of McFarland? Had he stayed back at the cabins to meet a quiet death at the hands of Wilson's platoon, or had he joined the hunting party and wandered into their trap?

The sheriff looked out at the remaining slickskins, but it was impossible to determine if McFarland was among them in the darkness.

"Wait!" he yelled, just as the first ghouls began to reach the slickskins.

At the sheriff's cry, everyone stopped. The ghouls stood a few feet from the slickskins, while the slickskins stared terrified at their assailants. It was a credit to the restraint of the citizens of Owen's Folly—and to their respect for the sheriff—that they held themselves back while fresh slickskin brains were within easy reach.

"Where is McFarland?" the sheriff yelled.

The slickskins looked at him, but no one said anything.

"I said, where is McFarland? Is he here, or is he at the cabins?" Furiously he reached into his vest and shoved the sketch into the faces of the cowering slickskins.

Again, no one said a word. They just stared at the sheriff.

"This is the last time I ask, or I swear to God we will tear you limb from limb. Where is McFarland?"

When the slickskins again neglected to answer, the sheriff sighed to himself. The hard way. So be it.

"Fine," said the sheriff. "Citizens of Owen's Folly, it's time for breakfast."

The ghouls all moved forward at these words, and soon there was so much blood that the rising sun found a fine red mist as it shone down on the village square. Arms flew from sockets. Heads popped like corks out of a gun. The screams, at first shrill and panicked, quickly gave way to the soothing moans of the undead.

Mungo hopped about with a wheelbarrow he had found somewhere, collecting as many brains as he could find. As he passed by the ruined chapel and its small cemetery just to the west of his tavern, something caught his eye. He lowered the wheelbarrow and went to have a closer look.

The sounds of ravenous feasting faded into the background as he approached one of the graves and crouched down to inspect it. He noticed a mound of dirt had formed as if a small animal were making an exit for its warren. As Mungo watched, all of a sudden a hand emerged from the mound of dirt. It flailed about, trying to gain some leverage.

Mungo gasped as he deciphered the inscription on the tombstone. He leaned forward and took the hand in his own. He noticed there was very little skin or muscle on the hand. He definitely felt some bone.

Gently he began to pull, and the mound of dirt grew larger. Then another hand emerged, and both hands produced arms. All at once a head burst through the soil, and Mungo was helping the creature step out of the hole from which it had just emerged.

When it had gained footing on solid ground, it began to brush itself off with long sweeps of the gaunt hands, and Mungo noticed that everything about the creature was thin and malnourished.

Mungo cleared his throat awkwardly. "Need any help there, sir?"

The ghoul pulled caked dirt from its eye sockets, revealing two dark blue eyes. It cleared its throat loudly and spat. "No, thank you. I believe I can take it from here."

As the dirt and mud continued to fall, Mungo slowly beheld the form of the man: he was very tall and thin, and one forearm was simply two bones connected to a hand. Scraps of cloth clung to him like flapping scabs, and a few wisps of long gray hair clung to his skull.

When he had finished removing the debris from his body, he extended his hand to Mungo and said, "Jedidiah Owen. Pleased to make your acquaintance."

A broad smile gradually made its way across Mungo's face. The founder of Owen's Folly, returned from the dead! Could he perhaps be persuaded to dine at Mungo's? It would be wonderful publicity.

But he quickly recovered himself and took Jedidiah's hand. "Mungo," he said reverentially. "I've heard so much about you, sir."

"I'm sure you have. But let's talk over dinner. I smell brains."

"Indeed you do! Right this way." And taking up the wheelbarrow with its precious cargo, he led the town's founder straight to his restaurant and sat him at the very best table.

Looking out the window, Owen was astonished to find his own likeness staring confidently back at him. A statue of himself in the village square? He'd missed this place.

The feasting went on and on, until the feasters, unable to feast anymore, slumped down next to the corpses in gore comas.

The sheriff looked upon the carnage and smiled. The citizens of Owen's Folly wouldn't be troubled by the slickskins again. It was a job well done.

He looked up as from the north cries arose from the villagers. They had come up from Mungo's cellar.

It was Wilson.

19.

BROUGHT TO YOU BY THE FINE FOLKS AT READING R.R.

Mysteries can be very mysterious. Take murder, for instance. Who killed that person? No clue. It's a mystery.
Codes are mysterious, too. Does KTMN stand for Kill That Man Now, or Kangaroos Trounce Mutant Ninjas, or Kindly Terminate Martin Nash, or Kids Terrorize Moody Neighbors?
No clue. It's a mystery.

The boy was covered in grime from head to toe save for his face, which he had obviously just wiped clean. He was flanked by the members of his platoon, and they seemed to walk toward the sheriff in slow motion, their steps elongated, their faces inscrutable.

When they reached the square, Wilson looked up at the sheriff's hard face. "Looks like things went more or less according to plan," he said quietly.

The sheriff nodded. "The people of Owen's Folly are very brave."

"That they are," said Wilson.

"And—and Jezebel? Did you find McFarland?" The questions came out in a rush, a muddle of fatal suspicions and desperate hope.

Wilson's lips tightened, and the sheriff thought he saw the boy's eyes water.

"The cabins were empty, sheriff. I'm sorry." And Wilson told his mentor of the strange disappearances of his platoon members in the tunnels, and their reappearance as a pile of lifeless corpses.

"They must have known of some side tunnels." Wilson's voice rose with passion. "They must have known we were coming."

Silent howls of rage poured through the sheriff's mind. The rising sun grew dark, dipped back down beneath the horizon. The world turned blood red. He wanted to tear through something—rip a life piece from piece until the only thing left was the memory of what the thing had once been.

It didn't help at all to know less than an hour ago he had been doing just that.

The sheriff placed his hand on Wilson's shoulder and looked him straight in the eye. Regrettably he could only look at the boy straight in one eye, as he only had the one himself. "It's not your fault, son. I don't know what McFarland plans to do with Jezebel, but there was nothing you could have done to stop him from taking her. You did everything you could, and that's enough."

The sheriff put his hands on his hips and faced eastward, his chin slightly raised. Wilson thought he would look smart in a cape gently blowing in the wind. "I can tell you one thing, Wilson. I will find Jezebel. I will find her if it's my final, dying act. And I'll take revenge on McFarland if it's my finaler, undying act. Come on, deputy."

"Deputy—?" began Wilson.

But the sheriff had already left.

In the center cabin Wilson, Dr. Callahan, and Mungo crowded around the sheriff, who was sitting in a wooden chair in front of a rough desk. He held in his hands a small scrap of paper that he had found tucked in the pages of a book on the desk. It read:

Make your break at Center Point Station. Pursuit hot on McFarland.

—L.L.

The sheriff read it over and over again. It was a telegraph marked with yesterday's date, but why was it hidden inside a book?

"It has to be from a member of McFarland's gang who has decided to defect," said Dr. Callahan.

The sheriff slowly nodded to himself, working it through. Hiding the evidence was a prudent move. But what was the "pursuit"? Wilson and himself? If not, who?

"Center Point Station is only a couple miles north of here," Mungo was saying.

"Why it sure is. It's just a hop, skip, and a jump," said Dr. Callahan. "Isn't that where Fred asked Margaret to marry him? They had been going from station to station eating the hobos, God rest their souls. Fred said Margaret never looked lovelier than she did with hobo blood smeared across her face."

The doctor wiped a tear from the corner of his eye while Mungo consoled him.

The sheriff looked at the men from Owen's Folly. "My deputy and I are off to investigate this note. There's a lady who needs our help, and she just might be at the station. I'm sure Wilson and I will be passing this way again soon, and we're going to need a place to eat and sleep, aren't we, Mungo? And who knows, if this battle against the slickskins goes well enough, well, Owen's Folly seems a real nice place to settle down."

At this compliment both Mungo and Dr. Callahan broke smiles and shook the sheriff's hand.

"You're a real gentleman," said Dr. Callahan. "If you ever need surgery or an amputation, please don't hesitate to come into my office. It'll be on the house."

"And you know you're always welcome at Mungo's—and I'm sure the whole village would say the same, sheriff. You too, Wilson. You really showed your character."

"Kind of you to say, sir," Wilson said, and it was clear that he was pleased.

Outside the sheriff and Wilson mounted their still-uneaten horses.

"Just go northwest about three miles," said Mungo. "You should run into a worn dirt track that will take you right to the station. You'll be able to make it by nightfall."

"Much obliged," said the sheriff, and he tipped his hat to the men.

They rode hard, and it paid off; they saw the old weathervane of Center Point Station just as the sun was starting to sink behind the mountains to the west.

"There it is," said the sheriff. "Be ready for anything."

Instead of making directly for the station, which was a simple one platform affair, the sheriff and Wilson first went to a small rise that overlooked both the station and the surrounding area. And it was a good thing they did, for they saw that to the east a man was arranging what looked like a black sack over the railroad tracks.

"That sure looks suspicious," Wilson said as they urged their horses forward to get a better look.

The sheriff brought them to a halt when they could see the man and his actions more clearly, but they were still far enough away that their presence wasn't obvious. What they saw sent chills through them both.

A man in a black jacket and hat was bent over the railroad track, but he straightened often and looked to the west.

When he did so they could see he had an equally black greased mustache that tapered into a curl at each end. The man fidgeted nervously with the facial hair, straightening it out and letting it go; each time it would curl back up into a tight circle.

The object on the tracks that was the focus of the man's attention wasn't a sack at all—it was the helpless form of Jezebel, damsel in distress, bewitcher of bachelors, martial arts master. Her arms were tied flat against her body, her legs bound, and a gag had been forced in her mouth. The sheriff's heart broke as he saw her struggle in vain to remove herself from the tracks.

"Sheriff," said Wilson, pointing to the west. "Look."

Smoke was coming toward them in ever-growing plumes of charcoal gray. The sheriff said the only thing that came to mind.

"Shit."

He looked back at Wilson and said in a determined voice, "Deputy, there are two jobs to be done, and two of us to do them."

"You got it, sheriff. Your deputy won't let you down."

"I know he won't," he said, spurring his horse forward. "And Wilson."

"Yeah, sheriff?"

"I want the slickskin alive."

As the sheriff had anticipated, the man fled when he saw their approach, and the sheriff watched Wilson expertly wield his animal to track the slickskin. He himself made for Jezebel as fast as his horse would gallop.

He neared her struggling body just as the train rounded a bend and entered a straightaway, coming toward them at breakneck speed. He only had a few moments.

The sheriff quickly dismounted and ran to the helpless woman. It was then that she saw him, and the alarm in her eyes was as clear and piercing as the insistent whistle from the oncoming locomotive. He grabbed the ropes binding her and pulled as hard as he could.

Just as the two tumbled away from the tracks, the train sped past.

The dust hung heavy in the air. The rhythmic sound of the train gradually lessened. The last rays of the setting sun shone upon them.

Looking down at Jezebel the sheriff saw that she was even more radiant than he remembered. Her dusty blond hair was splayed out like a great, luminous fan, and her eyes were as gray as the truth. He was once again drawn to her lovely mouth that went almost all the way back to her ear, and the dark gap where her nasal cavity had been hinted at beautiful secrets she had to share. He thought of chicken and potatoes, for some reason.

He removed the gag from her mouth.

"Hi, handsome," she said. "Aren't you a little short for a lawman?"

"What? Oh, the badge. I'm the sheriff. I'm here to rescue you."

"You're who?"

"The sheriff. Surely you've heard of me?"

"The sheriff? The sheriff of what? Don't you have a name?"

"I probably did once, but I forgot it. People usually just call me the sheriff."

"The Man with No Name. Catchy." She spat out a stray piece of gag. "Well, the sheriff, you cut that whole train rescue bit a little close, didn't you? Would you mind untying me?"

Wilson told himself that it shouldn't be hard to capture a slickskin on foot. Just tell the horse where to go, knock the slickskin out, and tie him up. You're a deputy now. You're not allowed to screw things up anymore.

The man in black fled across the desert, and the deputy followed. The man picked his way among the rocks and vegetation that littered the landscape. It wouldn't be long before Wilson had him.

When he was near, Wilson called out in as manly a voice as he could muster, "All right, do yourself a favor and stop running. It'll be easier for you."

The man seemed to take no notice. If anything, he ran faster.

Wilson shook his head and spurred his horse to pursue. My missions are always so complicated, he thought.

Then he had an idea. Taking a length of rope he had coiled, Wilson tied a quick knot. "This is your last warning," he called to the man, who by this time was right in front of him.

The man still ignored him.

Wilson took up the rope and whirled it around his head until it became a blur. When he felt the time was right, he cast the loop of rope at the man. Bullseye! He had caught the man right around the torso, and his arms were pinioned to his sides. Wilson thought with a smile that must be a little how Jezebel felt when she was tied up. Without the impending train, of course. The man was getting a taste of his own bondage.

Incidentally, a word of advice for those finding themselves pursued by the undead on horseback: do whatever possible to distract them. Most of them will already be driven half-mad by the thought of being in such close contact with a living animal (the horse), and anything that can be done to heighten or complicate these feelings can only serve to aid those being pursued.

1. Empty any and all backpacks, knapsacks, suitcases, or other type of bag of any meat whatsoever. Ghouls certainly prefer raw flesh, but the sight (and smell) of

cooked—or even dried meat—may serve as the disorientation called for in this situation.
2. Do not run in a straight line. The undead always take the shortest possible route to their destination, and they do not alter this strategy on horseback. Zigzagging and using the landscape as cover will buy precious time.
3. Do not attempt to hide from the undead; they can smell human flesh better than a bloodhound. Holing up in a small cave or ditch will only ensure the ghoul has an easier time ending the pursuit.
4. The ultimate goal for the pursued must be either to effect a permanent escape from the ghoul, or to kill or incapacitate the ghoul. Finding a horse or other means of transportation usually means freedom, as ghouls aren't usually the best horsemen. Attempting to kill the ghoul, while obviously putting an end to the pursuit, is very risky, as achieving a headshot on a target on horseback is very difficult indeed. Rather, consider this fact: a ghoul with no arms is unable to effectively steer a horse.

Wilson cautiously approached the man, taking nothing for granted. When he was close enough, he admired his finely greased curly mustache.

After the man was securely tied up and hoisted onto the back of his horse, Wilson allowed himself a prideful smile. He rode back to the sheriff.

Jezebel was perched on a rock like a great, noble bird when Wilson got back with his prey. His breath still caught in his throat even though he'd seen her a few times before; Jezebel was the very portrait of elegance. Seeing her long blond hair taken up with the wind, he thought Helen of Troy must have looked something like her. The sheriff was a lucky man.

"And just how do you expect me to travel," she was saying, "if there are only two horses?"

"Well, I'm happy to let you share with me, just until we get you settled back in at—where'd you say you were from?"

"I didn't," she said, beating dust out of her dress rather violently.

Wilson let out a cough into his gloved fist.

"Wilson!" said the sheriff. He saw the man struggling against his bonds on the back of his deputy's horse. "I see you've accomplished your task admirably."

As Wilson dismounted, the sheriff walked over to the man and heaved him off the horse. He hit the ground hard.

"I believe you've met my deputy, Miss Jezebel." She nodded toward the boy with a smile.

"Now let's see what Mr. Train Engineer can tell us about all this nonsense." The sheriff loosened the man's gag. And got his hand bitten.

Jezebel gave a little laugh.

"How about that, deputy?" said the sheriff, shaking his hand gingerly. "Ever hear of a slickskin biting one of us?"

"No, sir."

"Me neither. Now let's give this another try." He looked down again at the man. "Now you no-good rotten gutless motherless scoundrel of a goat, you listen to me. There will be no more biting, you hear me? I've got some questions I'm going to ask, and you're going to answer them. Is that clear?"

The man turned his head away.

The sheriff let out a sigh. "So be it. Guess we're doing this the hard way. Wilson, grab ahold of him under his arms. Yes, just like that. This is a tactic I learned back in the East. They call it 'enhanced interrogation.' Pay attention—you never know when you might need to use this. Now hold him tight."

The sheriff took the man's right calf and held it up. Then he pulled.

The man's right leg came clean off at the waist. Blood gushed out like an overturned pail of milk. The man screamed.

"All right. Feel like talking now?"

The man continued screaming.

"Fine. Wilson, keep hold of him."

The sheriff pulled off the left leg. A second stream of blood, even heavier than the first, spewed forth.

"How about now?"

The man continued screaming.

"Have it your way. Wilson, this next part gets trickier now that we don't have as much leverage. You have to kind of hold him by the one armpit and by the neck at the same time. Yep, that's exactly right. You're a natural, boy."

Wilson blushed.

The sheriff tore off the man's left arm. More blood.

Jezebel wandered over to the legs and started to nibble, very ladylike, on the thigh meat.

"And now?" asked the sheriff. "Anything you want to share with us?"

The man was howling in pain.

"All right, then. It's like you don't even understand me. A shame. Wilson, I have to ask you to move down here a bit and hold him by the trunk and neck once more. Just like that."

Off came the right arm. Blood everywhere.

"Now, sir, if you've refused to talk up to this point, I'm going to assume that you won't talk now and that we should just finish this. Wilson, hold the trunk, please."

The sheriff placed his hands on either side of the man's head, just above the neck.

"All right, here we go."

"Wait!" shouted the man. "Wait! I'll talk! I'll talk!"

The sheriff looked puzzled. "Really? Every other time I've done this slickskins don't say a word. Come to think of it, I don't think I've ever had a slickskin say a word to me. You, Wilson?"

"No, sir. I usually just eat them."

"Exactly right. What makes you any different, if I may ask?"

"I speak Zombese. So I can understand you."

"Zom-what?"

"Your language. Zombese."

"What do you mean, my language? What was that word again? Could you spell it?"

"Forget it!" said the man, who appeared to be in some discomfort. "You've got to get me to a doctor. I'm going to die!"

"All in good time, friend. First you have to answer a few questions for us."

"Like what?"

"Like, I like to know who I'm talking to."

"Name's Nelson."

"Well, Nelson, what were you doing tying up this young lady and leaving her in front of a locomotive?"

"I was saving her."

"Saving her? From our vantage point it looked like you were trying to get her run over. Isn't that right, deputy?"

"Sure is. Can't see it any other way."

Nelson became even more agitated. He bobbed his head up and down, splashing into the large pool of blood forming beneath him. "But you don't understand! You don't know where they were taking her, what they were going to do to her."

"You're right," said the sheriff, "we don't. Why don't you enlighten us?"

"McFarland...McFarland and Anderson and their men were hired to bring in two ghouls. To capture and bring them in for tests...experiments. They both got their ghouls, one of which was him"—he nodded at Wilson—"but we were ambushed by a horde of undead and had to split up again. Don't know what happened to Anderson's gang, but we high-tailed it out of there."

The sheriff gave a wry smile. "Hear that, Wilson? I'm a 'horde of undead.' Never been given such a compliment. Go on, Mr. Nelson."

"Well, McFarland took us to a hideout belonging to some friends of his to regroup."

"At Owen's Folly?"

"That's correct. But the ghouls there were acting up as well. We'd pretty much left them alone, but something was working them up into a frenzy, we could tell. McFarland had us move on, going through some tunnels near the cabins. There were even undead in the tunnels. They were everywhere. McFarland had the idea to pick off a few and leave them in a heap to try to confuse them. Anyway, we got out of there as quick as we could and made our way north. That's when I took that ghoul and left the group."

"And why on earth would you do that?" asked the sheriff.

"Well, I overheard McFarland talking with One-Eyed Lester, his right-hand man. We call him his right-eyed man, actually, as that's more accurate. But McFarland told Lester about why he was hired to bring in some ghouls."

"You didn't know before then?"

"No. We follow McFarland's orders, no questions. He pays us well, and there's always food. And whiskey."

"I see. And what did McFarland tell this one-eyed fellow?"

"He said we were taking the ghoul to Dr. Gimmler-Heichman. Well, we had heard that name before, but it didn't mean anything to us. There was some sort of commotion when we split with Anderson's group about it, but we didn't give it a second thought. Like I said, we aren't paid to think twice. But McFarland was talking about the kinds of things Gimmler-Heichman was doing to the undead. Grafting limbs where they don't belong, attaching animal parts to humans. Some say he's trying to find the secret of the undead so he can use it to his advantage. McFarland said there was even a rumor he even wanted to start an all-ghoul brothel.

"That's when I made up my mind. I can't abide humans messing with the laws of nature. I don't know what causes ghouls in the first place, but I do know it isn't for us to fiddle with. Who knows what worse monstrosity could be created."

"Monstrosity?" asked Jezebel.

"Present company excepted, of course. So when the gang moved west toward Tucson and camped for the night, I made my move. I threw this here ghoul onto my horse—much like your deputy here threw me an hour ago, and rode as far as I could, not really knowing what I was going to do. I considered letting her go, but then I thought of all the pain she must be in, being undead and all, so I decided to do the humane thing. That's when you folks showed up."

Nelson told the end of his story with less and less vigor and increasing breathlessness. The blood that had been spurting from his stumps was now merely a trickle. He was very pale.

"I appreciate your information, Mr. Nelson. But just one question. Who is L.L.?"

Nelson hesitated and looked vaguely up at the sky. "L.L.? I don't know what you mean."

"Interesting," said the sheriff with a smile. "Looks like you don't have too much longer." He turned to Jezebel. "He put you in this mess. What do you want to do with him?"

"Oh, I've got an idea," she said wickedly.

As they rode west into the night they talked about what Nelson had told them.

"What do you think this Dr. Gimmler-Heichman is really up to?" asked Wilson.

"I don't know—but it's up to us to stop it," the sheriff replied. "You see, deputy, with great power comes great responsibility."

"Wow—did you just think of that yourself?"

"Sure did. There are a lot of people in this world who can't fend for themselves for one reason or another. Maybe they're poor. Maybe they have to take care of their families. Maybe they're idiots. But if you find yourself with the ability to do something for other people, well, it's your responsibility to do it. For all those people who can't."

Wilson nodded. "That makes sense, sheriff. How do you suppose we can find Dr. Gimmler-Heichman?"

"Easy. We follow McFarland. We find McFarland, we find Gimmler-Heichman."

"Sounds like a plan to me," said Jezebel, from behind the sheriff. She glanced at the back of Wilson's horse. "How's he doing?"

Wilson looked over his shoulder at the rump of his horse. "He's doing just fine. Give him a few hours."

Strapped to the back of Wilson's horse, once again, was Nelson. This time, however, he was very much dead.

20.

Kung Fu, Hustle

Violence is never the answer. Actually, revise that. Violence can always be the answer.
What was the question?

The sun had just begun to emerge, a giant ball of blood that sent long shadows of darkness toward their final destination.

"Bosch's work is a little too optimistic for me," Jezebel was saying as they followed McFarland's trail. "I mean, who's to say this isn't really hell and the afterlife is just more of the same? Hell, hell, then hell, I say."

"I suppose," said the sheriff. "Have you seen his triptych *The Garden of Earthly Delights*?"

"That's exactly what I'm talking about it. Worse, worse, and worst. What does Hieronymus Bosch know that we don't? Why does it have to get worse? How do we know things can get worse? Life's pretty shitty right now, if you ask me. Always has been. The dead are walking the earth, for Christ's sake."

"I interpreted it more as an allegory for the dangers of human excess," said Wilson.

The sheriff and Jezebel exchanged a smile.

"Oh, Wilson," said the sheriff, "you've still got a lot of living to do."

The sheriff was pleased that he and Jezebel had shared that connection. He knew in his rotten, putrid heart of hearts that she was the one for him (he was more certain of it than certain the sun shines), but he was anxious about her reciprocating the feelings. From the moment he had rescued her, she had played coy, which as any bachelor with any experience with the opposite sex can tell you, means one of seven things:

1. The woman is madly in love with you.
2. The woman is not interested in you but has low self-esteem.
3. The woman has some sort of physical abnormality, such as a facial tic.
4. The woman is drunk.
5. The woman is bored.
6. The woman is drunk and bored.
7. You are mistaken.

Despite the low 14.2857% chance, the sheriff was desperately hoping for the first option.

Just then they heard hoof beats on the path behind them.

"Looks like we've got company," said the sheriff. He was in the process of leading them into the brush when that company arrived in the form of four angry-looking men.

"There they are," said one. "We'll get them for killing Billy."

"Poor Billy!" said another. "He was too young to die."

Jezebel hopped off the back of the sheriff's horse, saying, "I'll handle this, boys."

"No," shouted the sheriff. "Jezebel, get back here. It's too dangerous—we don't know a thing about these slickskins."

She stood silently before the four slickskins on horseback, waiting.

"Well look at that one! She's just standing there waiting to meet her maker."

"Correction, Ed. She's met her maker, and he sent her back. Let's send the devil a message that we don't want any returns. Let's have a little fun with this one."

The four men dismounted. When one of them took out a pistol, the others made him put it away. Instead, they took up their rifles like clubs.

"Please, Jezebel," pleaded the sheriff. He began to dismount.

Jezebel smiled, holding up one hand to wave away the sheriff and holding up the other to beckon the slickskins. There was a coy twinkle in her eye.

They advanced on her all at once, and when they were within distance she performed a powerful roundhouse kick on the man to the left. It was a strong kick, evidently, as the man's head separated from his body and hit the head of the man next to him. The three remaining slickskins stood dumbfounded for a moment, staring at the fountain of blood that had a moment ago been their friend.

Then they regained their resolve and turned back to Jezebel. The man in the center swung his rifle at her head, but she deftly sidestepped the attack. As the man's momentum carried him away from her, she stomped savagely at the side of his knee, snapping his leg in two and causing him to fold up like a bad hand of cards.

"My knee! My knee!" he screamed, holding the joint that was now at right angles from where it should have been.

Jezebel looked annoyed. She took up the man's rifle, jumped high into the air, and brought it down into the man's chest. It broke through the man's ribs, went through his heart, and drove into the ground beneath him.

The remaining two men seemed much less eager to continue the attack. They both produced their pistols and aimed carefully at Jezebel's head. Just as they pulled the triggers, however, Jezebel dropped down and performed a sweep kick, upending both of the men, who now found themselves flat on their backs.

Jezebel again leaped into the air, flipped twice, and landed with one foot atop each man's crotch. As their cries of agony rose to the heavens (or hell—or a revised version of hell), she decided to show mercy. She grabbed each man by the back of the neck, and brought their heads crashing into one another, exploding their skulls.

As the men's bodies fell back down to earth, she turned back to her companions. They were both still on their horses, their mouths hanging open.

"Wh-what...?" stammered the sheriff as Jezebel walked away.

"I wanted my own horse," she said over her shoulder, giving him—once again—a coy smile. Then she picked out the best of the lot.

That night they decided to build a campsite, as all the fresh meat was much too tempting to simply leave behind.

"Could I have just a bit more intestine?" asked Nelson.

Wilson knelt next to him and placed some of Ed's lower intestine into his mouth. They had propped Nelson up against a rock so he could enjoy the feast.

"Still don't remember anything, do you, Nelson?" asked the sheriff. "The letters L.L. don't ring a bell, for instance?"

"I'm afraid not, sheriff. All I can tell you is I regained consciousness while riding—or, rather, being strapped to—this young man's horse. I don't remember a single thing that happened before that moment. To tell you the truth, I wouldn't have even remembered my name is Nelson had you not informed me of such. I have been quite famished since awakening, however."

"You'll get used to it," said Jezebel. She turned to the sheriff. "Have you ever heard of someone losing all their memories? I mean, is that normal?"

"It isn't exactly normal, but I have encountered it before. In our case, it is both a blessing and a curse, I think. He may have had valuable information to share with us, but he may also have been a bit miffed about the loss of his limbs."

"Is there any brain left, young man?"

Wilson dutifully deposited some brain into the gaping maw underneath that still glorious mustache.

21.

AURUMANIA

Since time immemorial men have been seeking the perfect gift to win the heart of a coveted female. Classic examples: diamonds, automobiles, expensive works of art (for the wealthy); chocolates, flowers, a voucher for a free drink at a local eating establishment (for the not-so-wealthy). But what is the true secret to a woman's heart?

Trick question! Women don't have hearts.

Sometime later, the three-and-a-half ghouls were back on McFarland's trail when they came across a welcome sight: a caravan of slickskins heading west.

"Hey, I bet I know what those are," said Wilson. "Those are those slickskin gold hunters, aren't they, sheriff?"

"Could be," said the sheriff.

"Should we go get us an afternoon snack?"

"I don't know, son. There sure are a lot of them, and only three and a half of us. Wouldn't take much for us to get into some serious trouble real quick."

Wilson tried to hide his disappointment. "You're right, sheriff. I don't know what I was thinking. I'm going to get myself killed one day."

"Nonsense," said Jezebel, putting an arm around the boy's shoulder. "You just have to know how to handle yourself, and when to take risks. I bet, for instance, that the sheriff here is so highly skilled that he could bring us back one of those ghouls, despite the danger."

She shot the sheriff another of her coy smiles. Bored or enamored? Or filled with so much hatred that she wanted to see his head blown off by the gun of a slickskin? What was she playing at?

"I—I don't know, Jezebel. I have no doubt that I could do it, but..."

"But nothing, sheriff. As a matter of fact, let me show you how it's done." Jezebel hopped nimbly—more or less—off her horse, and started walking toward the stream of slickskins. "Just follow the slickskins," she yelled over her shoulder. "I'll find you."

And with that, she was gone.

"Well," said Wilson.

"Indeed," said the sheriff.

They followed a path parallel to the slickskins, and it wasn't twenty minutes later that Jezebel returned to them, a slickskin male slung over her shoulder.

She threw the corpse down to the ground. "See," she said, and looked at the sheriff with a smirk. "Easy."

Wilson dismounted and made for the fresh meat, but Jezebel stopped him. "It's the sheriff's turn," she said. "We wait until he brings back another, then we eat." She picked up the body once more and hoisted it onto the back of her horse, then mounted. "That is, if he's able to bring another back."

She urged her horse forward, and the sheriff barely had time to dismount and hand the reigns to Wilson before he was left behind.

Tracking slickskins is easy. They're really very stupid, for one thing. They never, ever suspect that anyone with ill intent could be—at that moment—just behind them, ready to end their life. Or, if they do (again all odds), it is invariably when there isn't in fact anyone with ill intent just behind them.

The problem at the moment was that if the sheriff sneaked up behind one of the slickskins in the caravan, there would be another one of them right behind. And that slickskin would of course raise an alarm, until a slickskin with a gun was alerted, at which time said slickskin would arrive and blow the sheriff's lovesick brains out.

Because that's what this was about; the sheriff had no illusions. He was in love, and Jezebel had challenged him to do this thing that, while immensely dangerous, he should by rights be able to do. He was a sheriff, after all.

What was her game? Did she want him to fail, to be killed by savages so she wouldn't have to put up with his overtures anymore? Or was this a test? Did she want him to succeed? Would she only give her hand to someone who could face danger and not look away?

In any event, he found himself walking directly toward the line of slickskins with no clear plan in mind, which was odd. The sheriff was a thinker first, a doer second. He couldn't let this love nonsense get in the way of a job. Or of his life, for that matter.

So he stopped. And planned.

Alex loved gold more than anything. Ever since he could remember, he'd been drawn to that dull shine. Back in the East he had attempted many different schemes to procure more of the stuff. He had:

- Taken a job at the bank. But he quit at the end of his first day, when Alex was told the employees did not get to take the gold home with them.
- Tried his luck at cards. But it appeared that almost everyone else could cheat better than he could.

- Become a dentist's apprentice. But the dentist caught him trying to put fool's gold fillings in the patients' teeth instead of the real thing.
- Tried to rob the bank he had worked at. But he didn't have a gun, and no one took him seriously when he asked for the gold.
- Attempted alchemy. But he seemed not to be able to get the equations quite right.

Then he heard about the gold in California. They were giving it away for free! All you had to do was find it! And if there was one thing Alex was good at, it was finding gold—he just couldn't manage to actually hang on to it. So when the next group of prospectors left for the West, he was with them.

The trip had gone well, and along the way he had met quite a lot of people who shared his fascination with *aurum* (as the wise Romans used to call it, and as he called it himself in the quiet of his thoughts), though he never lost sight of the fact that they were his future competitors. As a matter of fact they weren't too far off now. What state were they in? Arizona. Hot.

What was that? Glittering there, just ten yards away from the trail? Alex looked around at his traveling companions, but no one seemed to have noticed it. He walked off the trail, bent over, and picked it up.

A gold nugget. Small, but good nonetheless. Funny that it should just be laying out there like that. That's what California was like, or so he had been told. Gold just laying out there on the ground, ready for the taking.

Maybe he didn't need to go to California after all. He looked around him, ducking a little so he wouldn't draw anymore attention to himself than he had to. Alex's breath caught. There it was: a second nugget, maybe fifteen yards farther away from the path. Had he found one of those veins everyone was talking about?

Three nuggets later, and Alex was in heaven. He had struck gold! He knew his prayers had been answered, and his heart beat with joy.

He was stuffing the seventh nugget into his pocket when the sheriff ripped that heart out.

Wilson never doubted the sheriff would return successfully from his mission—not when he left, not when he took rather longer than expected, and not when he heard stumbling footsteps coming their way.

So when the sheriff arrived and dropped his slickskin on the ground, much as Jezebel had done a little while before, he gave the sheriff a nod. The sheriff had said he was going to do something, and he had done it. It made sense.

"Well done," said Jezebel. She walked over to him and touched his cheek. "I like a man who can keep up with me."

A good sign, thought the sheriff. A very good sign.

Jezebel walked over to her horse, retrieved the slickskin corpse, and threw it down next to the one the sheriff had just brought. "Let's eat."

The sheriff and Jezebel started in on the corpses as Wilson lowered Nelson to the feast.

It wasn't long before Jezebel said, "Wait. Where's this one's heart?" She was talking about the slickskin the sheriff had brought back.

The sheriff looked a little bashful, but then he produced something from the inside of his vest. It was the slickskin's heart.

"I was saving it for you," he said, offering it to Jezebel.

She took the heart and ate it in two bites, then kissed the sheriff with the passion of a thousand stallions, her mouth smeared with heart-blood.

The Zombie Sheriff Takes Tucson

Sometime later, as Wilson took Nelson on a long ride to nowhere, the sheriff and Jezebel hopped on top of the remains of the slickskins and made sweet, sweet love.

22.

A Macabre Watermark

Nothing says you care like sending someone a kitten. Absent the availability of kittens, one may turn to the time-honored tradition of sending one's thoughts in writing that is barely legible, whose ink is smeared, and that is thoroughly wrinkled and crumpled from the however-many-miles journey it took for it to travel from point A (you) to point B (her).

This madness must stop. It is unreasonable to expect a person (usually a gentleman) to expend countless hours crafting a delicately worded letter, stumble to the post (especially difficult with only one leg), and scrounge around for enough change to pay for its sending.

The solution? Silence. Pure, sincere, nerve-quieting silence.

When two people are bonded by friendship or romance, that bond can only be strengthened by the absence of communication, for as has been proven again and again, if left with an absence of data, the mind tends to imagine the best.

I myself have four dear friends I haven't spoken with in nearly a decade, and we've never been closer.

But there's always kittens, too.

By my calculation it is approximately 110 miles as the crow flies from Phoenix to Tucson. For most of the 60 or so miles I have so far traveled, I have been sorely reminded of the lovely amenities Phoenix has to offer, not the least of which include the services of a certain washerwoman who made sure I had a clean pair of underpants each morning.

It is disconcerting to realize that I may fail to reach Tucson before my stock is depleted.

Of all the quirks a man may have, demanding clean underpants every day isn't such a bad one, is it, Nancy? I could have a penchant for eating cats or collecting snow globes, which, while of course being much more socially distasteful, would be a desire much more easily fulfilled, sadly. At least my peculiarities more or less conform to society's expectations.

What is it you always say? Be careful what you wish for—it just might eat you? I kid. In seriousness, though, the meeting for which I have long been preparing has been weighing on me all the more heavily now that I have almost caught my prey. The encounter may turn ugly; the sheriff has always been a ruthless fighter when he believes he is on the right side of the law. But I must show him—as I continue firmly to believe—that he is not, or, rather, that I am.

It is such a bother indeed to have to sleep outdoors with nothing but the stars for shelter. One must always be on guard, especially out here in the West, for roaming ghouls that might happen onto a camp. It has been much debated whether a fire is on balance an intelligent choice while out in the wilderness. On the one hand, it provides warmth, illumination, and protection—as well as the illusion of a more domestic setting. On the other, it is possible that a fire could attract ghouls from miles around. I have opted for a modest fire, shielded on two sides by a formation of rock. I have tried sleeping in the wilderness without a fire and have found I just can't do it. Besides, I know I will be sleeping so lightly that the movement of the moon will awaken me, let alone the infernal racket the ghouls put forth when they moan. For the moment, the fire is helping me to craft this somewhat pointless letter to you while I wait for sleep to come.

There are some positives to sleeping out of doors, of course. The air is much fresher. The scenery is usually stunningly beautiful in these parts. There is no raucous laughter filtering into one's room from below as if the floorboards didn't exist at all. But here I speak of my recent experiences, and those, while mostly pleasant thanks to the caliber of people I have met along the way, are nothing compared to the luxuries of my true home.

How is it, back home? Are the buildings still made of brick? Is justice still upheld by lawmen and meted out by courts of law—rather than at the end of a rope, as I have become accustomed to out here? It must seem to you I have fallen off the face of the earth and been deposited into an earlier time, just as it seems to me that you are in some futuristic land where transgressions are met with precise consequences and even the lowest of society may use the public toilets.

All this is assuming, of course, that there has not been a repeat of the events of four years ago.

I hope your salary is sufficient for the admittedly miraculous services you—

Please forgive the red blotch at the top of this sheet. Hearing that all too familiar moaning that I often perceive even in my dreams, I performed some surreptitious surveillance, which yielded two horribly decayed ghouls that were very near to my position. One was a fat little fellow, probably just off a meal and looking for dessert, and the other was a female with only a few scraps of clothes left on her body. She was grotesque in every sense.

But it was a modest exertion. The woman broke nearly in two with just a swipe of the cane, while the fat one popped like a balloon. I moved the campsite a bit to escape the splatter and some of the smell. Alas, this nearly finished letter could not be moved in time, so you now may enjoy a macabre watermark.

Look at how I jest. When did it become so, that we accept with a toss of the head these grim reflections of ourselves that just minutes, hours, or years before were walking, welcomed, among us, drinking with us, sharing our conveyances, bearing our children? What does it now say that I may turn a phrase like that, write off the encounter—the life and death encounter with a somehow living thing—with just a wink? Has humanity sunk so low that instead of respecting those who have gone before us we laugh at their misdeeds and misfortunes, laughing and laughing, as there but for the grace of God go we?

But look how I ramble. You know I tend to become verbose when I lack sleep. So let me end gracefully, lest I provide you with an entire tract on our humanity or the lack thereof.

Brian South

The mint cookies you sent were delightful. I just finished the last of them yesterday. Please give your Aunt Agatha my kindest regards.

23.

Chester's Brigade Redux

Sequels rarely have the same spice as their predecessors. Entering a new world for the first time provides a previously unseen magic that often entrances, shocks, or challenges. The second and subsequent trips into that world, however, show that the luster of such experiences quickly wears thin.

Dinosaurs become re-extinct. Child wizards merely learn new spells. Going back to the future seems questionable at best. Very few kids are really that good at karate. There are only a finite number of ways to rob a gambling hall, with a finite number of accomplices. How much grease is too much grease?

These considerations and others must be taken into account when revisiting a place that once held such a special place in one's heart.

The next morning they were enjoying a breakfast of cold slickskin when Wilson's ears pricked up. "Did you hear that?" he asked.

The others shook their heads, even Nelson—who lost his balance as a result.

"It sounded like a cry for help." Wilson stood and faced west. "There it is again. It's coming from that direction."

They hastily broke camp and mounted their horses. It was a good twenty minute ride before the others were able to hear what Wilson heard. It was a sorry sound: a low moaning or wailing. It sounded like a person in pain.

Soon they saw the source of the pitiful cries: it was a ghoul crawling along the ground. It was missing its right leg and most of its left arm, and as it crawled it left a trail of bright red blood like an oil slick.

"No—it couldn't be," said the sheriff, dismounting. He inspected the ghoul more closely.

"It is. Chester! What's happened to you?" He knelt beside Chester, as the ghoul raised himself up and rested on its elbow.

"Sheriff...waylaid in valley. Brigade needs help...McFarland." This was all he could say before he collapsed in exhaustion.

The sheriff turned quickly to Wilson. "Deputy, go get Doc Callahan. Bring him back as fast as you can. Tell them we have many wounded and we badly need his help."

Wilson had already begun to steer his horse south. "Yes, sir," he said with determination.

"And Wilson, this may be your most important assignment yet. Don't let me down."

"Never." He was off, Nelson still strapped to the back of his horse.

The sheriff and Jezebel were able to revive Chester and place him rather precariously on the sheriff's horse. He wouldn't say much more than he already had, only that what was left of the Brigade was back the way he had come. They followed the path of his blood.

What they saw when they reached the remnants of Chester's Brigade was horrific. Body parts were everywhere, and the ground seemed to be painted red with blood. Clumps of lifeless bodies littered the area, while here and there a ghoul struggled feebly to stand. Few if any were unhurt.

The worst, however, was the moaning. The Brigade members let out pathetic, painful cries that were similar to

Chester's earlier moans, but worse by a factor of ten. They sounded like wounded animals pleading desperately for mercy.

He saw Jezebel's face set like stone, and she and the sheriff went from ghoul to ghoul, trying to find something they could do. Rarely was there anything within their limited medical skill set; the only help they could provide for the wounded was to put pressure on cuts to stop the worst of the bleeding. They weren't built for healing; they devoured.

After he had gone through about half the wounded the sheriff realized the most terrible aspect of the scene. These ghouls weren't dying. They would have to live like this, with the full knowledge of what they had been, and unlike Nelson none of them deserved it. Most could barely crawl, let alone walk.

In front of him he saw a woman shredded from the torso down, clawing her way forward, her entrails following behind her. A few feet away he saw Jezebel gently lifting a man's head to give him a drink of blood from her canteen. Aside from his head, the man was little more than a set of shoulders and an arm.

Wilson must have taken the sheriff's exhortations to heart; he was back with Dr. Callahan by the time the sheriff and Jezebel had performed their clumsy triage of the wounded. Upon entering the valley, the deputy's face blanched, and tears welled up in his eyes.

The sheriff seemed to read the boy's mind. These were people he had spent his whole life with, people he had abandoned to go adventuring with the sheriff. "There isn't anything you could have done," he said to his deputy as the doctor began examining the ghouls. "This was a horrible, purposeful attack. If this was McFarland, he knew what he was doing."

All told, of the fifty original members of the Brigade, perhaps a dozen remained.

The sheriff, Wilson, and Jezebel stayed with the Brigade as its surviving members recovered. The first night Chester was well enough to tell the sheriff more fully what had happened.

"We were a well-oiled killing machine," he began. "Your visit to the Brigade gave us the inspiration we had been lacking, and we put it to good use. We trained for days on end and had taken on slickskins we encountered in our wanderings three different times, each to great success.

"One of our scouts had informed me of a village, Owen's Folly, that was being terrorized by a group of fiendish slickskin bandits. Supposedly the 'skins were real smart ones, going straight for the brain. Don't know why that intelligence doesn't get passed around in the slickskin community, but I'm not complaining. We were told these bandits had killed all the law enforcement in town and the citizens had resorted to using untrained militiamen for defense.

"Well, we took a vote, and it was unanimous. We had to help them. The Brigade had never taken on slickskins nearly this well-trained, but we all felt it was our duty. We mobilized and moved toward the town, and were about two miles away when it happened.

"I've never seen slickskins so savage. They seemed to take a sadistic pleasure in killing and dismembering ghouls. I don't know how many of them there were, but they seemed to be everywhere—hacking with axes, bludgeoning with bats, lashing with chains, using pistols at point-blank range. It was the most horrific thing I've ever witnessed."

Chester dropped his head into his remaining hand and began weeping. Jezebel put an arm around his shoulder.

"But that's not even the worst of it," he continued. "When they had done their nasty work, and we few were writhing on the ground at their feet, the boss said in this booming voice, 'Now, we've got two of your little group to make up for the ones that were taken from us. I know you folks ain't completely dead, but I'm fairly certain you won't be after us.'"

"He laughed, and his men laughed too. I couldn't even raise my head to get a look at them, but I could feel their anger and frustration. They wanted us to hurt. The worst part of the whole thing was I don't know who they took—I don't know who from the Brigade is dead or captured.

"'So we'll be taking these two,' he said, 'and you can tell him McFarland says not to follow us this time, because if he does, he's dead and they're dead. Again. Besides, I have a feeling he might be a little late. He'll have his hands full with you all.'"

"Again they all laughed, and this time their laughter faded away into the darkness. When I came to, I saw that I had to get help, so I set out to find some, and that's when you found me."

"Jesus," said Wilson.

"You said it, kid," said Jezebel.

"Are we off for them, sheriff? Should I saddle the horses?"

The sheriff sat in thought for a long while, so long in fact that they all wondered if he had drifted off and was thinking of something happy and safe from his childhood. But he hadn't.

"No," he said. "We can't catch up with them now, just like he said. I'm afraid it's too late to reclaim your friends, Chester. But I can promise you this: it isn't too late for revenge."

24.

My Darling Jezebel

Men and women rarely get along, as they usually want completely different things. When women want the couple to get to know each other first, men want sex. When women want go out with other couples and have fun, men want sex. When women want to settle down and raise a family, men want sex. When women want sex, men want sex.

Really the only time men and women get along is when women want sex.

The very first thing the sheriff did was send Wilson—once again—back to Owen's Folly to retrieve Mungo and Bub. He wouldn't tell anyone what he was planning, just that he needed men he could trust. When Jezebel asked him why he couldn't use females he could trust, he became frustrated and muttered something about feminists and political correctness.

As the sheriff wandered away to hold his own counsel, Dr. Callahan continued mending the limbs of the Brigade members. Most of the fixes were purely cosmetic—reattaching an ear, popping in a dirty eyeball—but the doctor was able to reattach the original arms of two of the wounded, and Dr. Callahan was somewhat optimistic that with time they might even regain the use of the limbs. For others, he fashioned false legs out of timber and sewed on spare arms of a length that nearly matched those of the originals. He even built a sort of wheelbarrow that Nelson could be strapped into and pushed around in.

For his work restoring so much for the Brigade, Dr. Callahan was voted a lifetime honorary member, which nearly moved the doctor to tears.

"I've never been voted an honorary member of anything," said Dr. Callahan, wiping his eyes.

"You've earned it, doc," said Chester, hobbling a bit on his new leg. "You've earned it, and more. We can't thank you enough."

Away from this heart-warming scene Jezebel approached the sheriff, who was still off by himself.

"You have a minute, sheriff?" she asked.

He started, as if he had been in another world. But when he saw who it was who had called to him, his face instantly grew brighter.

"Of course, Jezebel, of course. For you, anything."

She sat on a rock beside him. "You're in love with me, aren't you?"

"No...I mean, I don't know what you're talking—" Jezebel gave him a knowing smile. He hung his head and let out a sigh. "Yes, I am. You know I am."

"Well I'm in love with you too, you big lug."

Jezebel thought it was cute—if a bit un-sheriff-like—to see him blush.

"Now that we've got that taken care of, to the matter at hand."

The sheriff instantly grew serious. "What of it?"

"I know why you sent for Mungo and Bub. I want in. This McFarland almost killed me, and he needs to pay."

"Jezebel, this isn't any sort of business for women."

"Don't give me that nonsense. You've seen what I can do, how I can handle myself. I have to be there when he goes down."

"Your dedication is touching. Really, it is. You're a credit to your sex. But we have all the fighters we need."

"All the male fighters, you mean."

"Jezebel, if something should happen to you..."

"Last chance. Let me join you. You'll be sorry if you don't."

"Last night we said a great many things. You said I was to do the thinking for both of us. Well, I've done a lot of it since then, and it all adds up to one thing: you're going back to Owen's Folly where you belong."

"But, sheriff, no, I—"

"Now you've got to listen to me. You have any idea what you'd have to look forward to if you stayed with us? Nine chances out of ten, we'd both wind up dead. Again. Isn't that true, Chester?"

Chester, trying desperately not to appear to be eavesdropping, was. "I'm afraid McFarland would insist."

"You're saying this only to make me go," said Jezebel.

"I'm saying it because it's true. Inside of us, we both know you belong at Owen's Folly. You're part of their work, the thing that keeps them going. If we leave here and you come with us, you'll regret it. Maybe not today. Maybe not tomorrow, but soon, and for the rest of your life."

"But what about us?"

"We'll always have Center Point Station. We didn't have, we lost it until we came to Chester's Brigade. We got it back last night."

"When I said I would never leave you."

"And you never will. But I've got a job to do, too. Where I'm going, you can't follow. What I've got to do, you can't be any part of. Jezebel, I'm no good at being noble, but it doesn't take much to see that the problems of two little ghouls don't amount to a hill of beans in this crazy world. Someday you'll understand that."

"Now, now." The sheriff gently placed his hand under Jezebel's chin and raised it so their eyes met. "Here's looking at you, kid."

Jezebel stood and walked away. The sheriff thought she was going without saying a word until he heard faintly, "I'll be at Owen's Folly when you're done." Then a galloping horse.

Meanwhile, Wilson was leading Mungo and Bub into the valley, and they became more and more sober as they surveyed the carnage.

"Someone could so heartless, to think," said Bub.

"It's one thing to kill a man," said Mungo, "it's another entirely to leave him in such a state as this."

They were looking at a ghoul who, thanks to Dr. Callahan, was able to walk by bearing most of her weight on a single pole attached to her torso. She used crutches to swing herself forward. Hours ago she could only crawl around on the ground.

"It's disgusting," said Wilson to Mungo and Bub. "And it's the work of the same man who was terrorizing Owen's Folly. McFarland. Somehow he got the better of Chester's Brigade, and he kidnapped two of them. He left the rest like this."

The faces of both men tightened, and intensity smoldered in their eyes.

"Hello," called a voice. "Thank you for coming."

It was the sheriff, walking slowly toward them. He had an odd expression on his face, like half of his soul had been taken away.

"I asked you here to help me capture, torture, mutilate, murder, and devour the men who did this. The law's the law."

25.

A Man, a Plan, a Canal: Tucson

When can a man find it in his heart to do the noble thing? When all the odds are against him, when he's done despicable, dastardly things, when he's outnumbered twenty to one and his enemies peer out at him with bloodlust in their eyes, when the only one to benefit would be someone who can't possibly repay him, does he still rise to the challenge, take valor by the hand, and smile at the confidence of his enemies and stride boldly toward death?

Usually not.

"Well, sheriff," said Mungo without missing a beat, "you know I'm on board for the eating part, especially if there's brains involved. And looking at what these animals did to these fine people, the capturing, torturing, mutilating, murdering, and devouring seems only fair."

"Agree," said Bub. "After what sheriff done for Owen's Folly, least can do to get help revenge on McFarland scoundrel. What have in mind?"

The sheriff led them to the small campfire he had made nearby. "One moment," he said, and he went back the way they had come.

Wilson sat stone-faced with the other two ghouls. He was still a boy, but he had seen enough horror in his life for an old man.

"What is it about slickskins," he asked his companions, "that makes them hunt us down like animals?"

"Their nature," said Bub. "Vicious, vicious, blood-thirsty beasty beasts."

"I wonder if it's because we eat them all the time," said Mungo. "No, that doesn't make sense. Slickskins hunt deer for food, and you don't see the deer in an armed revolt against the slickskins. It's just the natural order of things; some animals eat other animals. Ghouls eat slickskins, slickskins eat deer, deer eat grass. The grass doesn't complain to the deer anymore than the deer complains to the slickskin. Perhaps it's time the slickskins just accept their place in the food chain."

"They had better," said Wilson, "or else we'll get more and more cases like this one." He nodded toward the site of the massacre, where ghoul blood still seeped into the sandy soil.

"We're going to make sure that doesn't happen," said the sheriff. Following him was Dr. Callahan, who already looked uneasy. The sheriff and the doctor sat beside the three ghouls.

"Let's talk. You've all seen what happened in that valley. Doc, you most of all. It's a terrible, terrible thing. I swore an oath long ago to see that evil-doers of every stripe are brought to justice, but this goes far beyond that. These were fine people I knew and loved, people who raised my deputy, made him the man he is today. These were good people.

"I've asked each of you to be here because I believe you are the most capable ghouls I've ever met. You defended Owen's Folly with courage, cunning, and heart. You've proven yourself to be fearless in the face of danger. And you're willing to do the right thing, no matter what the cost.

"Now Wilson and I are heading to Tucson. That's where McFarland was going; he's probably already there now. We're going to deal with McFarland once and for all, and make him answer for the horrible things he's done here and at Owen's Folly.

"But there's an even greater evil, one that we know less about. We've been hearing about a man, a Dr. Gimmler-Heichman, who has been performing experiments on ghouls. That's who McFarland is headed to, bringing two ghouls from Chester's Brigade in tow. We don't know what sort of experiments this man is conducting, but we've heard rumors. Wilson and I plan to stop those experiments.

"And here's the thing: I don't want an army of ghouls with me, because Tucson is swarming with slickskins—it's infested with them. But we could use a small, elite team that can move about undetected. I'd like you folks to be that team."

The three ghouls from Owen's Folly looked at one another wordlessly. They knew what a noble thing the sheriff was proposing, but to varying degrees each of them—especially the doctor—thought of himself as something other than a soldier.

Mungo was the first to speak. "You know I'm in, sheriff. I would go to the ends of the earth if you said it was for a good cause, and this cause is certainly that. Besides, I've heard rumors that Tucson brains have a special zest to them that makes an excellent curry. Dying to try it."

"Mungo, you're a brave soul," said the sheriff. "Thank you kindly."

Bub and Dr. Callahan sat thinking. Mungo was the closest thing to a real fighter in Owen's Folly. He had been trained in various methods of surprise attacks, and he had a knack for dismemberment. But what about them? Bub was the town barber, and Dr. Callahan's skills lay in mending wounds, not inflicting them.

"Well," said Bub, "you know I not much fighter. I mean, I good at it, but I rather eat someone than kill themselves. Don't know though I could look myself in the trimming mirror again if turned down, the sheriff. Besides, cut my customers while shaving them often— shouldn't be bad for you."

Wilson visibly brightened at the news Bub was joining them. While Wilson was a more natural soldier, he had taken quite a liking to him during their time together at Owen's Folly.

"I thank you, Bub," said the sheriff. "It means a lot to us."

That left Dr. Callahan. And while the rest of the group was sitting awkwardly, waiting for his decision, the doctor was thinking of a time in his childhood when a giant bear had attacked and killed his kid sister. He hated that bear. He hated it so much, he hunted it down and ate it. After picking out the bits he was pretty sure were his sister. But the fact of the matter was that he was moved to such anger that he could actually take a stand, actually go against his pacific nature and turn his rage into righteous determination. And, if he was truly honest with himself, he was quite good at killing, too. He knew that the sheriff's cause was just. He knew that McFarland and his men were evil. But what really got his ire up, his blood boiling, was remembering all the stitches he had just sewn, all the wounds he had cauterized, all the crude, artificial limbs he had just constructed. Those people would never live lives as full as they once did, to say nothing of the many others who had died at McFarland's hands. They would forever bear the mark of what had been done to them.

"Doctor?" the sheriff was saying. "Doc?"

"Eh, what?" said Dr. Callahan.

"It's just that you were sort of...roaring. And your hands are bleeding."

Dr. Callahan looked down at his hands and saw that the sheriff was right. His nails had dug into his palms so deeply that bright blood was flowing freely from the wounds.

He smiled at the men around him. "I think you have your answer, sheriff."

26.

Tucson Two-Step

It is indisputable that the progress of technology, while making life simpler in many ways, has likewise made people much more stupid.

Primitive man benefited from the invention of the wheel in that he was able to more easily move items from place to place; conversely, he lost the need to calculate the trajectory of a catapult, something that wasn't reacquired for thousands of years.

When Steve's brother, Johannes, developed the printing press in the fifteenth century, humans no longer had the need to hand copy long works of writing. Penmanship has never recovered.

Now the ability to purchase audio recordings of other people reading from those books has finally negated that pesky task of thinking all together.

Soon, according to anonymous sources, engineers will unveil the ultimate technological marvel. Called the DeathTrap 800 (title still tentative) this machine will allow a user to stay in bed all day long and have sensory data of a selected fictional program pumped directly into his or her cerebral cortex. With some slight modifications, users will have the ability to completely switch off the awareness that they are not a part of the fictional program and are indeed strapped to a bed and being fed nutrients through a tube. Pre-orders are now being accepted.

* * *

Like a toddler mimicking his older, more socially aware brother, Tucson had many of the same features of Phoenix, but it didn't have the same bluster and luster. The streets weren't lit well at night. It was dirtier. It only had one whorehouse.

When Abernathy checked in at Miss Tabitha's Hotel and Eatery, a beefy man in suspenders with too much hair on his arms gave him his room key. "103," he said. "No fighting."

Abernathy put the key in the pocket of his duster and smiled kindly. "Let's hope not."

The man didn't return the smile.

"Say, where's Miss Tabitha, anyway? That's her name over the door, isn't it?"

"She's dead," said the hairy man. He spat into a corner.

"Very sorry to hear that, er..."

"Edgardo."

"Very sorry to hear that, Edgardo," said Abernathy. "She sounded like a lovely woman."

"She was horrible. I'm glad she's dead."

"Well. We all have to go sometime, I suppose. Thank you kindly for the lodgings."

The man grunted.

"Pleasant day," said Abernathy, putting on his hat and tipping its brim.

The man grunted again.

Abernathy left the man his card:

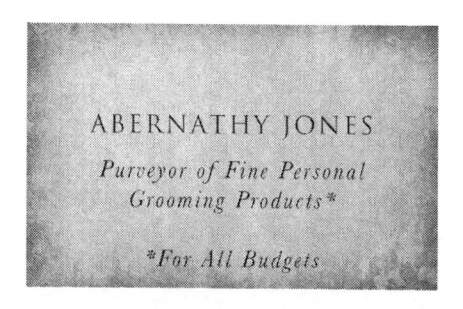

> ABERNATHY JONES
> *Purveyor of Fine Personal
> Grooming Products**
>
> **For All Budgets*

As he walked to the post office to check for messages from Nancy, Abernathy reflected on all that had come to pass in his life, leading him to this very spot, at this very time. He thought of the meeting he would have tonight, and he wondered how he would fare. He wondered about a great many things.

At the post office he found three letters from Nancy waiting for him, each mainly confirming past messages he had sent to her, and one package. As he browsed through the letters, one item stuck out from the rest: Dr. Gimmler-Heichman was in Tucson.

The thought both intrigued and terrified him. There was no doubt the man had done some brilliant work on the biology and psychology of ghouls, but many said that he had taken his experiments too far, that his work had taken him places no man should ever go. He remembered reading in the *Atlantic Daily* how Dr. Gimmler-Heichman had actually begun to train ghouls to do his bidding using a complex combination of drugs, electric shocks, and raw meat. Supposedly he had trained a ghoul to mow his lawn on command—all he had to do was ring a bell.

The grainy picture in the article had shown a smiling Dr. Gimmler-Heichman with his arm around the ghoul. The ghoul didn't look pleased.

He considered paying the man a visit. Maybe Dr. Gimmler-Heichman could give him some advice for his meeting tonight. But he decided against it. There was no telling what the scientist was working on at the moment, and the last thing he wanted was to be turned into some pseudo-undead version of himself. Scientists creeped him out, besides.

Abernathy took a healthy walk around Tucson and made a brief stop at the general store. Afterward he returned to Miss Tabitha's—or, more accurately, what was once Miss Tabitha's—had a bite to eat, and returned to his room. There he unwrapped the package Nancy had sent. A note on top read:

> Took some serious doing to find these. Enjoy.
> —N.

In the square box were a stack of wax discs that proclaimed:

BOOKS ON PHONOGRAPH:
Foreign Language Edition
Learn Zombese with Ease!

Abernathy added another silent thanks to the already innumerable collection he had offered up to Nancy. She truly was a miracle worker.

He took the records to the phonograph player he had bought at the general store, and the rest of the evening he spent learning a new language. He was so engrossed he almost missed his meeting.

27.

The Saviors

There is a saying, "You can't teach an old ghoul new tricks." It is unclear who said it first, but someone must have, as it's been making the rounds lately. More to the point: this saying is wrong. One can most certainly teach an old ghoul new tricks. It's the young ghouls that have so much trouble, as they are notorious for not yet having learned the adaptability that is the hallmark of the old ghoul. Young ghouls are too busy attending networking events, conducting protests, and voting Republican.

A more accurate saying might go something like this: "You can't teach a young ghoul new tricks that don't involve the slaughter, dismemberment, or disembowelment of slickskins."

This saying is quite true. It just doesn't have the same ring to it.

After taking his leave of Chester and what was left of the Brigade, and entrusting Nelson in their care, the sheriff began in earnest to prepare his posse, a task which would take several weeks. He had covered the basics of slickskin attacks when he trained them in Owen's Folly, and now he moved on to more advanced tactics. The sheriff's strategy was not to try to train each of his team in all areas; rather, he made sure each of them mastered at least three of the six ghoul combat disciplines while having a strong grasp on the basics of hand-to-hand combat. This way he wouldn't be teaching civilians more of a crash course than he already had to. He posted the following assignments on the trunk of a tree:

- Mind games: Mungo and Bub
- Covert operations: Wilson and Dr. Callahan
- Animal husbandry: Wilson and Mungo
- Surveillance: Wilson and Bub
- Non-traditional limb elimination: Bub and Dr. Callahan
- Elementary bomb-making: Mungo and Dr. Callahan

The sheriff was surprised that the three ghouls from Owen's Folly were such quick learners; when he ran exercises in the village they showed promise, but now they had taken their dedication to a whole new level. Wilson soaked in everything, as he always did.

By the end of the first week they could probably have gone to Tucson, but the sheriff didn't want to take any chances. They would train for three weeks.

They even developed a little jingle.

"Wherever there is injustice, you will find us!" Mungo would say.

"Wherever there is suffering, we'll be there!" Dr. Callahan would continue.

"Wherever liberty threatened, you find..." Bub would chime in.

"The Salvadores!" they all finished together. They also created a little dance, but the sheriff and consequently Wilson were embarrassed and refused to be around when it was performed.

The reason it was decided to name the team the Salvadores was because Mungo had once taken a culinary vacation to northern Mexico, and he thought giving the group some multi-cultural flavor would add a little personality, as well as strike multi-ethnic fear into their targets.

"You really went to Mexico?" Wilson asked him.

"Oh, yes," replied Mungo. "Food tourism is going to be the next big thing. You have to stay ahead of the trends if you work in such a cut-throat industry as food service."

"Very interesting. What did you learn there?"

"For one thing, the Mexican slickskin flesh has a sort of tangy aftertaste to it. Very flavorful, very delicious. The brain is more or less the same as your typical southwest American slickskin, with just a hint of pepper. I tried some excellent brain fajitas at a fabulous restaurant outside of Tijuana. Everything is locally sourced within thirty miles—very low impact, very green. They have an herb garden in the back, and they raise their own slickskins."

"Raise their own slickskins! I've never heard of such a thing. That must take quite a while."

"Sure does, and it's more expensive than you could believe. Of course, it didn't used to be nearly so costly, before the whole PC controversy over force-feeding and harvesting at a young age. Now you'll find quite a lot of the higher-end restaurants only using free-range slickskins, no additives, no synthetics. Completely organic."

"Sounds delicious," said Wilson.

"Oh, my boy, you have no idea. I was all set to open my own operation in Owen's Folly, but that damned McFarland and his gang showed up. Couldn't get the necessary supplies to line up the resources. Of course once you get it going it's more or less self-sustaining, but that's the trick, isn't it? That's the first thing I'm going to do when we're done with our little piece of vengeance here, is to set up a quality restaurant in town. Might even get a Michelin star one day."

Wilson was clearly impressed. "That's a lot of dedication, Mungo."

"We all have dreams, boy. It's only a matter of going out and grabbing them. You can always find a reason to put off what you really want to do with your life, but there's never a good one. What's your dream?"

Wilson thought a moment. "I want to be him," he said, pointing at the sheriff as he instructed Dr. Callahan and Bub in the best way to bite through an Achilles' tendon. "Everything he stands for, I respect. You can call it hero worship if you like, but I call it an apprenticeship.

"That is the most genuine, hard-working, and loyal man I've ever met. You saw what he did for Owen's Folly, and you've heard the legends about him. I'm here to tell—most of those legends are true.

Mungo nodded. "The world would be an entirely different place if we all aspired to be like the sheriff. And Wilson, it isn't just an apprenticeship. The sheriff made you his deputy. Don't take that lightly. Do you see a badge on any of our chests? We're risking our lives for the man, and all he gives us is a firm handshake, which is more than enough thanks from a man like that. But if you listen to what he says and do the things he does, you'll turn out like the sheriff much sooner than you think."

The sheriff was impressed with how effective Mungo was at slickskin mind games. He would walk through the training course, and nine times out of ten he wouldn't be able to tell where the chef was going to pop out. The sheriff knew he was dealing with a true master of terror when Mungo suddenly appeared from beneath the dress of a slickskin mannequin he had made. He explained to the sheriff how he had learned the art of fear-inducement while brain-hunting for his father's restaurant. He was certainly a natural at it.

Bub, on the other hand, was not meeting with the same level of success.

"No, no, Bub," said the sheriff, after he had fallen out of a tree and landed on his head for the second time. "You've got to use your girth to your advantage. You've got a big, fearsome frame on you—make it work for you."

"All right—how this?"

The sheriff walked back through the practice course, wondering where Bub would emerge from this time. He was about halfway through the course when he noticed the slickskin mannequin begin to move. Expecting Bub to merely mimic what Mungo had done earlier, the sheriff looked down at the dress, only to find Bub lumbering toward him. It wasn't a mannequin. It was Bub. In a dress.

"I think you're making some progress," said the sheriff, chuckling. "I'm going to be having nightmares about that for years."

Bub was also progressing nicely at non-traditional limb elimination. He found that his training as a barber translated well to brutality. As he explained to Dr. Callahan, his fellow student in the discipline, "I make same motions I do as barber; just make them more violently."

He demonstrated this strategy for the sheriff and the doctor when he sneaked up behind a cactus dressed as a slickskin and shaved off its entire cheek. "Stubbly," said the barber, bringing his thumb up to his mouth.

Dr. Callahan was also an excellent student at limb elimination, and for similar reasons. He took his medical knowledge of joints, tendons, and muscles and used it to his advantage.

"You see, sheriff, if you make a small but deep cut just so"—he slit a mannequin's upper thigh from behind—"the subject will collapse completely. And I challenge you to find me a slickskin who can shoot straight with a crippled leg underneath him that's gushing blood."

The doctor did worry the sheriff when it came to bomb making, however.

"Now, doc, just like I showed you. Sprinkle just a touch of the gray powder into the mix," the sheriff whispered as the doctor bent silently over a slickskin skull alongside a variety of powders.

The doctor glanced at the sheriff and nodded.

"Now the last pinch."

Dr. Callahan took a small amount of powder and dropped it into the concoction.

Instantly there was a terrific plume of smoke that enveloped the entire area, blotting out the sun. The sheriff coughed and waved his hat in front of him, searching in vain for his incompetent student.

"Doc? Doc?" he called. "Doc, are you okay?"

From the direction of the skull Dr. Callahan coughed and stumbled, collapsing at the feet of the sheriff.

"Good thing we didn't use the real explosive powders," said the sheriff.

"If it's okay with you," coughed the doctor, "I'll let Mungo take care of the bomb making. I'm a doctor, not a—" The remainder of his protestation was cut off when he passed out.

The sheriff never had to worry about Wilson's aptitude; he quickly mastered everything the sheriff put before him. Covert operations seemed to come naturally to the boy, while Dr. Callahan kept sneezing loudly as he was storming a mock slickskin shack. Surveillance was a piece of brain for him, too—multiple times the sheriff had found that his deputy had been watching him surreptitiously for what could have been hours. Wilson even took over some Bub's training.

It was animal husbandry that the deputy took a shining to the most, however. The sheriff was teaching Wilson and Mungo strategies such as how to make a swarm of rats precede you into combat, or how to get bats to circle over your opponent's head. Imagine his surprise, then, when at the end of the first week Wilson came riding in on an enormous javelina.

"What in world...?" said Bub, who was desperately trying to fit inside a hollowed-out cactus.

"I'll be damned if it isn't a skunk pig he's riding," said Dr. Callahan.

But the sheriff just laughed as Wilson paraded around atop the giant peccary, which was rubbing its tusks together as if warning the other ghouls not to get too close to its new friend.

They ate it instead.

28.

BLOOD ON THE MOON

Reunions between old friends are joyous occasions, as they allow each party to relive a time when it was clear someone else in the world truly knew them, accepted them, and would stab someone in their bodily defense; when friends reunite there is a rekindling of past identities: a recollection of better, more idealistic selves that are valorous and upstanding and completely unlike the banal mediocrity that both personalities have become; rather it is an affirmation of what one once willed oneself to become, an acknowledgement that reality or fate has blocked any sort of progress toward that end, and yet a small spark—a minute, almost insignificant flicker—is at this rendezvous rediscovered, telling us that once, one day, maybe not that long ago, we had the possibility of being great, and perhaps—just perhaps—that greatness is attainable still.

It was late. Later than Abernathy usually liked to be out at night, ghouls or no ghouls. Tonight there were ghouls.

He had left his horse behind and now he was walking on foot with nothing but his cane and leather valise. The full moon cast a silver brilliance all about the rugged, broken landscape, but more brilliant still were the harsh, razor-sharp shadows cast by the unique rock formations of the area, splayed out like vast swathes of inky black paint marring the land.

Abernathy thought to himself that a smarter man than he might read into the imagery around him something of the eternal struggle between good and evil, civilization and chaos. But, not being a smarter man than himself, he contented himself with the knowledge that reading into things too deeply can cause one's brain to hurt, thereby leading to increased stress and anxiety. Abernathy reveled in his unhurt brain, and in his relative lack of increased stress and anxiety.

The meeting he was now approaching had caused him enough stress and anxiety already.

He could see a small fire—surely a good sign—atop a hill that he was quickly nearing. It wouldn't be long now.

The gravelly path he traversed made the only sound he could hear, an echoing crunch that seemed to carry for miles. He gripped his cane tighter.

But then there was another sound, one that began so faintly that at first he wondered if he was actually hearing it. Soon enough, though, there was no doubt about it: a steady chorus of moans was coming from the hill now directly in front of him. He was close enough that he could see the wood of the fire crackling and sending up sparks high into the night. But he couldn't see the things that were making the moans.

Abernathy left the path and climbed the hill slowly. When he reached the fire he saw through the flames that a man—no, a ghoul—was sitting on the other side of the fire.

All around now the moans seemed to be coming from the shadows themselves. No matter where he looked he couldn't make out any sign of other ghouls. It was unnerving.

He looked for a place by the fire to sit but there wasn't one. So he stood, leaning a little on the cane.

"Evening, sheriff," he said.

"Abe," said the sheriff, nodding his head. "Been a long time."

"I came here, came to Tucson, to—"

"I know why you're here," said the sheriff, cutting him off. "You're here to kill me."

Abernathy was so shocked he couldn't respond at first. "But—"

"I don't need to hear anything you have to say. I agreed to this meeting to give you a warning. Those moans you're hearing? They're a special bunch. You may have heard about our work."

Abernathy gulped and nodded.

"Well, if you don't want to be part of that work, I suggest you go back to where you belong."

"But I'm not here to kill you. If you'd only let me explain. It's such a simple matter."

"Not here to kill me? What's that for then?" asked the sheriff, gesturing at Abernathy's cane. "Bad knees?"

"You know what this is for," said Abernathy. "You know damn well."

"Oh, I know, deputy. I was there when you had it custom made in Boston, after the turn. Never did understand your aversion to firearms."

The sheriff's words conjured images for Abernathy that had long been buried: A young man—a kid, really—plucked off the streets by a lawman with a tin badge. Finding a role model, a mentor. A father. Training morning, noon, and night: horse-riding, apprehension, the law. Talks out in the wilderness, on politics, on philosophy, on life. The onslaught of the undead—men, women, and children all—crashing through sitting room windows, devouring any animate thing that came their way. The fires, the moans, the blood, the cries, the terror, the rage. The quiet. Learning to live in a world forever changed. Protect the living not only from outlaws, but from the undead. Ghouls roaming the countryside, wandering the streets. Then, the unthinkable. A routine mop-up, a ghoul too close. A bite on the arm. Panicked eyes, soft voices. Pleas, refusals. A friendship broken.

"That's why I'm giving you a chance here, Abe. For old time's sake. Go now, or never go. The posse's hungry, and I won't be able to hold them off too much longer. I think you'd find they're a handful, fancy cane or no." Shadowy forms began to take shape to Abernathy's left and right. The moans grew louder.

"But if I could just explain—"

"Deputy." The sheriff's tone left no room for debate. "Not another word. Just turn, and go."

Though Abernathy had no choice, his mind rebelled, shouting inside the skull the ghouls wanted so badly that he should face the sheriff, do what he had to do, finish this for all time. But as he watched his feet take him one step at a time back from the fire and his past hero, he knew that staying would mean his death.

The sheriff had been no ordinary man in life, and he was no ordinary ghoul in death. It was no bluff that the ghouls he had chosen to surround himself with were indeed elite, Abernathy knew.

He told himself he had made the right decision. He told himself all the way back to the hotel. He just didn't know if he believed it.

29.

THE WILD BRUNCH

Brunch is such an odd thing. It was created by fat, lazy people who were too lazy to wake up at a reasonable hour and too fat to wait until the next proper time for dining.

Other qualities may be ascertained of brunchers. They have no regard for the sanctity of the correct time for eating dishes—scrambled eggs share the plate with a turkey sandwich, porridge is consumed with ham salad. Those indulging in brunch invariably have nothing better to do with their lives. They linger on their quilted blankets, gazing up at the clouds as if there were no money to be made, no responsibilities to be met.

And then they go have lunch.

The sheriff's reunion with Abernathy had more of an impact on him than he'd care to admit, but he was able to harness that energy by redoubling their training efforts.

At the end of the second week of training the sheriff was confident in each of his charges' basic mastery of their assigned disciplines, but he didn't want to leave it to chance.

So one morning he saddled up the horses and the Salvadores fell into formation.

"Gentlemen, I can't tell you how both impressed and grateful I am at your remarkable progress. You've conquered every task I've set before you—with one or two explosive-related exceptions. This final week of training we are going to put your new-found knowledge to the test. Our surveillance specialists, Wilson and Bub, will set out immediately and find us some slickskins ripe for killing. Once they've located these 'skins, they'll report back here, and we will devise our plan of attack. In the meantime, Mungo and Dr. Callahan, why don't you find some more skulls. Animal will be fine. Understood?"

"Yes, sir!" they all responded.

"Then make it so."

Wilson and Bub had been riding along a faint northeastern trail when Bub asked him, "Tell something, deputy. Do you think I good as sheriff says? Mean at fighting?"

Wilson turned to him with a smile. "Bub, let me put it this way. You are head and shoulders above Dr. Callahan, and I would trust the good doctor with my life."

"You think really I got what takes?"

"That and more," said Wilson.

Suddenly the deputy pulled up and cocked his head to one side.

"What was that?" he said. "Did you hear anything?"

They sat stock-still on their horses, hardly breathing. Actually, they weren't breathing at all. Ghouls can do that when they need to.

"There it is again," said Wilson.

"Think heard it," said the barber. "Almost like—singing."

The first thing the sheriff had taught them about surveillance was that you can control how quiet you are, but you don't have that kind of control over a horse. They dismounted and tied their horses to a tree, then silently crept in the direction of the voice.

"Home! Home on the range!" sang the voice, now clearer. "Where there's beer and the prostitutes sway!"

"My god," whispered Bub, "that horrible. I mean, really, really bad singing. I've heard bad singing. This worse."

"Where often is heard, a really loud turd!" To their great discomfort they could make out the singing very easily now. They were close. "And the pies are—What are the pies again?"

"The pies are infested with clay."

"And the pies are infested with—Are you sure that's it? It's not quite as catchy as the rest of it. I mean earlier you've got beer and prostitutes and turds, and you follow it up with clay pies? It just doesn't make a lot of sense."

Wilson and Bub peered over an outcropping of rock to see the bearers of these voices directly below them. There were two slickskins sitting against a wagon eating a late morning meal of sausages and what looked like gruel. No one else was in sight.

"Well that's what we came up with. Why do you want to be changing everything now, when it's already done and dusted?"

"I'm sorry, isn't the title 'Sam and Andy's Musical Extravaganza'? Not 'Andy's Musical Extravaganza'? I do believe there's a Sam in there."

Wilson gestured to Bub to back away slowly. Back at the horses, he said, "I think we've found our slickskins."

For millennia soldiers have used crude drawings in the ground as a means to communicate an area's layout, and this is exactly what the Salvadores found themselves crouching around now.

"Here is the overlook Bub and I used to reconnoiter the slickskins," said Wilson, placing a rock next to some squiggly lines, "and here is where the 'skins' camp is. They've got a campfire here, their horses tied here, and this is a wagon. They call themselves 'Sam and Andy's Musical Extravaganza.'"

"Sounds like some sort of travelling musical troupe?" said Mungo.

"No," said Bub. "These slickskins anything but musical. Wilson I talked about it riding back. Sing so bad has to be sort of cover. Might even be in area to spy us."

The men looked at one another uneasily. This was supposed to be a training exercise.

"Well we'll have to be extra careful, right?" asked Dr. Callahan, trying to hide his nervousness.

"We've got nothing to worry about," said the sheriff. "You men have outperformed everything I had hoped for you. If these slickskins have been sent here for us, well, they're about to meet us."

The posse all seemed to relax at the sheriff's words. He was right, after all. They had trained their undead butts off. It was time to show the world what they could do.

The two slickskins were just finishing their leisurely brunch. While they were the best of friends they admittedly quarreled now and again, especially when it had to do with the show. It had been Sam's idea. Last spring he had turned to his best friend in the whole world over a draft in the saloon and said, "You know what, Andy? I think I got me an idea to make a little money."

Sam was certainly the brains of the operation. He wrote the songs, booked the gigs, and managed the show—and played the washboard with some back-up vocals. It was a genius plan; they would travel from town to town, bringing with them a radical new kind of entertainment: clever and biting parodies of popular tunes and traditional melodies. And this genius plan would have worked, save for one crucial detail.

Andy couldn't sing to save his life.

At first Sam thought he must have had a cold or an inner ear infection. He had heard the man sing dozens of times at the saloon, and his rousing songs were met with cheers from the men, and when he sang ballads there wasn't a dry eye in the establishment. But now, every time Andy sang from their special repertoire, his pitch was as volatile as a drunken sheepdog, his rhythm as irregular as a lactose-intolerant housewife, and his memory for lyrics as reliable as a politician the day after an election. Besides that, he was deaf in one ear and halfway there in the other.

And then the truth struck Sam: the hard, sad truth of why he—he and all the men in the saloon all those times—had been suckered into believing Andy had the honey voice of a be-chapped angel.

He had been blind drunk. A dog in heat would have sounded as good—and quite possibly, better.

By the time the full revelation had sunk in, Sam was far too invested in the show to be able to make a graceful exit. Fliers had been printed. Music halls rented out. A wagon customized. He couldn't make a break for it until he'd recouped at least some of his investment.

So, the revised strategy: edgier, raunchier lyrics that the audiences would pay more to see and more saloons as venues in the hope that Andy's voice would be shielded by that same veil that prevented Sam from learning the hideous truth from the beginning.

This brunch, a business brunch as he called it, was to be the rebirth of the show: a calm, subdued setting that had little chance of injuring Andy's sensitive ego, and a run-through of the tunes with the new lyrics. All in all, it wasn't a complete disaster. While Andy couldn't comprehend the meaning behind many of the new lyrics, he knew in some way that what they were doing was mischievous, and he enjoyed mischief very much.

So it came as a surprise that when Sam had wandered a little ways away to answer the call of nature, Andy should show such despair at their situation. As a matter of fact, his sorrow seemed to extend so far that he was actually moaning!

Concerned for his friend, Sam made his way back to camp to find him sitting by the fire, just where he had left him.

"Things will turn around, Andy, you'll see. You shouldn't beat yourself up over it."

While the soft wailing seemed to be gaining in intensity, Andy looked up from his musings and said, confused, "Who's beating who up?"

"Maybe we'll get you some voice lessons or something, just so you can carry a simple tune."

Andy just stared at Sam with the look of a man who has just been told his pet pig has won the Miss Arizona beauty pageant. But by now the horrible moaning had come so near that even he had started to hear it.

"Hey," he said, "do you hear that moaning?"

Their first indication that something was terribly amiss—besides the painfully obvious chorus of moans that heralded death and destruction—was when something that looked like a half-decayed boar's skull was hurled into their campsite. It flew past the wagon, over their campfire, and over their heads before coming to rest at a large rock wall at the back of their camp.

Sam and Andy looked at one another wordlessly, the expression of confusion mixed with a touch of panic mirroring one another's face.

"Wh-what's that?" said Andy, nodding to the skull. "And why's it smoking?"

Before Sam had a chance to tell him that it appeared to be an animal skull, probably that of a javelina, that had been partially eaten and/or decayed with the passage of time, and that the odd wisp of smoke emanating from it most likely meant something within the skull was burning, hopefully nothing too dangerous, but who knew, skulls weren't supposed to smoke under any circumstances and they'd best be getting out of there immediately, the skull exploded.

Sam and Andy were thrown to the ground, and Sam got a nasty scrap on his knee, but save for this minor injury all that was seriously jostled was their nerve.

As the rock and skull dust hung in the air, Sam and Andy looked at one another for a split second wordlessly, the sound of the javelina skull explosion still echoing inside their heads and out. In that instant the two shared an unspoken understanding that notwithstanding any previous musical disagreements, they would do everything in their power to help each other escape with their lives.

Armed with this knowledge, the two rose to their hands and knees and began crawling—Sam toward the wagon and Andy toward the horses tethered next to it. They crawled very quickly; it becomes easy to speed crawl under certain circumstances, as anyone who has ever been accosted by mysterious moaning and projectile boar skull explosives can attest. They were even able to harness the horses to the wagon without any further trouble, and Sam had begun to let a glimmer of hope enter into his mind that they might be able to escape without further harm—despite the near-constant moaning—when they heard something moving in the wagon.

There was not supposed to be anything moving in the wagon. It carried various implements for their act—costumes, bowling pins, snake oil—and before this moment none of the items had shown any sort of tendency to move of its own volition. Sam was just moving to unharness the horses and cut their losses when he saw from the corner of his eye Andy moving toward the back of the wagon.

"Andy, no!" he shouted, but it was too late. He saw the wagon doors open and heard a terrible roar and a scream, but he was prevented from seeing what caused either. Against his better judgment he slowly crept around the side of the wagon to have a look.

There on the ground, beneath the open doors of the wagon, lay Andy. At first Sam thought he was fine, since he seemed to be conscious, but then he noticed the lower portion of his leg was missing beneath the knee.

"What—" began Sam.

"Mountain lion," said Andy in a calm tone. He pointed over his head toward the campsite. There, sitting before the still-smoldering fire, reclined a mountain lion, hungrily munching on Andy's shinbone.

"Let's get out of here," said Sam, helping Andy up.

"What about my leg?"

"Leave it."

It didn't seem possible, but the moans were growing louder.

Andy put his arm over Sam's shoulders, and Sam supported him around the waist, and the two hobbled as best they could away from the carnage of the campsite. Sam told himself he really should know better, but once again he began to have hope they would escape whatever it was that was out to get them, since the moaning seemed to be lessening the farther away from the campsite they traveled.

But he was wrong. Again.

They were passing through a small clump of cactus when all of a sudden two of the cactus exploded, or seemed to, anyway. In their place were two of the most horrifyingly disgusting creatures Sam had ever seen. Their shape was vaguely human, but their skin had decayed so much that it was hard to tell with any certainty exactly what they were. Their bodies were made up largely of red, brown and green sores, some of which persistently leaked blood, pus, or mucus.

Andy gave a shout, and whether he fainted due to fright or blood loss, the end result was the same: Sam was left propping up a limp body while two hideous ghouls slowly stumbled toward him. He tried to hoist Andy over his shoulder, but it was no use; Andy was a big man, and Sam was not used to working with his hands. Dragging him was out of the question, as the ghouls were slow, but not that slow.

He slapped Andy's face repeatedly, glancing up every second as the two ghouls progressed to within a few feet of them. The moaning was deafening. "Andy, Andy! God damn it, wake up!"

But it was no use. Andy didn't wake up.

"Sorry, partner," said Sam, and he started to run. Behind him he heard the ghouls reach Andy's body, followed by the sounds of tearing muscle and the slurping of blood. Sam didn't look back.

He made his way back to the campsite, as he figured the use of one of the horses would increase his chances of escaping any other ghouls that might be around. He didn't know whether mountain lions could outrun a galloping horse, but the answer wasn't going to change his mind.

Sam feverishly unharnessed one of the horses, and foregoing a saddle he hopped on and dug his heels into the flanks of the animal as hard as he could. He shot forward—straight into the arms of three more ghouls. The ghouls instantly snapped the legs of the horse, causing the unfortunate steed to come crashing down and spilling Sam onto the ground. He had only enough time to turn over before they were on him.

One of the ghouls thrust its hand into Sam's abdomen. It was a curious sensation. Sort of like having one's intestines flossed, but a bit more painful. The ghoul fished around a bit, found what it was looking for, and emerged with Sam's intact stomach. He seemed to examine it for a moment, then he squeezed the contents of the sack into his gaping mouth. Out came the brunch that Sam and Andy had just enjoyed.

"Hey!" said Sam, "I was eating that!"

Then he died.

The Zombie Sheriff Takes Tucson

* * *

"Sloppy, but effective," said the sheriff. The Salvadores were sitting around the slickskins' former campfire, enjoying a meal of slickskin and mountain lion as the sheriff debriefed them.

"Mungo, the explosive device was properly made, though a little light on the powder, given the circumstances. Dr. Callahan's inexpert throwing caused further problems. The slickskins were merely alerted to our presence, rather than being blown to bits."

"But sheriff," interjected Mungo, "how can we eat them if they explode? The best we could do is make a heavy jam."

"Mungo brings up a good point," said the sheriff. "It is imperative when a mission is underway that you constantly keep in mind the main objective. In this case, the main objective was to hone our operational techniques on living targets. So while a miss did not lead to the failure of the mission, an accurate toss and explosion was preferred.

"To your other point, exploded slickskin does not make a very good meal, even as a sandwich spread. Too much shrapnel.

"Animal husbandry, well done. The choice of a mountain lion can be a tricky one; you must always weigh the pros of its viciousness and terror-inducement against the cons of its ravenous appetite. In this scenario, it was the right choice. You even caught a break when it partially immobilized one of the targets.

"The only team to earn perfect marks this afternoon is mind games. The near-constant moaning, while a traditional and perhaps over-used choice, had the intended effects of terrifying the prey, causing them to make unbalanced decisions. Your ambush placement was impeccable; you were able to foresee the slickskins' reactions very well. Nice job, Mungo and Bub.

"Surveillance and covert ops, most of the data that was collected was accurate, and we didn't give ourselves away too early or make any dumb mistakes. Good work.

"Finally, non-tradition limb elimination. Bub, what was that thing with the stomach? That was a touch of genius—I've never seen that before, and I got a front row seat. But that pizzazz didn't excuse what happened before it. Taking the horse down was one thing, but how about some effort on the 'skin before you kill him? I mean, except for his stomach, he was in one piece!"

Dr. Callahan and Bub hung their heads, but they could tell the sheriff wasn't overly displeased with their performance.

"All in all, you men showed a lot to me today. You've trained your butts off. And you're ready.

"Let's find McFarland."

30.

Fear and Loathing in Tucson

There is a sport ghouls play that would terrify slickskins so completely if they knew of it that no one would wander outside his house without a full arsenal of weapons ever again.

The ghouls call this sport brainball, and in practice it is similar to the slickskin sport of football (what uncultured Americans call "soccer"). After a successful hunt, a group of ghouls get together and form four teams. Each team has a "ball"—a severed slickskin head—that is marked by a bandanna with their team's colors, and the objective is to kick the head into another team's goal, which comes in the form of the hollowed-out remains of the slickskin who so generously donated his cranium. The first team to kick its head into the matching 'skin corpse wins the game. The prize is rich indeed: the winning team is rewarded with the brains of all four slickskin heads.

Brainball may seem a simple game, but in practice it usually takes hours to complete, given that most participants can move only as quickly as a slow walk, and when players fall to the ground—as they often do—it can take minutes for them to regain their feet (if they have them).

The greatest of all brainball players was able to perform feats that have made his name a legend from sea to sea. George Better, according to popular lore, had so much control over his team's head that he could make it taunt his opponents at will. He was said to have the ability to eat the brains out of the opposing teams' heads without them realizing it—and without cracking open the skull.

After his encounter with the sheriff, Abernathy's normally buoyant temperament sank as though laden with the corpses of a thousand ghouls. He took a case of whiskey into his room and stayed there for days at a time, not showing his face to anyone. It was so out of character for him that Edgardo, the beefy innkeeper, came to check on him. The only response he got was a card slipped under the door:

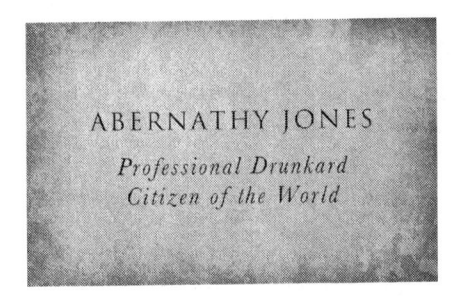

> ABERNATHY JONES
> *Professional Drunkard*
> *Citizen of the World*

The man just shook his head and went back downstairs.

Inside the room a haze of smoke danced thickly, distorting everything in sight. The light of a gas lamp fought valiantly to make sense of the place, but it was an impossible endeavor. Abernathy sat in bed, propped up by two pillows, a thin, poorly rolled cigar burning sluggishly between his lips. Beside the bed was an ashtray wherein lay the remains of perhaps a dozen more of those cigars, which he favored for no particular reason at all. He wrote furiously on a sheet of paper that rested on a writing board propped up by his knees.

> Nancy, I'm not a man who likes to admit failure often, if ever, but the fact of the matter is that I may have

met my match this time. My information was correct: I tracked the sheriff to a small village outside of Tucson, where he has been agitating the local ghoul population. I was able to get a message to him, and he agreed to meet with me. The meeting, however, didn't go according to plan, not even a little. The sheriff was determined to warn me off his trail. He threatened me, which though I should have expected it, still wounded me, still sent a shock of betrayal through my core. I tried telling him time and again my purpose for being there, but he would have none of it. Governed by some sense of twisted justice over the circumstances of our last parting, he was convinced that my intent was to kill him. The sheriff told me if I continued in my aim that he wouldn't be able to hold off his minions—or whatever he called them—and surely I would meet my end. I don't doubt that he meant it.

I'm at a loss, Nancy. You weren't there to see the sheriff how he used to be. Strong. Charismatic. A moral pillar. The transformation is complete. But, then again, perhaps it isn't. I could tell he still had his strength—he certainly looked like he could tear someone limb from limb, and probably has many times. And his charisma wasn't a question—just look at what he's been doing to organize the undead in the area. He's a born leader. As for the morality of the man, well, that's a question I don't pretend to know how to answer. Who's to say my perception of morality is clearer than his? Because I could tell he did have a set of morals, Nancy. I could. Why else would he let me go? It would be like the portly innkeeper downstairs meeting a juicy steak face to face and telling it to get out of here before things go south. It takes willpower, and courage. That's morality.

But I'm rambling. I'm sure you're used to that, but I try to rein it in when I can. I don't know what my next move is. I came out West with a job to do. Do I just give it up because the man I respected most in the world threatens my life? Maybe. I don't know. Maybe I'll be seeing you soon, Nance.

A week had gone by before the suspenders-bearing innkeeper with the beefy arms decided enough was enough. Though Abernathy Jones had paid in advance and admittedly he seemed like a nice enough fellow and there hadn't been a hint of fighting coming from his room and the personal grooming products he had supplied Edgardo were doing wonders for his sex life, something was amiss. No one holed up in his room for weeks at a time. It wasn't natural.

These musings ran so persistently through his head that Edgardo slammed down his newspaper—he was trying futilely to read the results of last week's geriatric soccer finals—and called over his beautiful daughter, Consuela.

"Consuela," he said, "go up to room 103 and check that nothing untoward is going on. You know how much I hate untowardness."

"Of course, papa," said Consuela.

Consuela had lived in Tucson all her life, and she had spent most of that life inside the building her father owned now that Mother had died. She pined every day, now that she had become a woman in age if not in fact, that she would be allowed to leave this place, and see the world. Or at least the rest of Arizona.

But despite her pining, Edgardo forbade her even to travel outside the hotel without a chaperone. The chaperone, of course, was himself. Consuela gradually had become resigned to her fate, but she still hoped that one day Edgardo would change his mind, or die.

"He is a nice man, Señor Jones," Edgardo was telling her, "but he is strange. Find out what is the matter with him."

Consuela made her way to room 103 and knocked politely. No response. She knocked again. Again, nothing. She tried a third time, much louder. Under the door slid a small business card, upon which was heavily printed:

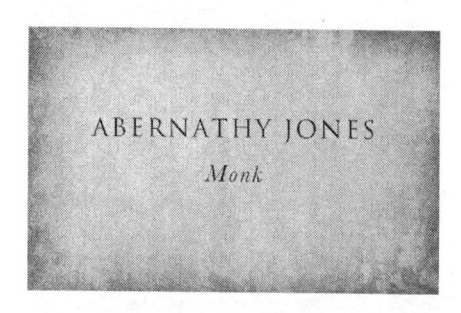

> ABERNATHY JONES
> *Monk*

Consuela furrowed her brow in confusion. Was this man Abernathy Jones really a monk? If so, why was he not at a monastery? She had heard that he had locked himself in his room with nothing but a few cases of liquor. Had he taken a vow of whiskey?

The thought struck her as the most pious she had ever considered. What a man! To test his liver like that, for so long, all in the name of...something! The dedication!

She knew, like she knew her real name was Rosalita and that Edgardo was not her true father but actually her uncle, that it was her destiny to assist this man in his monk-like pursuits, wherever they may lead. Her heart filled with the glory of...something!

Consuela rapped on the door with renewed vigor, shouting, "Señor, señor, it is I, Consuela. I have been called here to aid you! To aid you in your quest for...something!"

There was a pause as she listened at the door, her breath held in anticipation. Then, another card:

> **ABERNATHY JONES**
> *Solitary Monk*

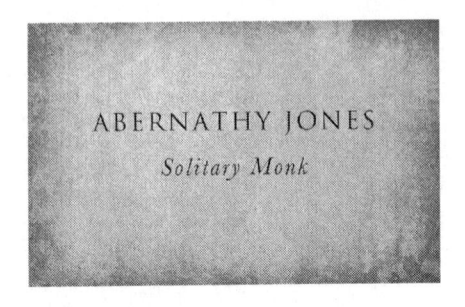

"Oh, but Señor Jones, I mean only to serve you. I swear I will never get in the way of your devotions."

Another pause. Another card:

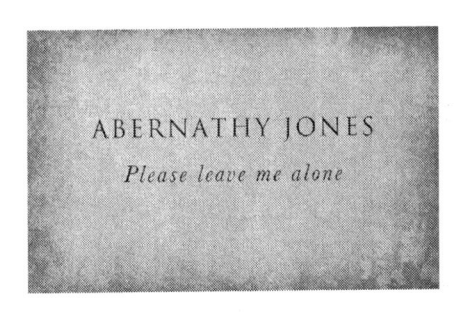

> **ABERNATHY JONES**
> *Please leave me alone*

When Consuela read those printed words a pang of sorrow coursed through her lovely body, and a great cry of frustration broke from her lips. Why must Señor Jones be so obstinate? She only wanted to serve him!

Her expression of frustration must have found its way into Señor Jones's heart, for even as the echo of the cry still hung in the air, the door of room 103 shot open, and there he stood, framed in the doorway.

Both Abernathy and Consuela froze. Neither had expected to find what was revealed when the door opened. Consuela imaged Abernathy would be a tired old man, made weak by his devotion to whiskey and to...something. Abernathy envisioned Consuela to be an overweight Mexican woman with four children trailing behind her.

Instead, they found each other.

"Well, hello there, um, miss," said Abernathy. "Would you, um, care to come in to drink...something?"

"Whiskey?" she asked.

"Yes. Actually, that's all I have. Is it too strong for you?"

"Not at all," she said and stepped inside.

31.

Wilson, P.I.

A true hero would never pretend to be something he's not. Heroes are meant to stand for something, to show the world their true colors in the face of great adversity. When a would-be hero acts with duplicity, he cheapens himself. A hero should always act with integrity.

The last known hero died 1,358 years ago.

The morning rose cool, with a gentle breeze caressing the cheeks of the Salvadores as they gazed curiously at the emerging sun. They had feasted all night on a mélange of slickskin, mountain lion, and horse, and to a man they felt more than a bit sluggish. But they knew they had work to do. As reluctant heroes, worn further down with every victory, the team wearily rose, one with the world around them, brushed off most of the gore and bone chips from their garments, and mounted their horses.

"That scoundrel McFarland has kidnapped his last ghoul," said Wilson. "McFarland, we're coming for you!"

"And after we take care of him," added the sheriff, "we've got a visit to pay to one Dr. Gimmler-Heichman."

The name of the scientist sent shudders through the Salvadores as they each in their own way imagined what hideous experiments the man must be conducting.

"He's evil incarnate," said the sheriff, "and he must be stopped. For now, on to McFarland."

The men rode west toward Tucson, the sun at their backs, stopping only when their horses needed rest, and once when they encountered a small family of picnicking slickskins, which added a few hours to their journey. But they rode hard, and soon they found themselves in the outskirts of Tucson, in a small village called Tanque Verde, according to a sign at the entrance. Like the rest of the area around Tucson, it was strictly a 'skin territory, and ghouls no doubt would be shot on sight. The Salvadores reined in just outside of town and huddled together to talk it through.

"We can't just storm into Tucson and hope we find McFarland and Gimmler-Heichman," said Dr. Callahan. "We'd be deader than those slickskin picnickers."

"Agreed," said the sheriff. "We need a plan much more subtle than that. Think about your training. What's the best way to gain information in hostile territory?"

The men looked at one another a moment before Wilson said, "Covert ops. Go undercover and pick up as much intel as you can without letting on who or what you are."

"Correct, deputy. What do you suggest in this scenario?"

"Well, the quickest way to find out where McFarland is would be to be amongst the slickskins themselves. Depending on how good the disguise is, one could get pretty close and perhaps overhear some valuable information."

The other members of the team nodded their heads in agreement. They all would have said the same thing, but Wilson was the quickest, or at least that's what they told themselves.

"And how many do you send in, and who?"

Wilson thought about it for a moment. "One. The smallest possible chance of detection. And if the operative is discovered, there is only one loss. As to who I would send, well, sheriff, you're the man for the job. You trained us on all the advanced areas of combat, and know them the best."

"Wrong," said the sheriff.

"Wrong? What's wrong?"

"It shouldn't be me who goes in. It should be you."

"Me? Why me?"

"You know covert ops better than any of us. You are quicker than any of us. And as a young man, you don't stand out as much. We send me or Bub in there, and we get discovered in a second. Most 'skins won't even pay any attention to you because you're young."

"What a hideous culture," said Mungo.

"Besides," added Bub, "if we lose sheriff, we lose leadering."

"Now you hold on right there," said the sheriff. "I wouldn't hesitate to go on this mission for a second if I thought I was the right man for the job. You fellows have trained hard, and each of you could lead the group, especially Wilson. If I'm ever taken out or incapacitated, I have no worries that you will be able to carry on with the mission just fine. In any case, it's going to be Wilson on this job."

He looked over Wilson's fairly typical ghoul appearance. "But you can't go in looking like that."

"What's wrong with the way I look?" asked the deputy.

"Well, for one, you're covered in blood. For another, no self-respecting slickskin wears clothes that dirty. It's a fault of the species; they're a vain group. If we wanted you to be a street beggar that might work, but for our purposes we need to find something else."

"I've got it covered," volunteered Mungo. "Be back before you know I'm gone."

"All right, Mungo, off you go," said the sheriff.

Mungo hopped on a horse and rode south.

"Now, while Mungo's out clothes shopping, let's talk a bit about slickskin behavior. What do you know about it?"

"They're fast," said Wilson. "And they don't always walk in straight lines."

"They rarely raise their arms when they walk," said Dr. Callahan.

"Cook their food before eat," added Bub. "Disgusting creatures."

"All very true, and things to keep in mind, Wilson. As your main objective is simply to listen, you hopefully will not need to interact much with the 'skins. But you can't do anything that'll make you stand out, either. And do you know what the biggest give away for ghouls would be?"

"Eating slickskins?" asked Dr. Callahan.

"Well, yes, I suppose that would be a fairly large giveaway," said the sheriff. "But I was thinking of something a bit more subtle, something you may not even realize slickskins don't often do."

"What is it, the sheriff?" asked Bub.

"Moaning."

The Salvadores gave a collective "ah!" as the information sank in.

"You mean to say slickskins don't moan?" asked Dr. Callahan.

"As far as I can tell, Doc, 'skins moan in two situations: if they've been terribly wounded, or if they've got a girl in the bedroom."

"Fascinating," said Dr. Callahan.

"And furthermore, you may be surprised to realize how often ghouls moan. You probably don't even realize we're moaning right now."

"By God, you're right!" exclaimed Wilson. "We are moaning!"

"That we are. Ghouls typically moan if there's any sort of food nearby, or if they're hungry."

"Which pretty much all time, right the sheriff?" said Bub.

"Right. The only time ghouls usually aren't moaning is when they're actually eating, and that's very different from slickskins. Wilson, this is the single most important thing you've got to be concerned about. If you give yourself away by moaning, or in any other way for that matter, you're a goner. No matter how fast you are, the slickskins are bound to be faster."

"I understand, sheriff," he said.

"Now let's try it. Try to stop moaning."

They all watched Wilson as he squirmed and sputtered. A few moans got out, but for the most part he was successful.

"Not bad, son. I think you've stumbled on the secret: if you don't breathe, you can't moan. But not breathing brings up another set of problems, since slickskins have to breathe."

"Imagine!" said Bub.

"So if they notice you not breathing, which should be no problem since we biologically don't need air to survive, they might discover you. It's a tight game you'll have to play."

Wilson practiced his moan suppression a few more times, but before long Mungo was back.

"Here you are," he said, throwing a garment to Wilson. "Should fit you perfectly."

"Mungo, this is a dress." Wilson held up the dress. It was indeed a dress.

"Well what's wrong with a dress? It's nice, isn't it?"

"It is nice, yes, but usually it's the slickskin females who wear dresses."

"I see. What about this one, then?" He tossed Wilson more clothes.

"This is more like it." It was a white dress shirt and brown vest. "I don't suppose you have any pants?"

"Pants? Oh, right." Mungo rummaged around in his saddlebag. "Here we are."

"All right, then," said Wilson, putting on the clothes. "Sheriff, I think I'm ready for the slickskins."

The Zombie Sheriff Takes Tucson

* * *

It had been dark for an hour by the time Wilson entered Tanque Verde's only saloon. It was a rough, dim place, the lanterns high overhead all but choked out by thick clouds of smoke rising from the vices of the patrons below. A long wooden bar spanned the length of the right side of the establishment, while eight or ten round tables accommodated mostly poker players to the left. In the back left corner a stairway rose to the second level, which was entirely open to the first floor; a railing was all that separated the boisterous crowd and the rooms for rent.

Wilson wasn't quite quick enough as he entered, and the swinging doors caught his sides before he was clear of the doorway.

"Slickskin," Wilson told himself, "think like a slickskin."

His failure to complete a proper ingress caused a few of the saloon-goers to notice him, and as he stumbled into the room he quickly decided that sitting at one of the few empty tables would serve his purpose better than a stool at the bar.

"Had a bit too much already, son?" asked an old man with a gray beard and kindly face.

A thin man he was playing cards with gave a laugh. "Looks to me like he's barely been off his mama's teat. What do you say, young man? Try your hand at cards tonight?"

"Ugggghhhh," offered Wilson, as he tripped past their table and sat at the one beside it.

"It appears the young newcomer is here for one thing and one thing only," said the old man.

"And no harm in that," said the other, and the men resumed their game.

Wilson surveyed the room surreptitiously. It was a common enough saloon—bar, poker tables, piano player in the corner—one might say it was even a little tame for a watering hole so close to the wilderness. The customers seemed mostly concerned with either drinking or playing cards or both, and it didn't appear to Wilson's untrained eye that anyone in particular was spoiling for a fight, which would surely have been the death of him.

"I said, what can I get for you?" said a woman standing at his elbow. Apparently he hadn't heard her the first go around.

"Ugh?"

"We've got whiskey, whiskey, and whiskey. Special today's whiskey."

"Ugh."

"One whiskey, coming up," said the barmaid, and she made her way to the bar.

The saloon was more or less full, and Wilson discovered he was lucky to find a table for himself. If anyone got too close, they might try to engage him in conversation.

"And I says to him, 'Ned, if you don't get off that horse this instant, there won't be any oats left.'" A raucous round of laughter followed this sliver of conversation that floated to him from the table behind.

"Jerry, that wasn't the way it was at all, and you know it. The horse wasn't even mine."

"What difference does it make whose horse it was? It was his oats, were they not?"

"Here ya are, big fella," said the barmaid, setting down a glass of whiskey.

"Ugh."

But she didn't go. Instead she coughed.

"Ugh," Wilson repeated, hoping his message would be clearer the second time.

"It's only, we don't run tabs here no more, not since old Tommy Three Guns came and went like a hurricane. I'll be needing you to pay up front, if you don't mind."

Wilson felt dread pour into him quicker than the patrons were consuming their drinks. What was he supposed to do now? Surely they'd throw him out once they realized he couldn't pay, and just as surely they'd realize his true nature when they did.

He lowered a heavy hand into his waistcoat pocket. At least if he gave a show of looking for money, maybe they'd have some sort of sympathy for him.

And then, had he not been surrounded by slickskins, a blessing for old Mungo would surely have left his lips. It was a coin. Whether the restaurateur had thought ahead to Wilson's present need or if he had simply collected the clothes of some well-to-do youth, Wilson didn't care. He would kiss the man when he saw him next.

Wilson slowly—as quickly as he could—raised his hand and deposited the coin into that of the waitress. She inspected the money, and when she did her eyes widened.

Wilson's heart sunk. The game was up. He had clearly given her some pitifully insulting amount, and he'd be thrown out just as sure as if he hadn't paid in the first place. He began to rise from his chair. His best chance was to try to get as large a head start as he could.

"Oh, thank you, sir! Thank you! This really is my lucky day. I was just telling Mary that I had a good feeling about tonight, and now I get a gold coin in my first hour on shift!"

The woman literally danced away with joy.

Had Wilson thought he could have still maintained his iron-clad control over his moaning reflex, he would have sighed. Crisis averted.

Wilson raised the glass mechanically to his mouth and took a sip.

And was instantly met by the most ferocious esophageal burning he had experienced since the time he had eaten the slickskin habanero vendor.

"Heugh, heogh, hhhhgh," sputtered Wilson.

"All right there, friend?" said a voice behind him.

Slowly, and with great difficulty, Wilson raised his hand in a dismissive gesture.

It took some time before the fire in his throat began to subside, but Wilson braved through it. He left the remaining whiskey alone.

"Terrible," the bearded old man at the poker table was saying, "just terrible to think my niece and nephew met such a fate. I swear by these blasted chips, the next ghoul I see I'll beat it out of him."

"Were they very old?" asked a squat little man at the table.

"No older than the young stranger sitting yonder. It was the Tuesday of the week before last. They found them along with the caretaker just north of that infested Owen's Folly. All that was left of them was their clothes and a few odd bones."

"Terrible," agreed the thin man next to him. "Any sign of the ghouls that done it?"

"Oh, it must have been some from the Folly. By all accounts the whole village is overrun with them. Crying shame, too. It was a nice place not too long ago.

"As nice as Barren Delta?" asked the squat man.

"Oh, now there's a place it would be a shame to see the ghouls take," said the thin man. "What a glorious town!"

As the conversation turned to the caliber of prostitution at Barren Delta, Wilson's attention turned once more to the barmaid.

"Oh, I thought for certain you'd have finished your drink, sir. I've brought you this, on the house, due to your unspeakable generosity. It's a double."

She stood in front of Wilson, waiting.

Slowly and with much regret Wilson took up his original drink and downed it, producing more of the searing flame coursing down his throat. The barmaid smiled. But she didn't leave.

Even more slowly, for all of a sudden it took much effort to steady his arm, Wilson took up the second drink, saluted the waitress with it, and drank all of it.

The saloon all at once began to sway as if Wilson suddenly found himself in the hold of a ship. Poker chips were tossed with piano keys, and the bar like a child's playground toy rocked first this way then that. Wilson vaguely had the impression of the barmaid leaving his presence, mentioning something about another drink.

He had to get ahold of himself. What would the sheriff say when he told him he had gotten drunk, and instead of finding information about McFarland, he got himself killed?

As Wilson shook his head in a vain effort to clear it, he heard bits of conversation from the unseen table behind him. Jerry, the man who had been telling some sort of joke before, was providing a lecture on livestock.

"You see, the best way to move cattle in these parts is to tell a story. Sure, cattle that come from Texas are a dime a dozen around here, but just see what happens when you tell them the cow's from Virginia. And how Virginia cattle are known for being some of the juiciest, most succulent cattle in the world, didn't you know? And look here, isn't this a chart showing this particular cow's pedigree up to its great-great-grandmother twice removed?"

"You sure are a clever one, Jerry."

"Thank you kindly."

"But I do have to work for my money, not like those bounty hunters in here a few weeks ago."

"Bounty hunters? I don't recall them."

"Sure, it must have been when you were out with old Mr. Williams's bride, wasn't it, Ned?"

"I don't know what you're talking about." Unseen laughter erupted, threatening to split Wilson's head in two.

"Well these bounty hunters come in acting like they just hit a lucky draw on the numbers, order rounds of drinks for the place. Sure, I wasn't turning down any drinks, but when we got to talking it was clear they weren't bounty hunters at all. What was their bounty? They were paid to bring in two ghouls. Any two ghouls! And only to Tucson. Well I tell you, I'd have spent an afternoon at the work and enjoyed the payoff by supper. These men from the wild acting high and mighty— What was that?"

Suddenly Wilson realized that in his drunken excitement he had forgotten to hold his breath. He had been moaning.

"Just thought I heard a ghoul, of all things," said Jerry. "If we start having ghouls in the saloon of Tanque Verde, I'll say we have much worse things to worry about, sure!"

Again, Jerry's audience obliged him with fawning laughter.

"Oh, miss. Do you mind? It seems our bottle's just about run dry."

Please, thought Wilson, please keep talking about McFarland. He was so close.

"But like I said, he kept buying, and we kept drinking, and bless him for it. Maybe I myself will take a warrant from the man's dispatcher, it looked like he was paid well enough, sure.

"Might be fun," said an unknown voice. "Go out of a Sunday afternoon and track down some ghouls. They don't give much resistance, after all."

"True enough. We certainly could do that if we had a mind to. Not sure where the man was headed, but he did make it quite clear he was from up north. Catalina, I think it was. Might be able to track him down that way."

Wilson could barely contain himself. What luck! He hadn't found where Dr. Gimmler-Heichman was located, but he had heard of Catalina, and if that's where McFarland lived, that's where the Salvadores would go.

But before anything else, he had to leave Tanque Verde, and leave the saloon. In his current state, that was saying something.

Just as Wilson had rather stiffly raised himself out of his seat, all sound in the saloon ceased. The last notes of the piano hung in the air. The clink of the poker chips was stilled, the rude laughter cut short. All eyes turned to the entrance as a man nearly the size of the doorway suddenly appeared. As he pushed open the swinging doors of the saloon a deafening peal of thunder sounded, and for an instant the man was turned into a black silhouette as lightning struck behind him. He took three measured steps into the saloon.

"Who done it?" he said in a voice as gruff as his beard.

When no one answered, he repeated his question. "Who done it? Who touched old Nelly?"

The room remained silent as the man took a few more steps into the saloon. "I can smell it on her. Someone's been riding her. Hard."

Wilson slowly lowered himself back into the chair, thinking that was no way to talk about a woman.

"She's been shitting nothing but oats since Tuesday last, and I only give her a special blend of grains—hardly any oats in it."

The man slowly scanned the saloon. "I know he's here," he said, taking a loud sniff. "It's the same smell as on my Nelly."

Finally he raised a finger—directly at Wilson. "You there, you're the one. You and I are going to have some words outside."

Wilson was filled with dread. How could his smell be on this man's horse? And what was he supposed to do now? He didn't have a gun, and even if he did, he wouldn't be nearly fast enough on the draw for a man like this.

But fortune was shining on Wilson that night. For as he began to rise, with of course all his undead slowness, he sensed that behind him a man had already stood.

The finger wasn't pointing at Wilson after all.

"Ezekiel, you've terrorized this town long enough," said the man, walking toward the door. "It's time someone taught you a lesson."

A deafening roar filled the saloon, and the man's body dropped just next to Wilson's table.

"Jerry!" cried Ned, and he rose to tend to his friend.

"Tut, tut," said Ezekiel. "That'll do. Leave him. Serves him right for touching old Nelly."

Ned glared at him. "You said you was going to talk to him outside. Not shoot him in the middle of the saloon."

"I got thirsty. Now go back to your drinks." Ezekiel waited until the man had returned to his seat. "And leave old Jerry for a little while. Let him think about what he's done."

With that, Ezekiel walked boldly to the bar, where he was instantly presented with a glass and a bottle.

The moment the man took his seat, the saloon came to life once more. Laughter at worthless jokes seemed to redouble, poker chips seemed to clink with a renewed sense of hope. The piano tune was played with an almost manic enthusiasm.

Wilson was doomed. Not only did he need to escape the saloon and the town undetected, but he was drunk. And now there was a luscious, sweet-smelling slickskin corpse not a foot away. What had he done to deserve these trials?

The blood oozed out of the man deliciously and pooled around Wilson's boots. The first faint whiffs of death found their way to Wilson's nostrils. The petrified look of horror on the man's face was as that of a town crier proclaiming the opening of a new all-you-can-eat buffet. And it was Brains Night.

All in all, it was simply unfair.

He made a conscious effort to steady himself. What would the sheriff do in a situation like this? He'd be a man, that's what he'd do. He'd do what needed to be done, for the good of all ghouls everywhere, no matter what sumptuous victuals lay literally at his feet...

Wilson felt his jaw set and his determination harden. With monumental strength of will he raised himself from his chair and took the first of what seemed like hundreds of steps toward the door.

"Leaving already?" said the barmaid instantly. "I'd a thought you'd want a couple more drinks on the house for your troubles."

"Ugh," said Wilson. The matter cleared up, the barmaid tended to her other tables.

Step after excruciating step of that odyssey from table to door was forever implanted in young Wilson's mind, but that night he earned the title of deputy, for he made it out of the saloon without arousing the suspicions of a single slickskin.

When the young stranger had made his rather awkward exit from the saloon, Ned, still heart-broken by the loss of his life-long companion, but equally terrified by the same man's killer who sat not twenty feet from him, risked a quick glance at his late friend's corpse, and with not a little amount of alarm, cried, "Hey! Where's Jerry's arm?"

32.

Hamburgers with Gimmler-Heichman

The less one knows about meat, the more one is able to enjoy it. Meat tastes wonderful, of course, but as with the lad hawking hard-to-find wares at unbelievable prices, it's best not to ask too many questions.

There is the story of Brian, a ghoul who was known for having the most delicate of culinary tastes. Whereas most ghouls become single-mindedly obsessed at the mere thought of slickskin meat, Brian would refuse to eat a slickskin who was any of the following: overweight, underweight, overly tan, had had alcohol within the past forty-eight hours, was from the state of Kentucky, had long hair, was missing any limbs, was over the age of fifty, or was a medical doctor. (When asked specifically about the last point, Brian explained that slickskins who mend other slickskins should be protected in order that the species should not die out.)

Brian's friends all thought him quite crazy—slickskin meat was slickskin meat, after all—so they decided to play a prank on him. One of them, named Johnston, proposed that Brian should prove to them that he could really tell the difference between any of the slickskins he proscribed and what Brian considered a "pure" slickskin. They would have a blind taste test. Confident in his abilities, Brian agreed.

The Zombie Sheriff Takes Tucson

The first dish Brian identified right away. "Certainly a slickskin with too long of hair. You can taste the mind-altering drugs."

The next he identified just as adroitly. "Overweight. Far too much fatty tissue.

"Kentuckian. When they're that inbred, the molecular structure starts to break down. Very stringy.

"Oh, my! What is that?" said Brian, removing his blindfold. "I've never had anything so delightful!"

Johnston and the rest of Brian's friends broke out into fits of laughter, and Brian grew more and more frustrated at not receiving an answer.

"Well are you going to tell me what kind of slickskin that is, or aren't you?"

"Joke's on you, Brian," said Johnston. "That wasn't slickskin meat at all. It was ghoul. My aunt was just run over by a stagecoach!" The friends resumed their raucous laughter.

Brian thought silently about what he had been told. He considered his friends, still laughing at his innocent faux pas. He thought about how delicious was the meat of Johnston's aunt.

He wouldn't have expected it, but his friends were rather tasty, too.

Nancy, I have wonderful news. Remember how I vowed never to love again after the tragic murder and dismemberment of my fiancée last year? Well, strike those words from my memoirs, because I've found someone new. Her name is Consuela, and she is one of the most delightful people I've ever met. Her outlook on life is as refreshing as a cool mountain breeze, and her breasts are the size of watermelons. Better strike that last part as well.

We met when she thought I was a whiskey-worshipping monk and practically broke down my door in the hopes of becoming my follower.

Consuela's father, Edgardo, owns the quaint little hotel (or *meson*, as he calls it) at which I've been residing here in Tucson, but he seems rather the protective type. Though Consuela and I have been seeing each other every day for a week, we haven't yet told her father, as we are both afraid that he may try to kill me and I would be forced to defend myself. Of course the property would then fall to Consuela, but we thought it best to take the more patient route.

Please double check that my divorce from that whore in Texas was finalized properly.

He and Consuela had just been seated at a table on the veranda of the trendiest restaurant in Tucson—there were only four restaurants—when a voice from behind called to him.
"Abernathy Jones," it said.
Abernathy turned to see a friendly looking man with salt-and-pepper hair and spectacles. He was wearing a white lab coat that was so blindingly white it looked as though it had been bleached several dozen times.
"Dr. Friedrich Gimmler-Heichman," said Abernathy, nodding at the man.
Dr. Gimmler-Heichman gave Abernathy a look of mild admiration and nodded at him.
"Miss Consuela," he said, "a pleasure."
Consuela looked at him suspiciously and gave him a fake smile.
"I've been meaning to stop into Miss Tabitha's to pay my respects," said Dr. Gimmler-Heichman, turning back to Ab-

ernathy, "but I simply haven't had the time. But when I saw you and your lady friend turn into this eating establishment, I thought Providence must have intended for us to meet. May I join you?"

"Who am I to stand in the way of Providence?" said Abernathy, pulling a third chair to the table. He handed Dr. Gimmler-Heichman a card:

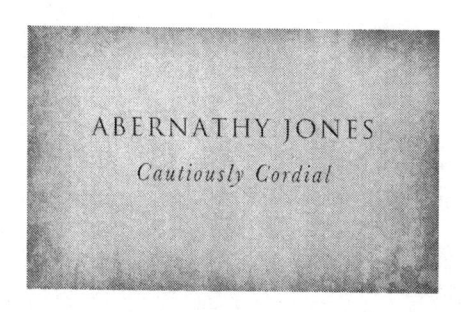

> **ABERNATHY JONES**
> *Cautiously Cordial*

"But why should you want to pay your respects to me? Have we met?"

"I don't believe we have met, Mr. Jones, but your reputation precedes you," said Dr. Gimmler-Heichman, taking the offered seat.

"And what reputation is that?"

"The one that says you're a man who doesn't let anything get in the way of his objectives. Including ghouls."

The waiter had come by, but no one had yet touched their menus. "Samuelson, three of your hamburgers, please. How do you like your meat, Mr. Jones? Medium? And you, my dear? Well done? I'll have mine blood rare, Samuelson, thank you." The waiter left after collecting the menus.

"What is a hamburger?" asked Consuela.

"Ah! An ingenious technique of preparing meat. The meat and fat are ground together and seasoned, then grilled and eaten as a sandwich. It is delicious."

"Objectives? What sort of objectives?" asked Abernathy, ignoring the previous line of conversation.

"Oh, one hears things, if one knows where to listen. Suffice it to say I believe I know the kind of man you are, and I am impressed."

"Kind words. But what can I do for you? Surely you don't just track down men you're fond of and order hamburgers with them?"

Dr. Gimmler-Heichman gave a sheepish grin that disarmingly made his face look as young as a ten-year-old's. "Indeed not. I have inserted myself into your dinner because I think I can be of service to you in your present pursuit."

"Oh? And what do you know of it?"

"I know enough to know that you have been tracking for months now a particular ghoul, that you have recently met with that ghoul, and that the meeting has gone poorly. I also know that you wish to meet with him again, but this ghoul will not do so willingly."

Just then the waiter brought their hamburgers, and while Consuela tentatively lifted the top of her bun and peered at what was underneath, Dr. Gimmler-Heichman hefted his very rare hamburger and without ceremony took an enormous bite out of it, causing a thin pink juice to drip down his chin and onto the plate below.

"You seem to know a lot about me," said Abernathy, as the scientist dabbed at his face with a napkin.

"As I say, one hears things if one knows where to listen."

33.

Lady Death

They say revenge is a dish best served cold. This isn't correct. Revenge is a dish best served lukewarm or at room temperature (depending on the room) with a side of sauerkraut lightly sprinkled with pepper, a generous helping of golden brown roasted potatoes, and a large loaf of marble rye, washed down with any kind of unfiltered wheat beer.

But whatever you do—and remember this, as it can be a matter of life or death—don't put any sort of fruit in the beer. Fruit doesn't belong in beer.

The posse sat around the camp. Dr. Callahan and Mungo were playing a game with some bones and a small slickskin skull—the rules of which neither ghoul was entirely certain—while the sheriff and Bub sat talking next to the fire.

"The danger, my friend," the sheriff was saying, "is living in a reality for so long that you forget other realities exist."

"Not sure follow you, the sheriff," said Bub, scratching his wispy hair.

"Look at it like this. Here's a man, any man." The sheriff drew a stick figure in the soil.

"And here's the world he lives in." A wide rectangle was drawn around the man.

"Next, our man decides to take a job. Let's say he's a banker."

"What kind banker?" asked Bub.

"Doesn't matter," said the sheriff. "Any kind of banker."

"But just argument's sake. Like to have full picture in my head."

"All right. He's a skull banker."

"For people deposit and withdraw skulls?"

"Yes."

"Okay. Proceed."

"So here, the man has chosen to limit part of his reality. A great deal, really—he sees himself as a banker, and he sees life as a banker sees it." The sheriff drew a smaller box within the rectangle, still enclosing the figure.

"You see, the man previously had all this space in his reality, but for one reason or another, that reality has been shrunk. Now let's say he makes another reality-changing decision. Perhaps he gets married, settles down, and buys a house." The sheriff drew the outline of a house around the stick figure.

"Now his viewpoint is even more limited. And say he has kids"—the sheriff drew an even smaller box—"that changes things as well."

"Oh gosh!" said Bub. "Look how limited his reality! How can hope to break out those limitations, the sheriff?"

"Well, Bub, that's the trick. The most challenging thing, once you've limited yourself so much, is to realize that you still have the ability to break out of those realities. Most people have a lot of trouble doing that. Once you do decide to remove some of those frames, you have to figure out which limiting realities you've placed on yourself are worth it."

"I see," said Bub. Then, after a moment: "What if want to remove all realities?"

"Bub, I believe that's what happens when you die," said the sheriff.

"Oh. Don't want to do that."

"Agreed, Bub. I think you should hold off on that one for the time being."

Suddenly the Salvadores realized as one that they weren't alone. Someone was nearing the camp. They spread out, as the sheriff had taught them to do, and took cover. Most even managed to suppress their moaning.

Mungo was closest to the form that began to take shape at the edge of their camp. It seemed to materialize out of the night air itself, first as a small child running carefree, then as a pale, blood-thirsty beast, and finally into what it was: a horse and rider.

But something was amiss: the rider slumped in the saddle, his head nearly resting against the steed's neck. Was the man wounded, thought Mungo. Then: surely this couldn't be Wilson, back so soon? They had believed it would take a week to get even a shred of information on McFarland.

Soon enough Mungo had his answers; as the horse drew nearer and he got a clearer view, he yelled, "Wilson!" The Salvadores quickly gathered round their returned member.

Indeed it was Wilson, and in poor shape. "No!" exclaimed Bub. "Can't be hurt!" The big barber pulled down his friend and laid him gently onto the ground. Wilson appeared nearly unconscious.

"Check, Doc," said Bub. "Want to know what's done to him, who's done it. McFarland have to wait."

The sheriff's laughter had just begun as Dr. Callahan checked Wilson for injuries, and by the time he had finished, it had grown to a great big belly-laugh.

"He's drunk," said Dr. Callahan.

"Drunk?" asked Bub.

"Drunk," confirmed Dr. Callahan. "He's drunker than Cooter Brown."

But the sheriff's laughter quickly ended, and he was soon kneeling at Wilson's side. "All right, deputy," he said. "What have you brought back to us?"

Wilson's head rolled toward his idol's voice, and a faint smile came to his lips.

"Catalina" was all he could say before he passed out.

The sheriff lowered the monocular and handed it carefully to Wilson, who took up the watch. Beneath them lay a familiar picture.

"Tell again why you think McFarland at whorehouse, the sheriff," said Bub.

"Well, Bub, in my experience, when a slickskin's flush with money, there's only two things he cares about: whiskey and women. And you can get whiskey anywhere."

"Ah," said Bub. "That right. Make good sense, the sheriff."

"Thanks."

The three ghouls were perched on the roof of the Catalina Bank and Trust, which had the distinct disadvantage of being directly across the street from Catalina's only brothel, Madame Delilah's House of Eternal Pleasure. The whorehouse was a large, two-story building, and every light upstairs and down was lit, giving onlookers a fairly clear view of the goings-on at Madame Delilah's, save for some sheer drapes. The view was so explicit, in fact, that Bub asked not to use the monocular, saying that "slickskin sex too animalistic for polite viewing."

They had been there an hour, and the sheriff and deputy took turns sweeping the windows in the hopes that McFarland would be seen.

"C'mon," said the sheriff. "He's got to be in there. I know he's in there." He took a rock and flung it blindly at the whorehouse.

"The sheriff, don't know I seen you this bothered," said Bub.

"This man killed a lot of people I cared about. Several times."

"I know has, the sheriff, I know—"

Just then Wilson gave a little sound of excitement.

"What's that, boy?" asked the sheriff. "Do you see him?"

Wilson steadied his hand for a closer look. "I think I saw..." He looked down at the drawing.

"Yes! That's him. That's definitely McFarland."

A couple passing in front of Catalina Bank and Trust found it odd that a red-tailed hawk would be calling this late into the night.

Missy, the new girl, left her post on the lower veranda and ran indoors.

"I think something's out there," she pronounced in a loud whisper to no one in particular. She looked a little crazed, but then again Missy had always seemed a bit off, making the bed after every romp and asking the men about their lives. That wasn't the way to be a successful whore, at least not in Catalina. Making a good living at whoring in Catalina meant one thing and one thing only: volume. Reel them in, take them upstairs, throw them back out. It was the eternal way of things (indeed, it was reflected in this fine establishment's title), and who was this Missy to come in taking an interest in people's lives? This was a business, after all. They weren't looking for a wife; they were looking for a screw.

The rest of the girls in the parlor paid her no mind. They fawned over their gentlemen, fixing them drinks, sitting on their laps, batting their eyes. The evening was just getting started.

One of the regulars, Rudolph Gosford, descended the stair with Amie, his favorite. Gosford liked to get his toss in early in the night, then have a light supper and play the violin.

"My dear," said Gosford, bringing Amie's hand to his lips, "it has been a dream. As always." Blowing her a kiss, he departed.

Missy rushed up to Amie, one of the few girls who would have anything to do with her. "Amie, please listen to me! I think there's something wrong outside."

"Sorry, what? I drifted off there a bit. Rudy gets a little rough on Tuesdays."

"I said I think something's wrong outside."

"Wrong? What do you mean?"

"I don't know...it's just a feeling. Something doesn't feel right."

"Well what do you want me to do about it? I've got bills to pay and a whole night ahead of me."

"I don't know. I just thought I should tell someone."

Their attention was immediately drawn to the open double-doors through which Gosford had just exited.

"Did you hear that?" asked Missy.

"I'm hoping I didn't."

They stood in the middle of the room like statues, not daring to flee, unable to verify their suspicions.

Suddenly a large torrent of blood came pouring in from the darkness, as if someone had tossed a great pail of the stuff directly at the two girls. Their clothing—every inch of it—was soaked, and oddly it reminded Missy of the time she'd seen a dunking booth at the fair. But with blood. At first they couldn't comprehend what had happened, but then they looked at each other, then at themselves, and finally the faint tang of metal reached their senses. It was, in fact, blood. A lot of it.

They screamed.

By now the other occupants of the room had become equally alarmed, with women standing wide-eyed in terror and men posing gallantly against an unseen foe.

Amie was still screaming when Missy noticed the figure coming for them. It loped forward slowly and with an awkward gait, and yet it looked somehow familiar. It reached them before either of the whores could gather the courage to move.

It was Rudolph Gosford. And yet, it was not. He was dressed exactly the same, and his features were as they were before, but Missy thought something was off.

His arm. The fresh wound still pumped out blood at regular intervals, and Missy also saw that partially obscured by his collar, a great chunk of flesh had been taken from the man's neck. What a wound! Blood was streaming out of it, down onto his clothes. Missy could see the muscles and tendons flex as he moved his remaining arm.

What was he doing with his arm?

Petrified, plastered in gore, Missy watched as, exactly as he had done not ten minutes before, Rudolph Gosford reached out for Amie's hand and brought it up to his lips. And bit it off.

Amie's once piercing scream now turned silent as she brought her arm up to her face and wordlessly examined the stump at the end of it.

Missy had seen enough. She backed away slowly, trying to keep anything moving within her field of vision, which was very difficult now that the room was suddenly swarming with clothed, half-clothed, and unclothed people running in every direction.

"The back exit," she heard a masculine voice shout, "it's jammed shut!"

Missy calmly walked to the fireplace and took up the poker.

"No!" commanded the sheriff, laying his hand against Mungo's forearm. "We need to verify the kill. And I'm the one who takes down McFarland."

Mungo nodded seriously and placed the armadillo bomb carefully back into his bag.

The windows of Madame Delilah's had all turned pink, as the Salvadores' creation feasted for the first—and probably last—time. The screams, a heavenly chorus to the five ghouls waiting outside, went on for quite awhile until they stopped with a muffled thud.

"I believe that's our signal, sheriff," said Wilson.

"I believe you're right, deputy."

Just as the posse entered the building a beautiful slickskin (as far as slickskins go) wearing nothing but underwear and holding what looked to be a poker ran past them into the night.

Bub, who had been salivating for quite some time now, turned and started to give chase.

"No, Bub," said the sheriff. "Remember what we came for."

The large room that opened before them was quite empty—except, of course, for the dozens of bodies in various states of disembowelment strewn across the room. A quick inspection showed that none of the dead was McFarland, but there was one interesting discovery: the sheriff kicked over one of the slickskin corpses to find a weathered man with gold teeth and only one eye. Wilson wandered over when he saw what the sheriff was looking at.

"You thinking what I'm thinking?" asked the deputy.

"One-eyed Lester," said the sheriff, "McFarland's right-eyed man. He can't be far off."

"Look over here, sheriff," called Mungo from a corner of the room.

The sheriff and the rest of the Salvadores joined the chef. There, at his feet, lay the dead undead body of Gosford, with a wound that cut halfway down into his brain, and an expression that told of complete joy.

"He died a happy man," said Dr. Callahan.

"Gosford, we hardly knew you," said Wilson, "but you were a true friend."

"Let's see to it he didn't die in vain," said the sheriff, moving toward the stairs. "The exits are all blocked, and all the windows were watched. McFarland's got to still be here.

"He's got a lot to atone for. Kidnapping my deputy and my lady love. Harassing the fine people of Owen's Folly. And massacring Chester's Brigade, the finest group of men and women I've had the pleasure of meeting these many years."

They paused at the sheriff's words, and each man thought of a loved one who had perished at the hands of the evil McFarland.

Enraged by these tragic memories, the five ghouls known as the Salvadores mounted the stairs and saw the four closed doors in the open hallway. The sheriff smashed open the first to find two whores quivering in fear, which in his rage he threw out the window screaming. The second door yielded a man—clearly not McFarland by the size of his girth—

who emptied a revolver into the sheriff's stomach. The sheriff smiled at the man, took him by the neck, and pulled off his head. He put the head underneath his arm, punched it in, removed the bone fragments, and scooped the brains directly into his mouth. He paused outside the third door, trying to sense movement within. When he barreled into the room, all that greeted him was an enormous stain of blood on an otherwise unoccupied bed.

He turned with a sly smile and nodded to his men. McFarland was in the fourth and final room. They took positions around the door, with Wilson just to the sheriff's right. The sheriff reduced the door to splinters, and they stormed into the room, only to find two more whores.

As the men quickly feasted on these newest victims, the sheriff considered what had just happened. McFarland had to be here. He had to be! There was no other explanation. Leaving the men to their meal, he quietly walked back out into the hallway and listened. Beyond the slurping and crunching of the fourth room, beyond the snapping of bones and the echoes of screams, he might just barely be able to make out...

Holding his breath the sheriff moved as quietly as he could back into the third room, with its blood-soaked bed. He stood motionless, his head tilted and his eyes half closed. Then with a speed that surprised even himself he darted to the side of the bed, punched his hand through the bloody straw mattress, and pulled back through it the struggling form of McFarland.

The sheriff held him by the neck so high that his feet didn't touch the ground. The sheriff smiled. With the other hand he reached into his vest pocket. He held the picture up directly next to the slickskin.

It was the spitting image.

"Oh, boys!" he called.

The Salvadores entered the room and were dumbfounded by what they saw.

Bub glanced back and forth between the drawing and the slickskin. "The sh-sheriff," he stuttered, "got him! Got McFarland!"

"I sure do," said the sheriff. "Now the question is what to do with him."

The sheriff threw the slickskin down onto the bed with such force that the legs snapped and the bed slammed down to the floor. McFarland looked more shocked than afraid.

"Tear him to pieces!" said Mungo.

"But, sheriff, we have to find out where Dr. Gimmler-Heichman is," said Wilson.

The sheriff considered the issue for a moment. "The deputy's right. We have to get that information out of him before we eat him."

He looked down at his nemesis and yelled, "Where's Gimmler-Heichman?"

McFarland, who by now had regained a great deal of fear, said nothing.

"Not you hear the man?" asked Bub, and he ripped off McFarland's arm and ate it.

"Easy, Bub," said Wilson.

Blood covered the rest of the mattress so that it might have been made up in red sheets instead of white. Its occupant roared in pain, and he tossed in his agony, but still he said nothing.

"He can't understand you," said a voice.

The five ghouls turned around as one, each taking up a defensive posture. But it wasn't a threat they saw there in the doorway. It was a gorgeous specimen of ghoulkind—flowing golden tresses, decaying cheeks of pale, sickly green, red-tinged eyes that told of insatiable blood lust.

"Jezebel!" exclaimed the sheriff. "My dear, what on earth are you doing here? I wanted you out of harm's way."

"If I had stayed out of harm's way, sweet thing, you'd never find out where Dr. Gimmler-Heichman is, or what he plans to do with ghouls."

"You know what experiments Dr. Gimmler-Heichman is conducting?" asked Dr. Callahan.

"I haven't been just sitting around while you boys have been playing commando," said Jezebel. And it was true—she hadn't been. Jezebel had quietly been gathering information from all around Tucson, everywhere from the odd wandering ghoul to established undead communities. She had stopped into dozens of saloons—and more often than not her blood beers were on the house or bought for her by an admiring gentleman. Piece by piece, she put together the puzzle of McFarland and Dr. Gimmler-Heichman, and her intel had led her to a small rented room above the general store in Catalina where McFarland had resided for the past week. She knew she had but to stay close to McFarland and she would find the sheriff and his men. And when she saw Madame Delilah's turn into a slickskin slaughterhouse she knew she would soon be reunited with her friends.

"Do you know where Dr. Gimmler-Heichman's laboratory is?" the sheriff asked her.

She looked at him and smiled. "I do. Besides, we wouldn't be able to get any information out of McFarland anyway. He doesn't speak our language."

"What do you mean? Wilson was able to understand him well enough."

"Most ghouls remember the language they spoke as slickskins, but when slickskins turn into ghouls, they inherently learn our language. That's why we can understand them, but they have no idea we're even trying to communicate."

"Fascinating!" said Dr. Callahan. "How did you make such an important anthropological discovery?"

"Like I said, I haven't just been sitting around."

A sound caused them all to turn back toward the room—where they saw McFarland struggling to open the window with his remaining arm.

He was quickly surrounded by ghouls, and Bub and Mungo held him.

"So, sheriff," continued Jezebel, "you can see that this most wretched slickskin has nothing to tell us, even if we could make him understand our request."

"Looks that way, doesn't it?" said the sheriff.

"Do you mind?" she asked, gesturing at McFarland.

"With my compliments."

As Bub and Mungo continued to hold him, Jezebel moved to face McFarland directly.

"I know you can't understand me, you slickskin piece of shit, but you have a lot of atoning to do—for kidnapping Wilson and me, for killing more ghouls than I could count, including the members of Chester's Brigade. And, well, this is the only way I can think of that even some of that atonement is possible."

Without hesitation, Jezebel punched McFarland straight through the bridge of his nose and between his eyes, burying her hand deep into his skull. With almost as much violence, she brought her hand back out, taking the wet, squishy mass of McFarland's brain along with it. She viciously tore the brain into six pieces and distributed them to each of the ghouls, who devoured them so greedily that small chunks of gray matter flew across the room, coating the furniture and sticking to the walls and ceiling. The brain was consumed before the lifeless—and faceless—body of McFarland dropped to the floor.

"Dr. Callahan, I believe you have a going away present for dear old McFarland," said the sheriff.

"I do?" asked the doctor.

"You do. In your bag."

Dr. Callahan nodded and produced the armadillo bomb along with a large grin.

"Just be sure to use the long fuse."

Madame Delilah's House of Eternal Pleasure, that fine and long-respected institution of Catalina, was blown to bits just as the six ghouls emerged from its hallowed halls.

The proprietors of Catalina Bank and Trust were still rejoicing months later.

34.

The End of Dr. Friedrich Otto Gimmler-Heichman (SPOILER), That Dastardly Devil of Evil

Endings are usually a letdown. One invests so much time, energy, and would-be child-support payments into some endeavor only to be left unfulfilled by its conclusion. How can a project possibly meet expectations when those expectations are for nothing short of the miraculous?

But every once in a great while—and it occurs so rarely that hardly anyone speaks of it anymore—an ending will take the expectations that have been thrust upon it and pay back those desires a hundredfold. The participant is then endowed with such wisdom, meets with such great success, that his life can never be the same. These endings are the stuff of legends, and when one encounters such an ending, it should be savored and cherished.

This is not one of those endings.

They decided it would be prudent to wait until the next nightfall to go after Dr. Gimmler-Heichman, as it was a well-known fact that slickskins were afraid of the dark and imagined horrible things going about in it, which of course was entirely justified since horrible things went about in the dark all time, eating people and frightening small children.

"A blind undead monk on the top of a very high snow-covered mountain told me it would be right around here," Jezebel was saying as they turned a corner, keeping to the shadows. Compared to the small towns and villages Wilson had encountered in his short life, Tucson seemed to be an endless murky sprawl, full of big, boxy buildings in which slickskins did who-knows-what.

He kept close to the sheriff, as he had visions of suddenly becoming surrounded by 'skins from all angles. Perhaps sensing this, or perhaps because it was the smart choice, the sheriff insisted on taking the safest route, even when it meant backtracking for what seemed like hours to a quieter, more secluded back alley or side street. The rest of the Salvadores, except for perhaps Jezebel—named an honorary member of the squad, despite the disadvantage of her sex—seemed equally hesitant, if not downright terrified, as in the case of Bub. The barber frequently made miserable attempts at staying behind, including insisting that his shoelace was untied, even though it was clear to everyone that Bub was wearing a Velcro shoe (there had only ever been one).

But despite Bub's terror, and the group's general hesitancy, they seemed to have arrived at their destination. Jezebel stopped in a doorway and pointed across the street to a set of stairs leading to a basement.

"There it is," said Jezebel. "The blind monk said I would find what I was searching for in the cellar of the blue jay's nest."

"What makes you think that's it?" asked Wilson. "I don't see any blue jays, or any nests."

Jezebel pointed at a sign that hung from the second story of the building, just visible in the moonlight. It read, "Jay and Nestor's Fine Furniture." The sign was painted blue.

"Good eye," said Wilson.

"Thanks."

The Zombie Sheriff Takes Tucson

The sheriff addressed the Salvadores. "Well, boys, we all know why we're here, and why Gimmler-Heichman needs to be stopped. Whatever you see in that horrible laboratory of his—and it may be beyond our wildest nightmares—remember the job we have to do. You've been a great gang—all of you. A great gang."

The sheriff tried to smile. "I'm going to tell you something I've kept to myself for years. None of you ever knew Jack Ripp. It was long before your time. But you know what a tradition he is around these parts. He could dismember a 'skin faster than you could say brains. The last thing he said to me, before he disappeared, was, 'Sheriff,' he said, 'sometime, when the team is up against it, and the breaks are beating the boys, tell them to go out there with all they got and win just one for the Ripper.'"

The sheriff's eye became misty and his voice unsteady.

"'I don't know where I'll be then, sheriff,' he said, 'but I'll know about it—and I'll be happy.'

"I can't tell you that this will be easy, because this man knows ghouls, and knows our weaknesses, but I can tell you this is right. If we don't stop him, he'll just keep on with these despicable experiments and his crimes against Nature.

"I want each of you to swear, even if you are the last of the Salvadores living, you will carry out this mission, and destroy Dr. Gimmler-Heichman." Each member agreed. "This is, perhaps, the most important thing you will ever do."

With those words he led the group boldly across the street and down into the cellar of Dr. Gimmler-Heichman.

The only light came from two grate windows that cast long, diagonal shadows the length of the musty laboratory. Only vague impressions greeted the Salvadores as they slowly made their way through the door and into the subterranean room: jagged machinery covered in rust, bones both exceedingly long and impossibly short, beakers giving off smoke despite no obvious heat source, shackles hanging from bare walls, shelves and shelves full of glass specimen jar containing body parts vaguely mammalian. And there was blood. Though the sheriff, keen as any shark, could smell the faintest hint of blood from miles off, here such a talent was unneeded; blood residue coated nearly everything. Dried blood on the instruments. Bloody fingerprints on an oaken table. A pool of blood on the floor. The ghouls' mouths watered.

All of their senses were on edge; they strained to hear, to see, to smell any sign of the evil Dr. Gimmler-Heichman and to bring about the end of that plague on ghoulkind. The silence rang in their ears. Each footfall, each unmuffled moan drew the attention of the entire party. But of Dr. Gimmler-Heichman there was no sign.

Then Wilson saw it: a flicker of motion that seemed miles away. He silently drew the sheriff's attention to it, and soon the posse was creeping down a narrow hallway off the far side of the laboratory. This area was even darker than the first. The ghouls held on to one another as they walked toward the source of the movement.

Finally they reached a small back room that was lit by a single guttering candle. What they saw there sent chills through every last one of them. It was a ghoul, clearly starving, chained to the wall with both hands over his head. There looked to be hardly any muscle left on his body. His clothing was tattered, and his face had a curious pink tinge to it.

"No! No!" The man shouted. "Don't you put me with them! It's cruel, you hear? It isn't right! Haven't you done enough with me already?"

"Easy there," said the sheriff. "We can get you out of here. What's your name, if you don't mind my asking?"

The man took no notice of the sheriff's words. He continued shouting into the darkness. "Have a heart, man! You can't do this!"

"That's Alexander," said Wilson suddenly.

"Who's Alexander?" asked Mungo.

"At least I think it's Alexander. It's hard to tell—he's much, much thinner, and his skin has turned an odd color. Alexander was a member of Chester's Brigade. If it is him, he must have been one of the ghouls McFarland kidnapped and brought to Gimmler-Heichman.

"Alexander?" said the sheriff. The man paid him no attention. "Alexander, can you hear me?"

Alexander continued yelling as loud as he could, not acknowledging the Salvadores in the least.

"What is it, Jezebel?" asked the sheriff. Jezebel had her hand to her mouth and appeared to be troubled.

"There's something about him. Something that isn't right."

"Do you think *this* Dr. Gimmler-Heichman?" asked Bub. The others gasped.

"No, Bub," said the sheriff. "That's stupid. Why would Dr. Gimmler-Heichman chain himself up in his own laboratory?"

"Oh," said Bub. "Right."

As Alexander continued shouting at persons unknown and generally ignoring the Salvadores, Jezebel was able to listen to him more closely.

"I've got it!" she said.

"What's the matter?" asked the sheriff.

"Alexander isn't speaking our language. He's speaking slickskin!"

"You're sure in for it now," said the shackled man, for the first time speaking to the Salvadores. He began breathing more heavily and his eyes took on a glassy look. "He'll sure be coming now."

"But what does it mean that he's speaking slickskin?" asked the sheriff.

"It means," said Jezebel, "that that"—she pointed to the man—"isn't a ghoul at all. He's a slickskin."

Everyone gasped again.

"Fascinating!" said Dr. Callahan.

The sheriff's voice was a mixture of skepticism and horror. "But—but how is that possible? And how do you know?"

"I know because no ghoul would be able to speak the language Alexander is speaking. We can understand it because we once spoke it as our regular language, but ghouls can't speak it. As to how it's possible, I have absolutely no idea."

Suddenly the dull echo of footfalls reached their ears, and it quickly became clear they were heading toward the Salvadores.

"Be ready for anything," said the sheriff. "Gimmler-Heichman is very, very dangerous."

But what began as a clatter of steps soon separated into two distinct gaits. "Sheriff!" came a cry out of the darkness. The voice seemed somehow familiar.

The mystery was solved when the two forms pulled up from their run just at the threshold of the room. Peering carefully at the shadowy figures, the sheriff was able to make out one male and one female form. The female looked vaguely Mexican, with a dingy dress and long dark hair. The other he knew instantly, if only from the items he carried. In his left hand was a leather valise, and in his right was a straight black cane with a brass handle. Both leaned forward slightly, attempting to catch their breath.

"Sheriff," said Abernathy Jones between gasps, "Sheriff, you have to listen to me. I have to tell you—"

Out of the corner of his eye the sheriff saw Bub and Mungo shuffle toward the new arrivals like bears to blood-flavored honey.

"I told you, Abe, the next time I saw you, you wouldn't leave the meeting alive. Now you have to decide."

"Decide what?"

"Do you want to be dead, or do you want to be dead-dead?"

Bub and Mungo, perhaps worked up by all the excitement, were making very good time. They were only a few steps away from the slickskins.

"Please, sheriff! I'm not here on business of my own; I'm here to warn you to get out of here!"

He threw a card at the sheriff in desperation:

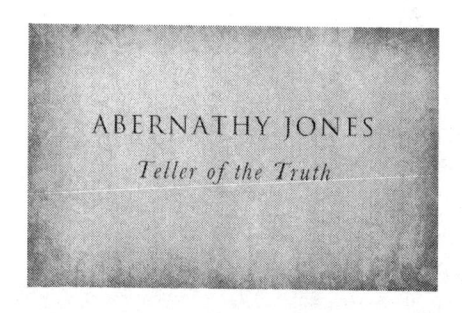

> ABERNATHY JONES
> *Teller of the Truth*

"You don't know what Dr. Gimmler-Heichman has been doing down here, what he's capable of."

"And you do?"

"He's been showing me some of his...experiments." Abernathy looked quickly at Alexander. "They aren't pretty."

Bub and Mungo had stopped within reach of Consuela now, perhaps waiting for the sheriff to give the word. Consuela, to her credit, had only wet herself.

"And you're risking your life to save a bunch of ghouls?" asked the sheriff incredulously.

"Well, yes. You aren't just a ghoul to me, sheriff."

Just as he uttered these words a sound came from the darkness as if rope was sliding through a tether, and a great metallic crash was heard. Wilson tried running back the way they had come, only to be stopped short by a gate of thick iron bars. He noticed with some satisfaction that Abernathy and Consuela were caught on their side of the cage. It was only a minor consolation.

The sound of slow, sharp clapping reached their ears from somewhere in the darkness, and all of them, both slickskin and ghoul, jumped.

"Very touching," said a cultured voice. "Very touching indeed."

Quiet footfalls gradually produced a figure out of the darkness illuminated only by the faint light of the flickering candle. He was a man of perhaps slightly below average height with a round bespectacled face atop which rested a tuft of rapidly graying hair. He held his hands behind his back as he stood on the other side of the bars, giving the sheriff and his posse a good look at his pristine white lab coat, made all the more pristine by the presence of layers and layers of blood covering everything in sight.

"Dr. Gimmler-Heichman," said the sheriff.

"My dear sheriff," said Dr. Gimmler-Heichman, scientific savant, malodorous malcontent, genial genius, giving a small bow. "It's such a pleasure to make your acquaintance at last."

"A pleasure? Meeting me?"

"Your modesty is touching—really it is. You see, I've made it my life's work to study the undead, and you are no ordinary specimen."

Abernathy led Consuela to a dark corner of the cell. No one paid them any notice.

"You aren't so ordinary yourself," said the sheriff. "But why would you want to study ghouls? I'm surprised you haven't been eaten yet."

"Oh it's fascinating, really. Language, customs, culture—you have quite the society, you ghouls. If it weren't for your nasty habit of eating people, I think our peoples might have been able to get along rather well."

"We would never live peacefully with you blood-sucking slickskins," said Wilson, bitterly.

"Don't you think 'blood-sucking' is a poor choice of words, my young deputy? But it's a moot point, isn't it? There shall be no peace, at least while current conditions persist. Which brings us to why we're all here together."

"Forget that," said Jezebel. "What have you done to poor Alexander?"

The unfortunate person in question had been staring uncomprehendingly down from his chains at the Salvadores during the conversation, but now he seemed to realize that the topic had turned to himself.

"You are going to let me out of here, aren't you, doctor? Now that you have them, there's no need to keep me, is there? No need at all."

"Funny you should bring up Alexander," said Dr. Gimmler-Heichman, ignoring that man's pleading. "For that's exactly why I brought you here."

"You brought us here?" said the sheriff. "Don't flatter yourself. We tracked you down from miles away, doctor."

"Of course you did, sheriff. Of course you did. But in any event, conditions exist as they do. Let me explain to you what has happened to dear Alexander. As you surmised, Miss Jezebel, he is, in fact, no longer a ghoul, but rather a slickskin."

"So it is true," murmured Abernathy.

"But how?" Jezebel asked. "How is that possible?"

"With this." Dr. Gimmler-Heichman had produced a syringe of what looked to be glowing green liquid. "And with this, I will save humanity. You admit yourself that ghouls and humans—slickskins, as you call them—cannot coexist peacefully. The one wants to eat the other, and the other wants to avoid being eaten. But the concoction contained in this syringe will change all of that.

"Our friend Alexander there is proof—living proof—of its effectiveness. Imagine it: a world rid of ghouls. Children will be able to play without being supervised by a man with a gun. The dead won't need to be shot between the eyes in front of grieving widows to make sure they don't try to eat them. The only moaning to be heard will be from the hospital or the bedroom. And the brilliant thing is that there need not be a single drop of blood shed on either side. An injection of this and within a few minutes a ghoul turns back into a human. Problem solved."

"Problem solved!" shouted Jezebel. "Problem solved? Has it occurred to you that perhaps the undead won't submit willingly to your glowing green goo? That maybe we like the way we are?"

"Of course it has. But I'm confident that when we have injected enough ghouls and the results are made clear to all, the rest of the undead will see reason. I have observed that your kind can be reasoned with, despite popular belief. A world without conflict is best for everyone, after all."

"You're mad!" said Bub. "You're mad scientist!"

"Oh, Bub, how I wish I could explain this to you in simpler terms, terms you could understand. But, come to think of it, I do have a way to explain it to you." Dr. Gimmler-Heichman moved quicker than thought, and before anyone could intervene he had pulled Bub's arm through the bars and pushed back his sleeve. "This won't hurt a bit."

"No!" shouted the sheriff, and he dove at Bub, knocking him back from the bars. But it was too late. The syringe in Dr. Gimmler-Heichman's hand had only a small amount of that strange green liquid left in it. The rest was in Bub.

"You monster!" cried Jezebel. "What have you done to him?"

"Done to him? My dear, I've given him the gift of freedom. I have freed him from the bonds of the undead. Or will have done, in a few moments. Once the mixture takes effect, Bub's blood will start pumping again as normal, his limbs and body will become much more pliable, and he'll no longer have that pesky craving for human flesh. In short, he'll be cured."

"Of course you didn't bother asking him if he wanted to be 'cured,' did you?" asked the sheriff.

"Oooh," said Bub, lying back against the wall. "Feel funny." He held his stomach as if he had eaten a bad slickskin.

"This is just awful," said Dr. Callahan. "I can't stand to watch!" The doctor walked to the far corner of the room—opposite Abernathy and Consuela—and hugged himself mournfully.

From high up came a voice they had all momentarily forgotten. "You're making another one, aren't you?"

Dr. Gimmler-Heichman addressed Alexander for the first time. "I am indeed, Alexander. How would you like a little company?"

"Company? You promised me you'd let me go. You told me you needed to run tests on me just until you could cure another ghoul! You have to let me go!"

"I'm sorry, dear Alexander, but I'm afraid I am going to have to hold on to you for a little while longer. There are tests and measurements to keep track of, you know."

"Ahhhhh!" Bub let out a sharp, piercing shout that startled everyone. He was holding his head in both hands and rocking back and forth slightly.

"That will be the blood kicking back in," said Dr. Gimmler-Heichman, glancing at his watch. "Right on schedule. Won't be long now."

As they all watched Bub, his transformation became more and more pronounced: his skin became less pale and more ruddy, and his muscles seemed to untighten and bend.

"And there we have it. Bub, you are now officially a slickskin again. Congratulations."

They all stared at Bub, wondering if the doctor's words were indeed true. Bub, meanwhile, was breathing heavily now, and his gaze was fixed on the stone floor as he slowly got to his feet. Finally he lifted his head to look at Dr. Gimmler-Heichman.

"Where...what—Oh my god!" This last cry was ripped from him as he saw the rest of the Salvadores surrounding him. "Get me out of here! How can you keep a guy in a cage with these things? Please, man, show some decency!"

"Bub, it's us," said the sheriff. "We're your friends."

"He can't understand you," said Jezebel softly.

By the time Jezebel had started to speak, they all knew in their hearts that what she was saying was true: they could see it with their own eyes. Bub was a slickskin.

"You son of a bitch," said Wilson.

Unbeknownst to him, Wilson was correct; Dr. Gimmler-Heichman was in fact the son of a bitch. His mother had grown up an orphan on the streets of Munich, and was a wretchedly horrible woman to all who crossed her path. The one time she was nice to a man, she ended up giving birth to little Friedrich H., which she was none too happy about. She never did it again.

While Bub heroically released Alexander from his chains and the two of them went on to build a very rudimentary barricade out of wooden benches in the corner occupied by Abernathy and Consuela, the sheriff, somehow keeping his rage under control, walked slowly and confidently to Dr. Callahan. Simultaneously, Jezebel questioned Dr. Gimmler-Heichman further on his latest experiment.

"Doctor," the sheriff whispered to the ghoul so only he could hear, "do you have any of those gray fox skull explosives left?"

"Stay away! We're armed!" shouted Bub from behind his barricade, despite the fact that no one had gone near the two benches they had propped up on their sides, and despite the fact that clearly neither of them was armed.

Completely ignoring the newly minted slickskins, Dr. Callahan turned slightly away from their captor to look into his bag surreptitiously. "One left, sheriff. But what's that got to do with the price of eggs? You don't mean to set it off here...?" He looked the sheriff in the eye and found nothing but hardened resolve.

"Remember what we agreed to out on the street. Remember the oath you took."

"I do, sheriff. My mama always told me to steer clear of trouble, but sometimes trouble's worth the trouble." Dr. Callahan's face set. "I'm ready."

"You know what to do."

Dr. Callahan had taken two steps when the sheriff said, "And doctor."

"Yes?"

"It's been a pleasure knowing you."

Dr. Callahan nodded and turned back toward Dr. Gimmler-Heichman, who was now in a heated argument with Jezebel on the morality of using unsterilized needles to perform euthanasia.

"But what does it matter?" Jezebel was saying. She had seen the sheriff and Dr. Callahan speaking in the corner, and she thought she knew what they were up to. She just had to keep Dr. Gimmler-Heichman around long enough for it to work. "They'll be dead in a few minutes anyway. Why bother?"

"It's the principle of the thing, young lady. As a man of science, I am bound to follow to the utmost the accepted methods and practices of the day. Besides, if I got into the habit of using unsterilized needles when it didn't matter, what's to say I won't be one day tempted to use them when it does?"

She saw Dr. Callahan moving slowly toward them. It was almost time. "It's a fair point, but if you are so obsessed with proper procedure, how do you explain the condition of your lab? There's caked blood everywhere."

"I assure you this facility is thoroughly sterilized after every use. It's clean enough to eat off of."

"Perhaps for me, but in your case I somehow remain unconvinced."

Suddenly she saw a spark in her peripheral vision, then a thin stream of smoke.

"What is that?" cried Dr. Gimmler-Heichman, clearly alarmed. "Surely you don't mean to—"

"It's enough to blow us all out of your little cellar laboratory and onto the street outside," said the sheriff over Dr. Callahan's shoulder.

"But ghouls using explosives? It's unheard of! How—?"

"Go to hell, doctor," said the sheriff.

And with those dramatic words hanging in the air, Dr. Callahan raised the gray fox skull with its lit fuse over his head and smashed it through the bars just at Dr. Gimmler-Heichman's feet. And—

Nothing happened.

Everyone froze, even Bub and Alexander. Dr. Gimmler-Heichman was reflecting on how fleeting life truly is and that it may be taken from us at any time. The sheriff was thinking he should have assigned another member of the Salvadores to prepare the explosives. Mungo was happy he was still alive, but was gradually realizing he was still trapped behind iron bars. Abernathy, draped over Consuela, was questioning, for once, if all this was really worth it. Jezebel was wondering how much force needed to be exerted to break those bars. Bub was experiencing an odd craving for meat. Wilson was thinking what the sheriff was thinking.

Consuela was beginning to think her father was right to shelter her from the outside world after all. Dr. Callahan was trying not to cry. Alexander also was trying not to cry. A javelina, looking down at the commotion from a small window to the street, was relieved the bomb had not exploded, as she had three little javelina to look after back home.

"Well," said Dr. Gimmler-Heichman, finally breaking the silence, "that was unexpected. Doubly so."

"You worthless sack of cartilage," said the sheriff. "Don't think this means you're safe. I promise you, I'll be eating your brains before sun up."

"My my, what a prognostication—and from such a precarious position, too. May I remind you that you stand where you stand, inside these fine iron bars, while I stand where I do, outside of them. It is a reality, my dear sheriff, that rather neatly reflects the greater reality of your kind in relation to mine; your days are most certainly numbered, whereas so long as the undead menace is kept in check, I am free to go where I please. Tidy, don't you think?"

While Dr. Gimmler-Heichman was speaking, three scraggly rats that looked like they hadn't eaten in days were making their way from the far wall of the cell to the bars the scientist was so fond of. They moved stiffly, as if they were very old rats. If rats used such implements, perhaps they would have benefited from a geriatric walker, or a motorized scooter. Alas, the rats were scooterless, but still they made their way to the bars and through them, and they hesitated when they reached the feet of Dr. Gimmler-Heichman. Their little rat whiskers twitched and their noses bobbed to and fro as they took in the man's scent. Then as one, still very slowly, they crept up Dr. Gimmler-Heichman's pant legs, two up his left leg and one up his right.

Dr. Gimmler-Heichman, unaccustomed to having rats in his pants, shivered and performed an intricate get-the-rats-out-of-my-pants dance. "What the devil?" he cried, trying to shake the rats from out of his clothing. But the rats persisted, and crept ever upward.

Then, when one of the rats reached Dr. Gimmler-Heichman's femoral artery, it bit down with all its little might. Blood gushed forth from Dr. Gimmler-Heichman's body and into the emaciated rat, swelling it up like a tick that bit into a hemophiliac who had just taken an anticoagulant.

"Oh!" cried Dr. Gimmler-Heichman.

The other two rats bit into the scientist as well, and with each bite Dr. Gimmler-Heichman's body jolted in extreme pain. Excess blood the rats were unable to ingest ran down his pant legs and pooled around his feet. Finally he dropped to the floor, slipping a little in his own blood. He raised his head to look questioningly at his captives for a moment, but soon the exertion was too much and his head fell back to the ground.

"Rats!" he said softly, and he lost consciousness.

The Salvadores were looking at one another with smiles, but they looked at Wilson most of all.

"Won't be long now," said Mungo, in a mocking voice.

And Mungo was right. Within half an hour, Dr. Gimmler-Heichman, or what had been Dr. Gimmler-Heichman, jerked his limbs a little, then sat up stiffly. He was wearing the most pleasant of grins.

"My dear friends," he said. He raised himself to his feet mechanically and took a few halting steps backward. His hand reached out and felt around on the wall, and then they all heard the sounds of old rope being tensed and a creaking pulley. Within moments, the bars had ascended back into the ceiling. "I do hope you'll forgive me for the atrocious way I've acted. I assure you I intend to make full and complete reparations as soon as humanly possible."

"Humanly?" asked Jezebel with a grin.

"Well, you know what I mean, don't you?" It really was a remarkable transformation. The color had drained from Dr. Gimmler-Heichman's face, and patches of his hair had begun to fall out. When he walked it seemed to be with a great deal of pain as he gingerly shifted his weight from leg to leg—but no sign of pain ever appeared on his face.

"I'm assuming those are your undead rats, Wilson?"

"They are indeed, doctor," said the deputy. "Larry, Curly, and Moe. Trained them myself."

The sheriff gave him an approving nod.

"Of course you did," said Dr. Gimmler-Heichman. He glanced over at the paltry barricade Bub and Alexander had erected and at the two cowering forms clearly visible beyond, and he gave a sorrowful shake of his head. "As for those reparations, no time like the present, as they say."

Dr. Gimmler-Heichman lurched forward and tore apart the benches with one swipe of his arm. As Abernathy and Consuela looked on, Bub and Alexander screamed in terror as the scientist came for them.

And they all lived happily ever after.

Epilogue

Sometimes things don't turn out as expected. The guy doesn't end up getting the girl. The doctor comes out, shakes hands, and says, "Congratulations. It's twins." A ghoul shows up and bites someone on their death bed.

Fact of the matter is, life refuses to be scripted, and even the wisest of men are made fools of more often than not. All this is important to remember, as it's natural to try to make sense out of life, to try to learn lessons from past mistakes.

Tragic thing about it is there are no lessons to be learned. Life just goes on.

Sometimes even after it's over.

The sun turned blood red as it shone through the plate glass window, casting shadows in large, upside-down block letters: BARBER. The sheriff looked pleased as he considered his freshly shaved face in the mirror, turning it from side to side. The towel was lifted off his chest, and the sheriff rose from the chair and walked to the open door.

He turned back, and standing in the doorway he was illuminated as with fire. "Till next time, Bub," he said.

"Till time, the sheriff," said the barber.

The sheriff took the eastern bridge out of town and followed the old path until he came to what looked like an abandoned cabin. He climbed the rickety stairs with increasingly heavy steps. He knocked on the door three times. In an oddly fitting juxtaposition, he felt like Death himself.

"Please come in, sheriff," said a soft voice from inside the cabin.

The cabin door creaked open to reveal hardly anything—no lights were lit in the cabin, and the only means of illumination came from the windows.

The sheriff walked through the threshold and saw Abernathy Jones sitting at an old wooden table. The table held the man's leather valise, as well as the black cane the sheriff knew so well.

"Please, sheriff," Abernathy said again, rising slightly from his chair, "come in and have a seat."

"I know what you asked me here for," said the sheriff, "and I've thought long and hard about it. I've decided it's your right. If after all our history and what you know of me, you still want to kill me, well, I won't stop you."

A faint smile touched Abernathy's lips, and he nodded to the sheriff. His hand left his lap and moved toward the cane—but rested upon the clasp of the valise instead. He unfastened the valise, reached into it, and what he pulled out utterly shocked the sheriff.

It was a packet of papers.

Abernathy placed the papers on the table, and the sheriff moved closer to inspect them.

After a moment the sheriff said, "You have got to be joking."

"No joke about it, sheriff."

"The White murder? But that case must have been closed ten, fifteen years ago."

"All the same. Some clerk in Boston noticed a witness's testimony hadn't been properly initialed and notarized, and the witness has since died. The courts are threatening to release Whittaker in the absence of proper documentation. So they tried tracking down the officer who took the original testimony, but he had been infected in a ghoul attack and then never seen or heard from again. And, well, I told the boys I knew I could find him, and here I am."

"You travelled clear across the country to get a ghoul to initial a set of papers for you?"

"Yes, sheriff. The law's the law, after all."

The sheriff shook his head in disbelief. He accepted a pen from Abernathy and began to initial the papers.

"Here...here...here...oh, and here...and the last one here."

When the sheriff had returned the pen, Abernathy produced a stamp press from his valise, stamped the papers, dated them, and initialed each one in turn. Finally, he looked through each individual page, scrutinizing every detail.

"Everything looks to be in order. I appreciate your time, sheriff. And I appreciate your not eating me."

"Don't mention it."

"If you ever have the need..." He handed the sheriff a card:

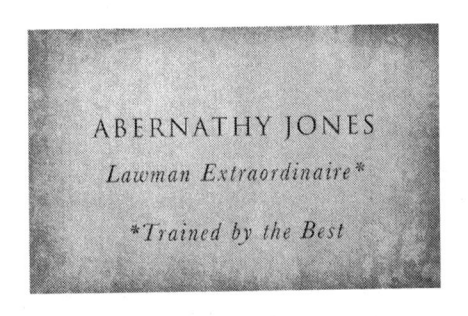

> ABERNATHY JONES
>
> *Lawman Extraordinaire**
>
> **Trained by the Best*

"Thanks," said the sheriff, meaning it. "I'll be in touch."

"Good. Well. This is good-bye, I guess."

"Guess so."

"All right, then. Good-bye, sheriff."

"Good-bye, Abe."

The sheriff began to walk to the door, but stopped just as he reached it.

"Good work, deputy," he said.

The Zombie Sheriff Takes Tucson

* * *

Nancy, I don't know how many times I've tried to convince you that there's good in people, even the most dastardly, but you're going to have to go on hearing the argument, for I've yet again confirmed my position. I've met a great many people since I was last able to write, and each one had his or her own unique way of expressing the kindness of the self that dwells in all living things. Some just took a little longer to show it, that's all. In any event, my recent adventures are a little too complicated and perhaps controversial to be relayed via post. For now please rest assured that the work I came out to the West to do has been completed to my utmost satisfaction and that I will give you a full report of the goings-on upon my return.

As I mentioned to you earlier, Consuela has turned out to be a refreshing travel companion; she seems awed anew at every geological or environmental curiosity we happen across. It's like traveling with a beautiful woman who's been sheltered her whole life and is experiencing everything for the first time. Actually, that's exactly what it is.

I don't think we'll take the most direct route home; you shouldn't expect us for perhaps another three or four months, as we've got a lot to see for the first time. I'm sending ahead those documents that were the purpose of this protracted mission by the most secure means possible. You should receive them in...well, two weeks ago, if my calculations are correct.

A.J.

PS—Please have no fear for my safety, Nancy. I am armed with the knowledge that even in death each soul has the capacity for generosity. And if that fails, I always have my trusty cane.

The sheriff made his way back into town just as the sun was beginning to set over the mountains. The gigantic plumes of black smoke coming from Tucson had begun to subside, and for the first time in a while one could see most of the sky again. In a few days—a week, maybe—some brave settlers, some from Owen's Folly, some from the remnants of Chester's Brigade, would venture into the ruins and start to reclaim what was rightfully theirs. Or at least something that was like what was once rightfully theirs. Someone had suggested the name New Charon's Gate, but nothing had been set in stone yet.

Soon the sheriff was once again among familiar surroundings. As he walked down the street he tipped his hat to those he passed. He was a very well-liked man.

He saw Nelson out for his evening roll. He nodded to him and his new wife, Esmeralda.

He nodded at Jedidiah Owen, rocking in a chair on his front porch.

He saw Dr. Callahan tossing horseshoes and drinking blood mint juleps with Mrs. Harrington. He winked at him when the doctor hit a ringer.

He passed through the village square, and was filled with memories.

He saw the abandoned shack where Dr. Gimmler-Heichman had set up his laboratory. He saw orange and blue lights flashing in the dirty windows.

He found himself next passing through the door of Mungo's restaurant, and as he did he took his hat in both his hands.

"Sheriff," said Mungo. "Beautiful evening, isn't it?"

"It sure is, Mungo."

"Can I get you a table?"

"Bar's fine for me, Mungo. I think a blood beer will do the trick. Oh, you don't happen to have any of those brain bites left, do you? I know it was a limited special."

Mungo looked at the sheriff with a twinkle in his eye. "I'm sure we'll be able to scrape up a few in the kitchen for you, sheriff."

He led the sheriff to the bar and poured him a pint of blood beer. "I'll see about those bites," he said.

Jorge caught his eye from the end of the bar and raised a full glass of blood beer into the air, toward the sheriff. Then he downed the whole thing in one go. An odd man, that Jorge, thought the sheriff, but the best slickskin I've ever met. Maybe second best.

The sheriff hadn't drunk half his pint when Alexander pulled up the stool next to him. "Sheriff," he said. He was already starting to fill out.

"Alexander. How are you getting along?"

"Just fine, sheriff, just fine. Beautiful out tonight."

"True enough," said the sheriff.

A basket of brain bites came, and the two ghouls shared the meal. The sheriff would have stayed longer, but he was anxious to get back home. He walked down the road and stopped in at the sheriff's department, but no one was there. The deputy must have already turned in.

Finally he arrived at his small cottage on the outskirts of town. Most of the shingles had fallen off, and some of the window panes had cracked. But smoke was coming from the chimney. It wasn't much, but it was home.

He called, "I'm home!" as he walked through the door, and when he walked into the kitchen Jezebel said, "About time, too. You haven't been to Mungo's already, have you? Dinner's been ready a quarter of an hour."

"Now what on earth gave you that idea," said the sheriff, giving a wink to Wilson, who was already seated at the kitchen table.

"Oh, no reason," said Jezebel, smiling and wiping the blood mustache off the sheriff's upper lip with her thumb.

"What's for supper tonight?"

"Wilson's favorite. Spleen stew."

"I told her the butcher's was having a sale," said Wilson, ladling himself some stew.

"And for once he was right," said Jezebel.

The sheriff took a seat and served Jezebel and then himself.

"It's good to be home," he said.

"Sheriff!" came a shout from the front of the house. The sheriff rose from his seat to see Dr. Gimmler-Heichman framed in the doorway. "Sheriff, I hate to bother you during suppertime, but I just had to show you this immediately."

"What is it, doctor?" The sheriff showed him into the parlor.

"It's this note," said Dr. Gimmler-Heichman, brandishing an envelope. "It came today in the mail. I truly do not know what to make of it."

He handed the letter to the sheriff, and this is what he read:

My Dear Dr. Gimmler-Heichman:

It is said that you have moved to Owen's Folly. If this is true, then our greatest fears have come to pass. I feel it is my professional duty to warn you, for old time's sake, that we will be arriving in one week's time.

Yours, very truly,

Leonard Larribee

"Leonard Larribee..." said the sheriff. "That sounds somehow familiar. I have it—the initials on the note we found in McFarland's cabin. L.L. It must be Leonard Larribee!"

"I'm afraid it is," said Dr. Gimmler-Heichman.

"Afraid? What do you know about this Larribee?"

"Too much. He has one goal in life: the eradication of all ghouls in the world."

"Only that?"

"Yes. But he means it, sheriff, and he has the funds to see it happen."

"How do you know all this? Why did he write to you?"

"He was my employer. In a past life, as they say."

"I see," said the sheriff.

"But you don't. You don't see at all. Leonard Larribee says he is coming here, and what he says, he does. And if he's coming here, that means he's going to destroy the whole village."

The sheriff's face tightened in a way Dr. Gimmler-Heichman hadn't seen since they left Tucson. "He's coming in a week? We'll be ready for him. You can count on that."

"But—what's the letter dated?" Dr. Gimmler-Heichman snatched the letter from the sheriff's hands and read the date in the upper right-hand corner.

"Doctor, you've turned white. Ghouls aren't supposed to be able to do that."

"The date," he said, pointing at the letter. "He'll be here tomorrow."

About the Author

Brian South grew up in Ohio, moved to Indiana, and finally settled in Illinois. He'll go wherever a good story takes him, be it the next state over, the comic book store, the humor section, or even the wild world of zombie fiction. He holds a BA in English from the University of Notre Dame, where he won the Richard T. Sullivan Award for fiction writing, as well as a Masters in Writing and Publishing from DePaul University. He and his wife, Sarah, live in the Chicago area with their three sons, Finnegan, Sawyer, and Oliver.

Connect with Brian South

www.briansouth.org
www.facebook.com/OfficialBrianSouth
www.twitter.com/stanhubrio

Made in the USA
Lexington, KY
25 October 2015